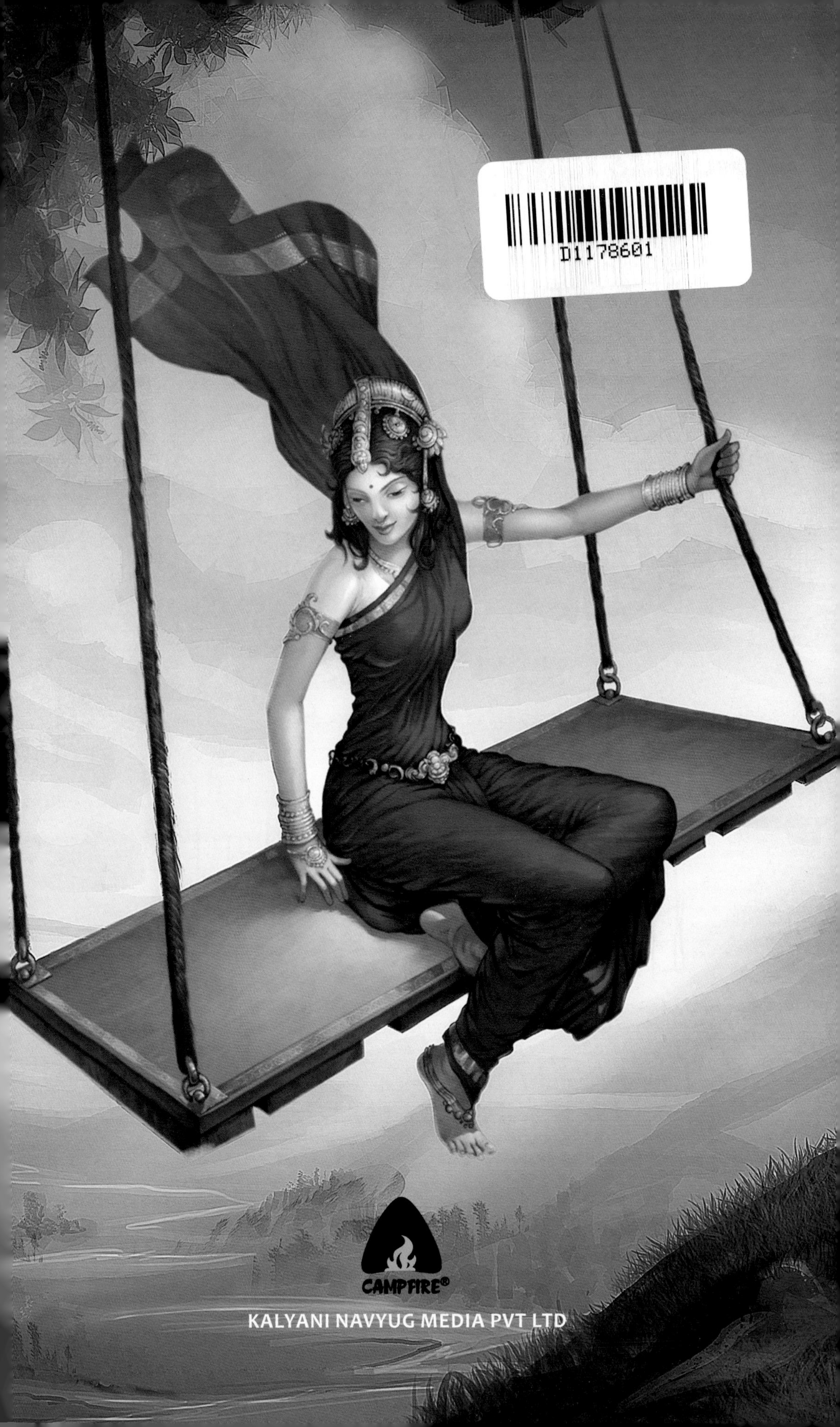

CAMPFIRE®
KALYANI NAVYUG MEDIA PVT LTD

Sita
Daughter of the Earth

ILLUSTRATOR **MANIKANDAN**
COLOURIST **ANIL C K**
LETTERER **LAXMI CHAND GUPTA**
EDITORS **EMAN CHOWDHARY & ADITI RAY**

COVER ART
ILLUSTRATOR **MANIKANDAN**
COLOUR & DESIGN **JAYAKRISHNAN K P**

CAMPFIRE®
www.campfire.co.in

Mission Statement

To entertain and educate young minds by creating unique illustrated books
that recount stories of human values, arouse curiosity in the world around us,
and inspire with tales of great deeds of unforgettable people.

Published by Kalyani Navyug Media Pvt Ltd
101 C, Shiv House, Hari Nagar Ashram, New Delhi 110014 India

ISBN: 978-93-80741-25-3

Printed in India

ABOUT THE AUTHOR

Born in 1980 in Dubai, Saraswati Nagpal was an early reader. On graduating from three-letter-word reading, she swiftly plunged into the world of legendary gods and godesses, living the fantastic stories in her head, and believing in them with the complete faith of a child.

She took to writing as a young girl, planning her first book when she was ten years old, though she managed only one chapter then. She wrote plays, stories, and poetry through high school and college. As a student of Indian classical dance and music, Saraswati presented myths through her stage performances, her favourites being the stories of Krishna and Arjuna.

A bit of a world traveller, Saraswati studied in Dubai, Delhi, and Iowa. Her parents and brother cherished her love for letters and always knew she'd be a writer some day. Saraswati counts every author she has read as an inspiration, moving her to tell stories. She can spend hours delving into the fantasy fiction of Trudi Canavan, Robert Jordan, David Gemmel, and Terry Brooks. Her dream is to write many magical epics and she is working hard at it.

Saraswati has been teaching young children for five years, and enjoys helping them weave their own stories through words, music, and movement. She finds the snow-clad Himalayas in India and the Drakensburg Mountains in South Africa most nourishing to the writing spirit, and currently spends her time between the two countries.

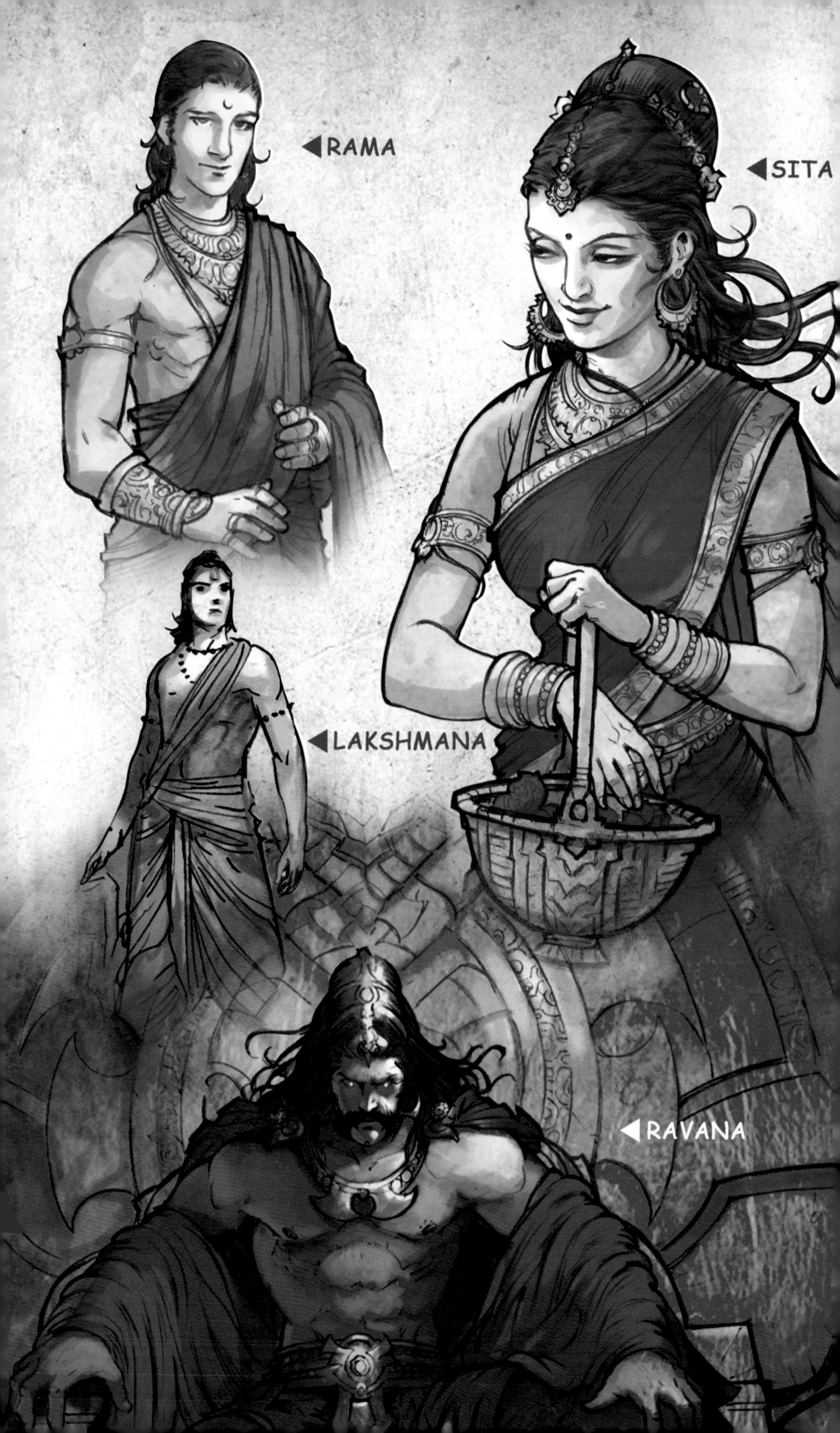
RAMA
SITA
LAKSHMANA
RAVANA

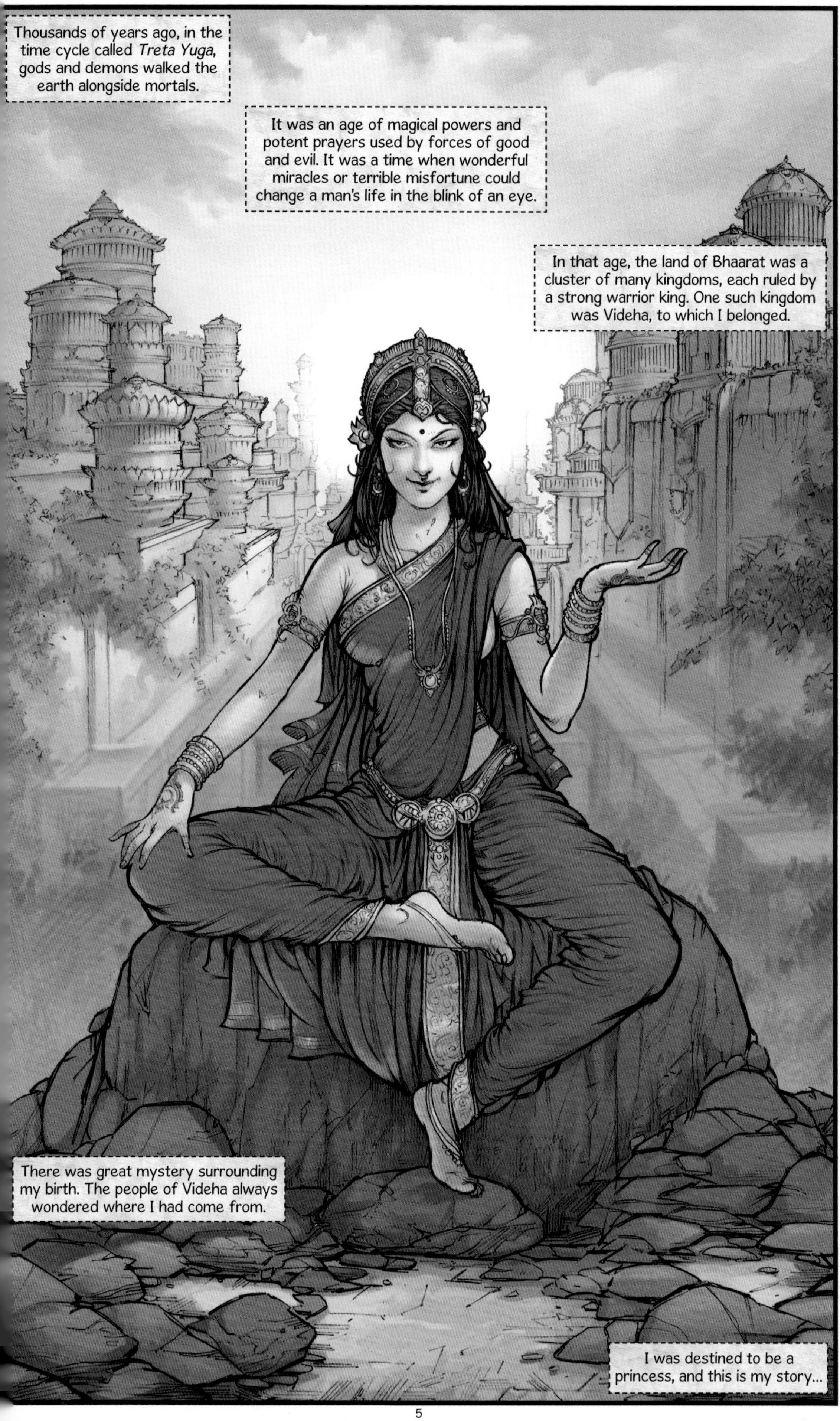
Thousands of years ago, in the time cycle called *Treta Yuga*, gods and demons walked the earth alongside mortals.
It was an age of magical powers and potent prayers used by forces of good and evil. It was a time when wonderful miracles or terrible misfortune could change a man's life in the blink of an eye.
In that age, the land of Bhaarat was a cluster of many kingdoms, each ruled by a strong warrior king. One such kingdom was Videha, to which I belonged.
There was great mystery surrounding my birth. The people of Videha always wondered where I had come from.
I was destined to be a princess, and this is my story...

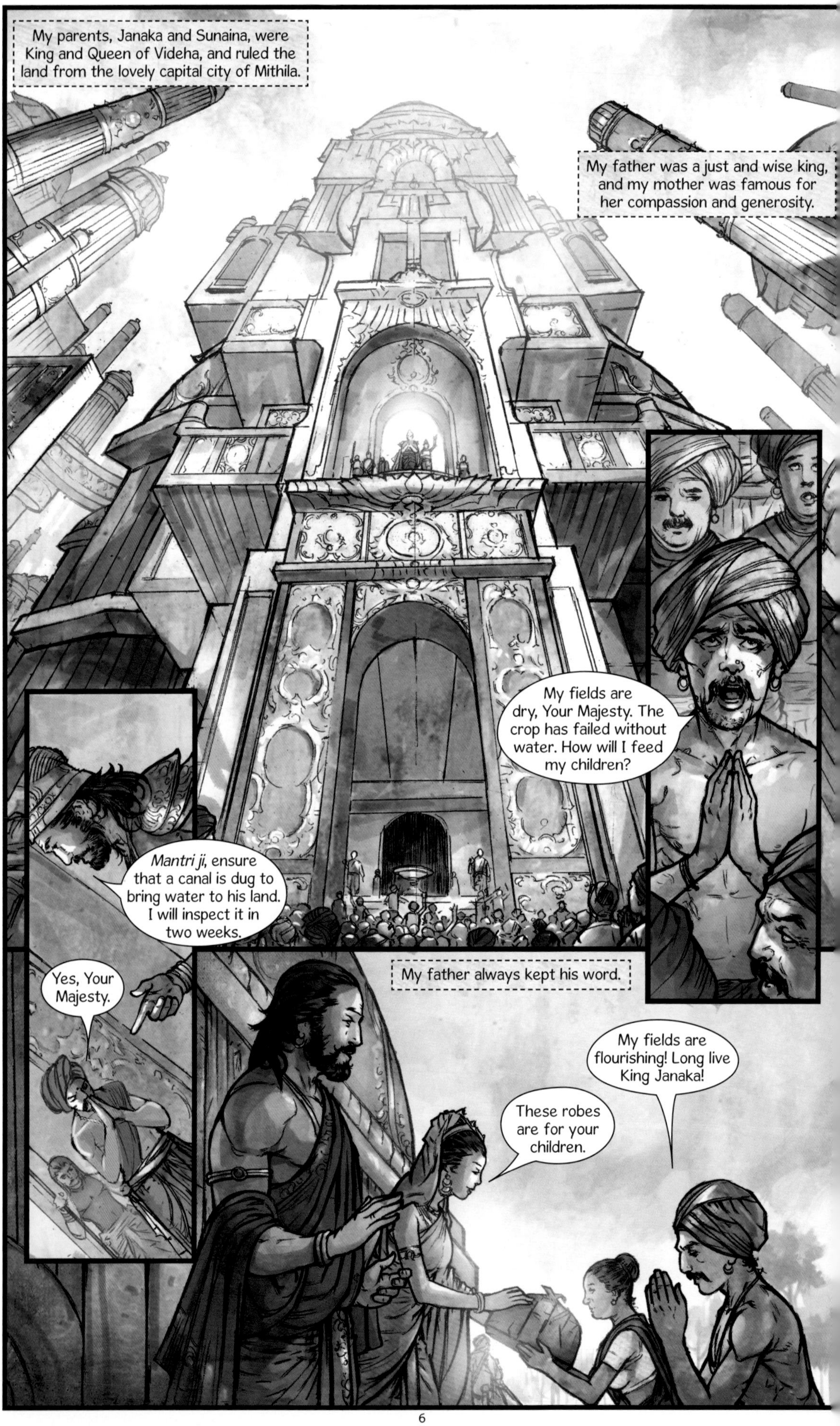
My parents, Janaka and Sunaina, were King and Queen of Videha, and ruled the land from the lovely capital city of Mithila.
My father was a just and wise king, and my mother was famous for her compassion and generosity.
My fields are dry, Your Majesty. The crop has failed without water. How will I feed my children?
Mantri ji, ensure that a canal is dug to bring water to his land. I will inspect it in two weeks.
Yes, Your Majesty.
My father always kept his word.
My fields are flourishing! Long live King Janaka!
These robes are for your children.

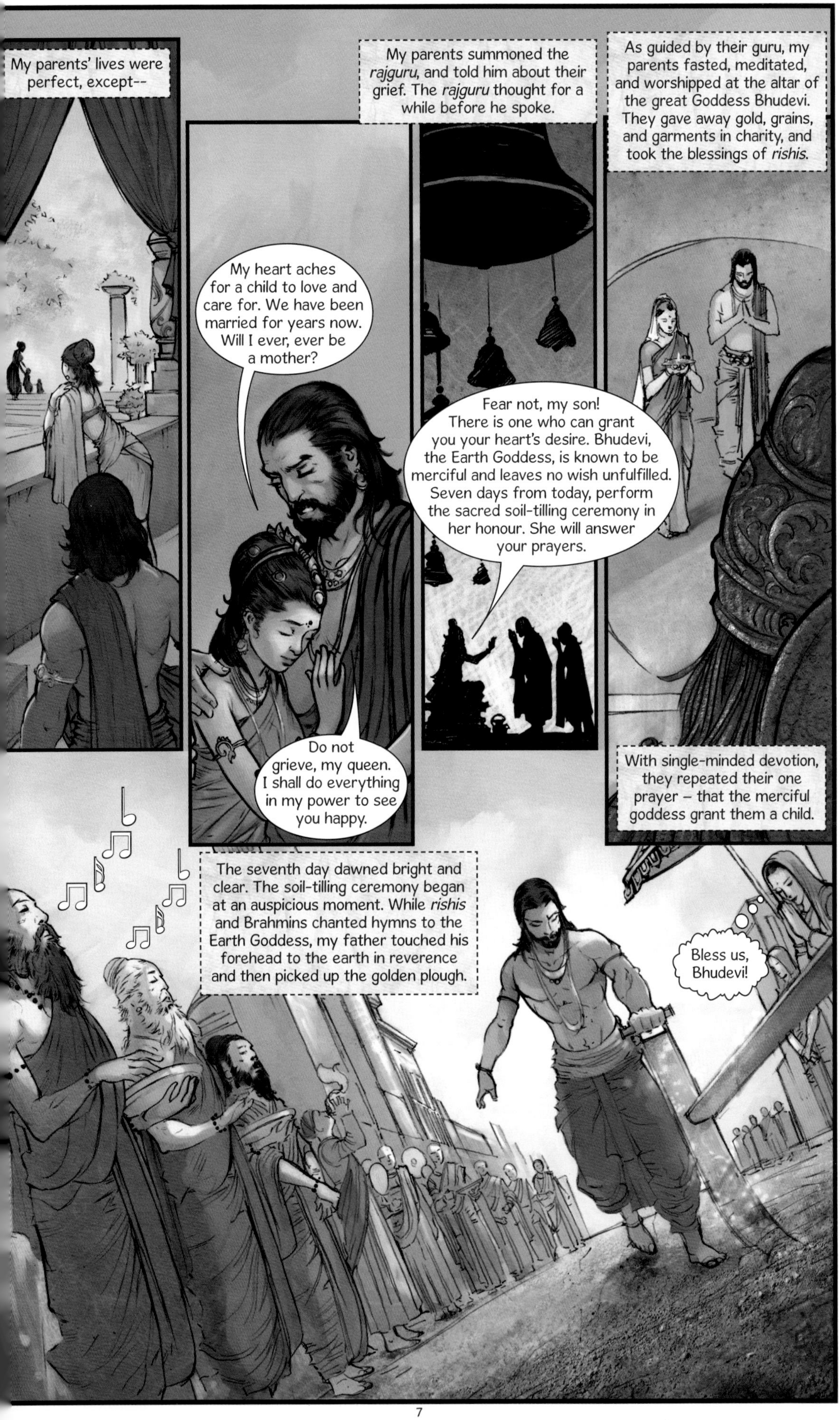

My parents' lives were perfect, except--
My parents summoned the *rajguru*, and told him about their grief. The *rajguru* thought for a while before he spoke.
My heart aches for a child to love and care for. We have been married for years now. Will I ever, ever be a mother?
Do not grieve, my queen. I shall do everything in my power to see you happy.
Fear not, my son! There is one who can grant you your heart's desire. Bhudevi, the Earth Goddess, is known to be merciful and leaves no wish unfulfilled. Seven days from today, perform the sacred soil-tilling ceremony in her honour. She will answer your prayers.
As guided by their guru, my parents fasted, meditated, and worshipped at the altar of the great Goddess Bhudevi. They gave away gold, grains, and garments in charity, and took the blessings of *rishis*.
With single-minded devotion, they repeated their one prayer – that the merciful goddess grant them a child.
The seventh day dawned bright and clear. The soil-tilling ceremony began at an auspicious moment. While *rishis* and Brahmins chanted hymns to the Earth Goddess, my father touched his forehead to the earth in reverence and then picked up the golden plough.
Bless us, Bhudevi!

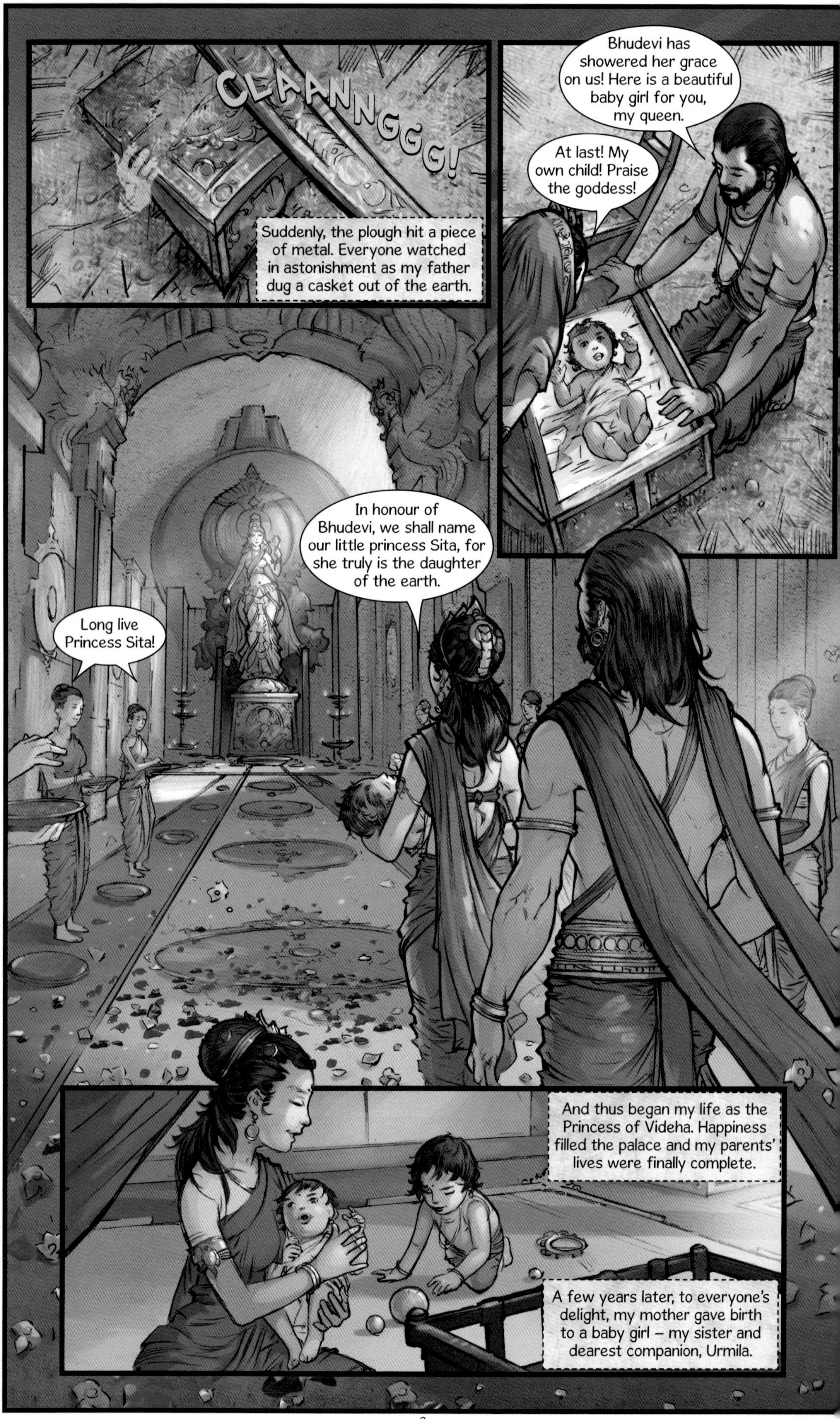
CLAANNGGG!
Suddenly, the plough hit a piece of metal. Everyone watched in astonishment as my father dug a casket out of the earth.
Bhudevi has showered her grace on us! Here is a beautiful baby girl for you, my queen.
At last! My own child! Praise the goddess!
In honour of Bhudevi, we shall name our little princess Sita, for she truly is the daughter of the earth.
Long live Princess Sita!
And thus began my life as the Princess of Videha. Happiness filled the palace and my parents' lives were finally complete.
A few years later, to everyone's delight, my mother gave birth to a baby girl – my sister and dearest companion, Urmila.

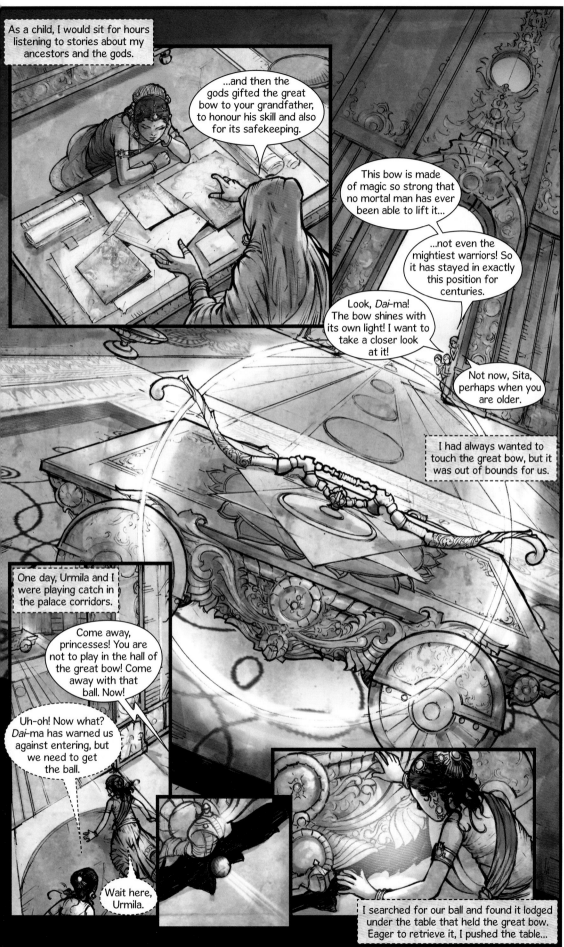

As a child, I would sit for hours listening to stories about my ancestors and the gods.

...and then the gods gifted the great bow to your grandfather, to honour his skill and also for its safekeeping.

This bow is made of magic so strong that no mortal man has ever been able to lift it...

...not even the mightiest warriors! So it has stayed in exactly this position for centuries.

Look, *Dai*-ma! The bow shines with its own light! I want to take a closer look at it!

Not now, Sita, perhaps when you are older.

I had always wanted to touch the great bow, but it was out of bounds for us.

One day, Urmila and I were playing catch in the palace corridors.

Come away, princesses! You are not to play in the hall of the great bow! Come away with that ball. Now!

Uh-oh! Now what? *Dai*-ma has warned us against entering, but we need to get the ball.

Wait here, Urmila.

I searched for our ball and found it lodged under the table that held the great bow. Eager to retrieve it, I pushed the table...

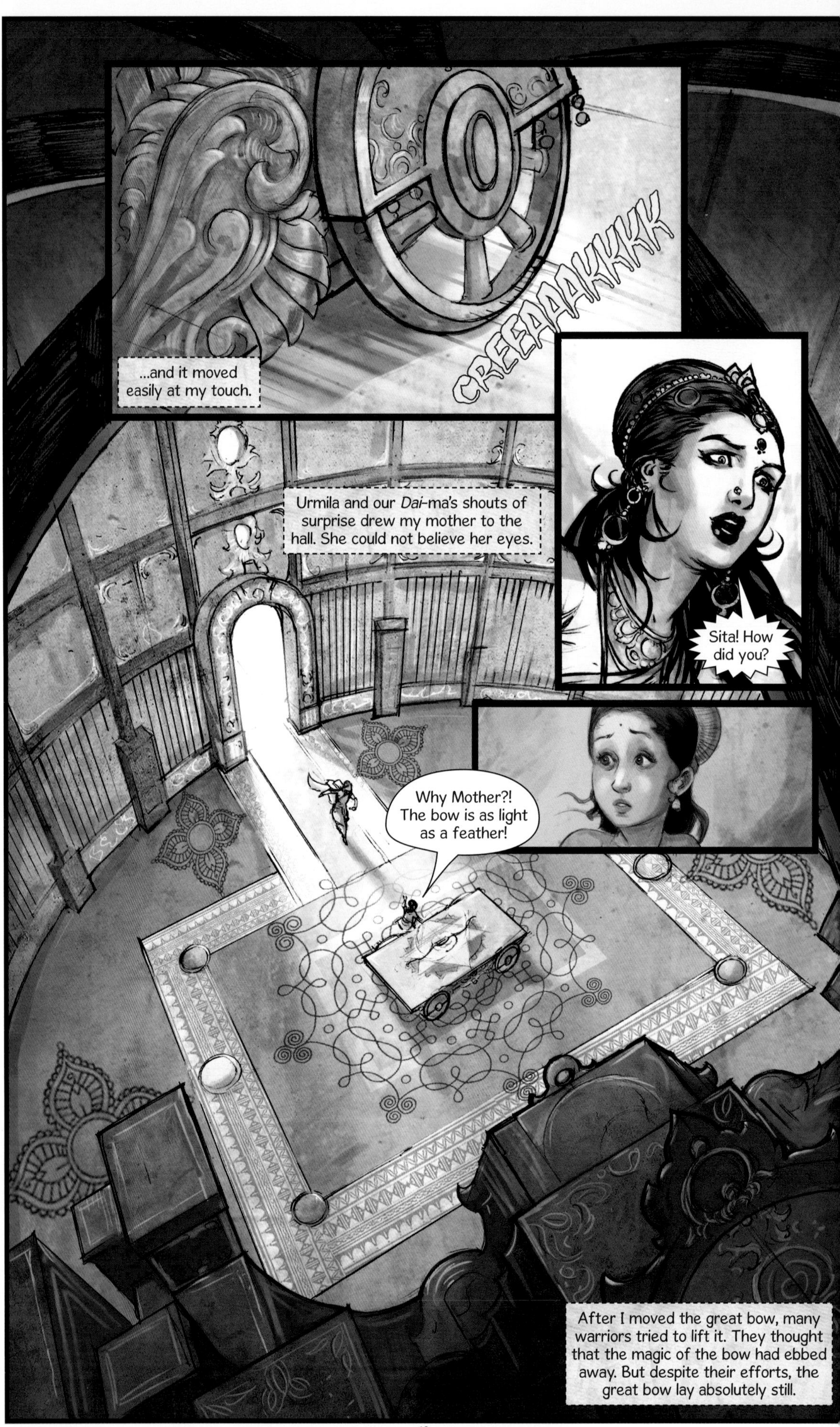
CREEAAKKKK
...and it moved easily at my touch.
Sita! How did you?
Urmila and our Dai-ma's shouts of surprise drew my mother to the hall. She could not believe her eyes.
Why Mother?! The bow is as light as a feather!
After I moved the great bow, many warriors tried to lift it. They thought that the magic of the bow had ebbed away. But despite their efforts, the great bow lay absolutely still.

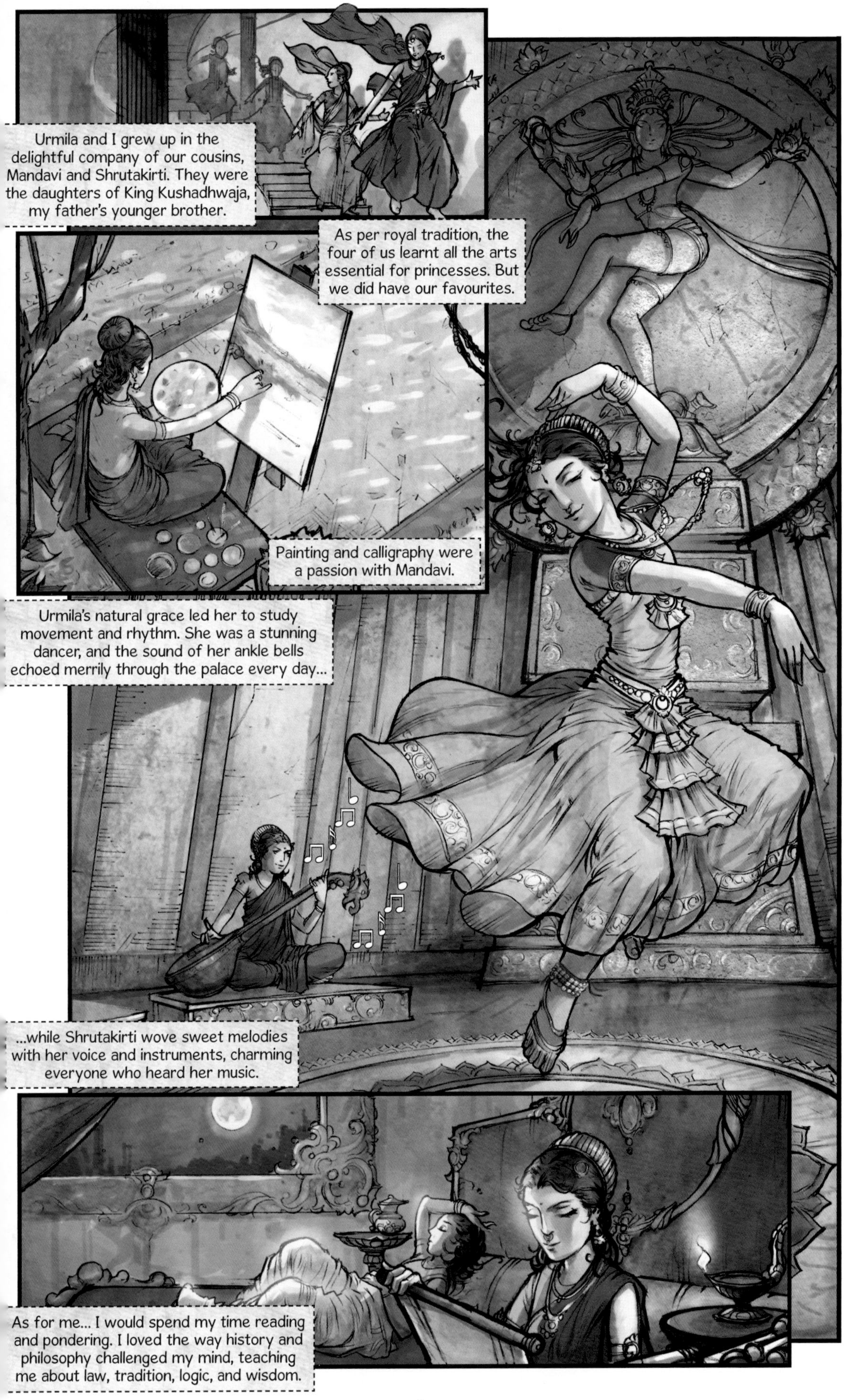
Urmila and I grew up in the delightful company of our cousins, Mandavi and Shrutakirti. They were the daughters of King Kushadhwaja, my father's younger brother.
As per royal tradition, the four of us learnt all the arts essential for princesses. But we did have our favourites.
Painting and calligraphy were a passion with Mandavi.
Urmila's natural grace led her to study movement and rhythm. She was a stunning dancer, and the sound of her ankle bells echoed merrily through the palace every day...
...while Shrutakirti wove sweet melodies with her voice and instruments, charming everyone who heard her music.
As for me... I would spend my time reading and pondering. I loved the way history and philosophy challenged my mind, teaching me about law, tradition, logic, and wisdom.

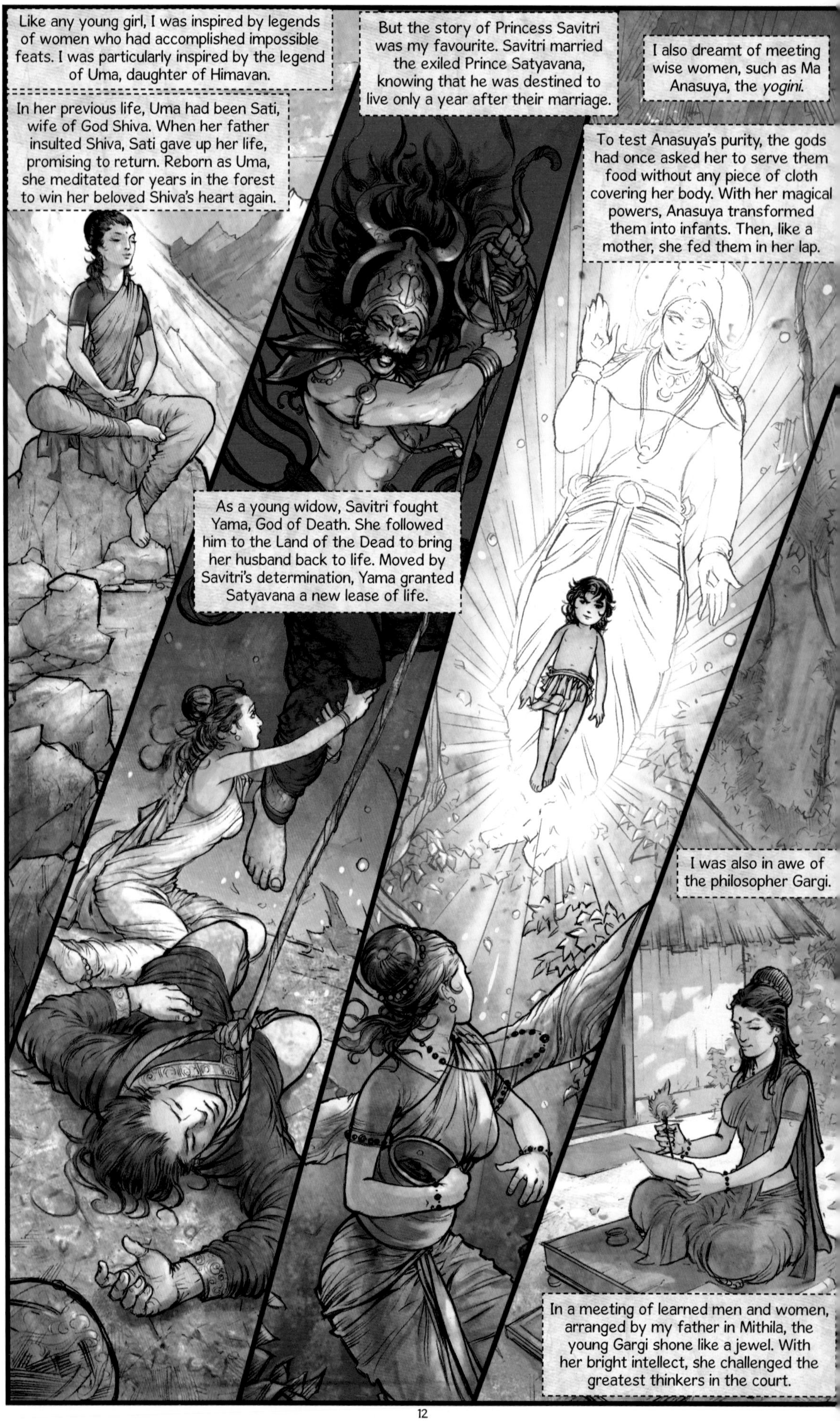
Like any young girl, I was inspired by legends of women who had accomplished impossible feats. I was particularly inspired by the legend of Uma, daughter of Himavan.
In her previous life, Uma had been Sati, wife of God Shiva. When her father insulted Shiva, Sati gave up her life, promising to return. Reborn as Uma, she meditated for years in the forest to win her beloved Shiva's heart again.
But the story of Princess Savitri was my favourite. Savitri married the exiled Prince Satyavana, knowing that he was destined to live only a year after their marriage.
As a young widow, Savitri fought Yama, God of Death. She followed him to the Land of the Dead to bring her husband back to life. Moved by Savitri's determination, Yama granted Satyavana a new lease of life.
I also dreamt of meeting wise women, such as Ma Anasuya, the *yogini.*
To test Anasuya's purity, the gods had once asked her to serve them food without any piece of cloth covering her body. With her magical powers, Anasuya transformed them into infants. Then, like a mother, she fed them in her lap.
I was also in awe of the philosopher Gargi.
In a meeting of learned men and women, arranged by my father in Mithila, the young Gargi shone like a jewel. With her bright intellect, she challenged the greatest thinkers in the court.

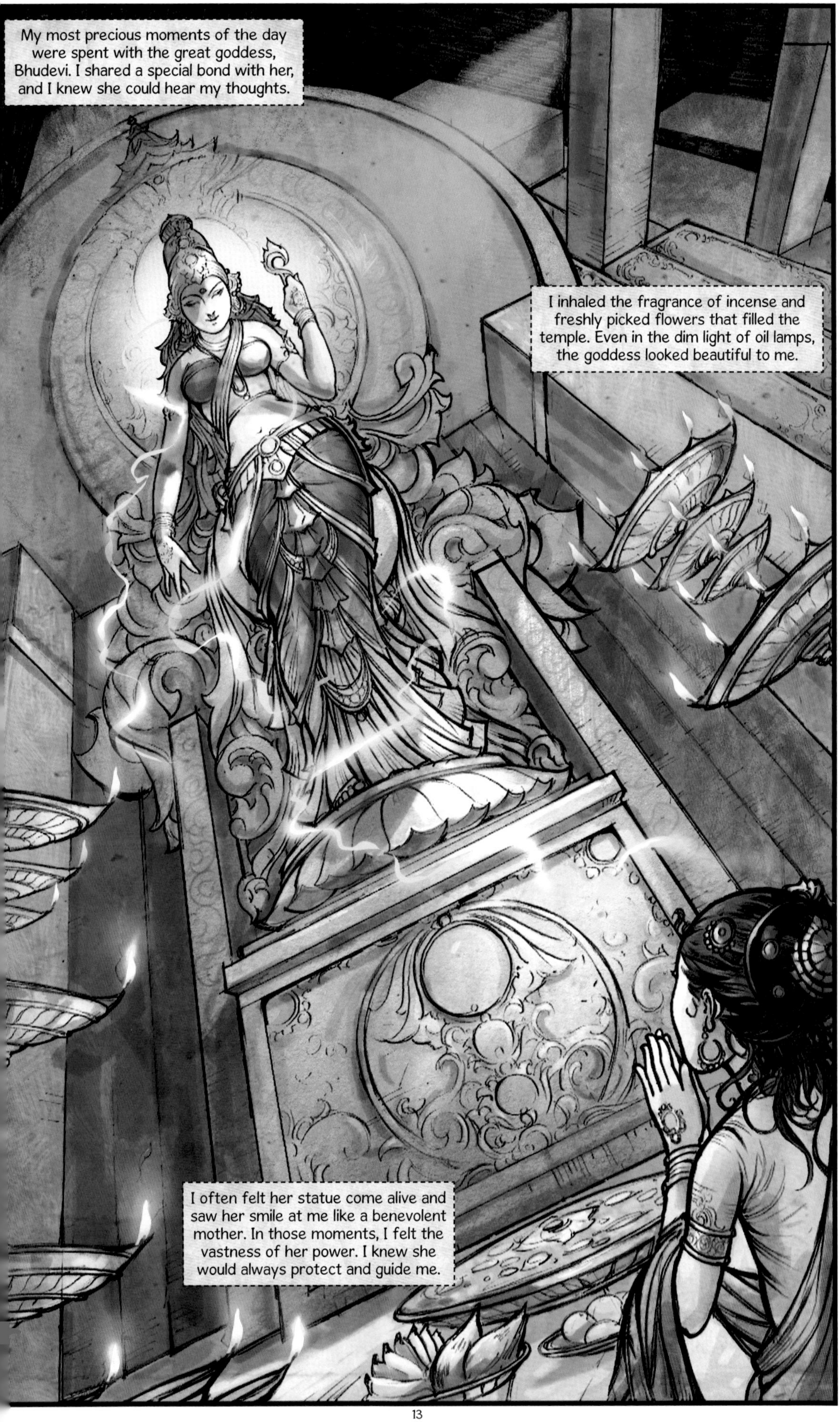
My most precious moments of the day were spent with the great goddess, Bhudevi. I shared a special bond with her, and I knew she could hear my thoughts.
I inhaled the fragrance of incense and freshly picked flowers that filled the temple. Even in the dim light of oil lamps, the goddess looked beautiful to me.
I often felt her statue come alive and saw her smile at me like a benevolent mother. In those moments, I felt the vastness of her power. I knew she would always protect and guide me.

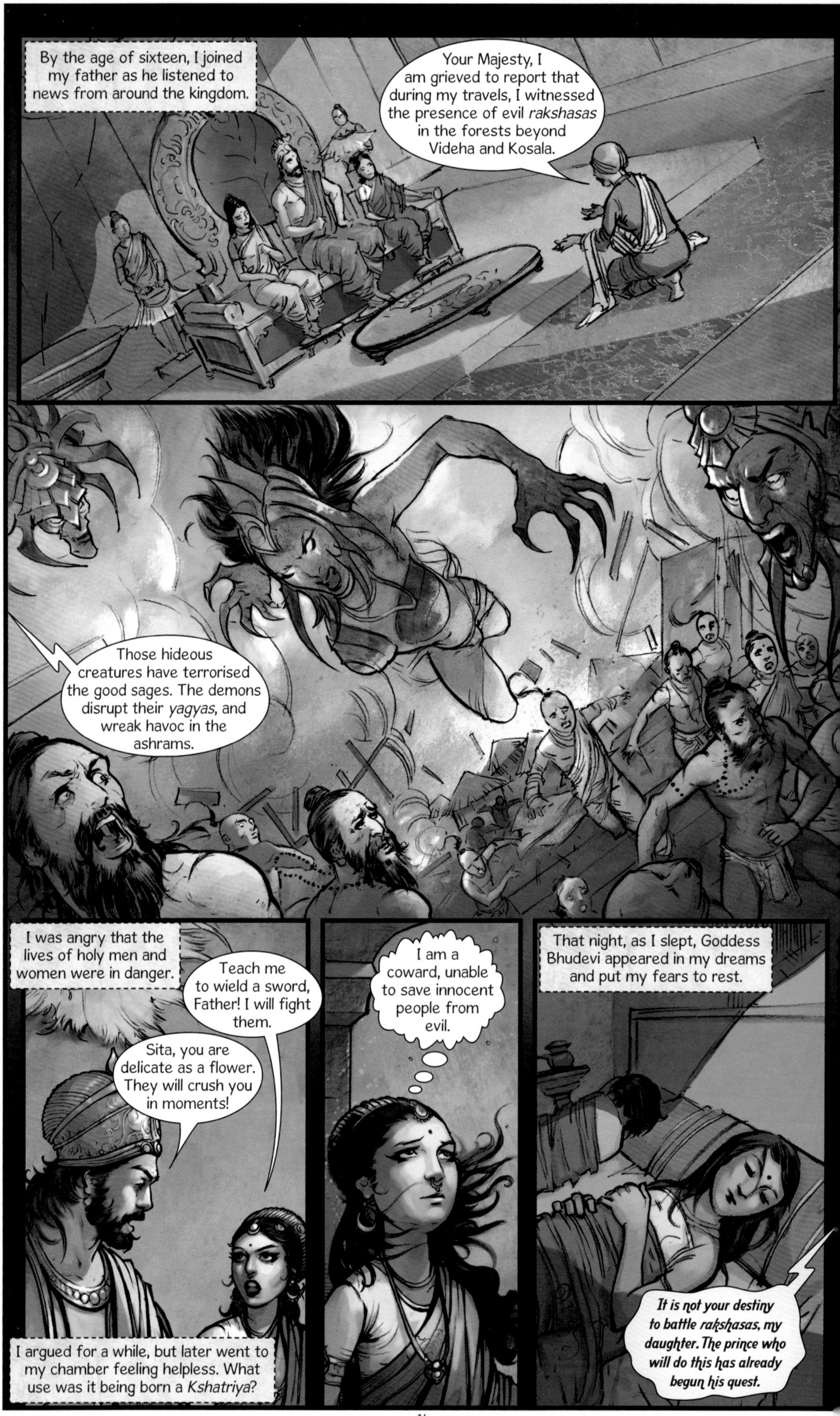
By the age of sixteen, I joined my father as he listened to news from around the kingdom.
Your Majesty, I am grieved to report that during my travels, I witnessed the presence of evil *rakshasas* in the forests beyond Videha and Kosala.
Those hideous creatures have terrorised the good sages. The demons disrupt their *yagyas*, and wreak havoc in the ashrams.
I was angry that the lives of holy men and women were in danger.
Teach me to wield a sword, Father! I will fight them.
Sita, you are delicate as a flower. They will crush you in moments!
I argued for a while, but later went to my chamber feeling helpless. What use was it being born a *Kshatriya*?
I am a coward, unable to save innocent people from evil.
That night, as I slept, Goddess Bhudevi appeared in my dreams and put my fears to rest.
It is not your destiny to battle rakshasas, my daughter. The prince who will do this has already begun his quest.

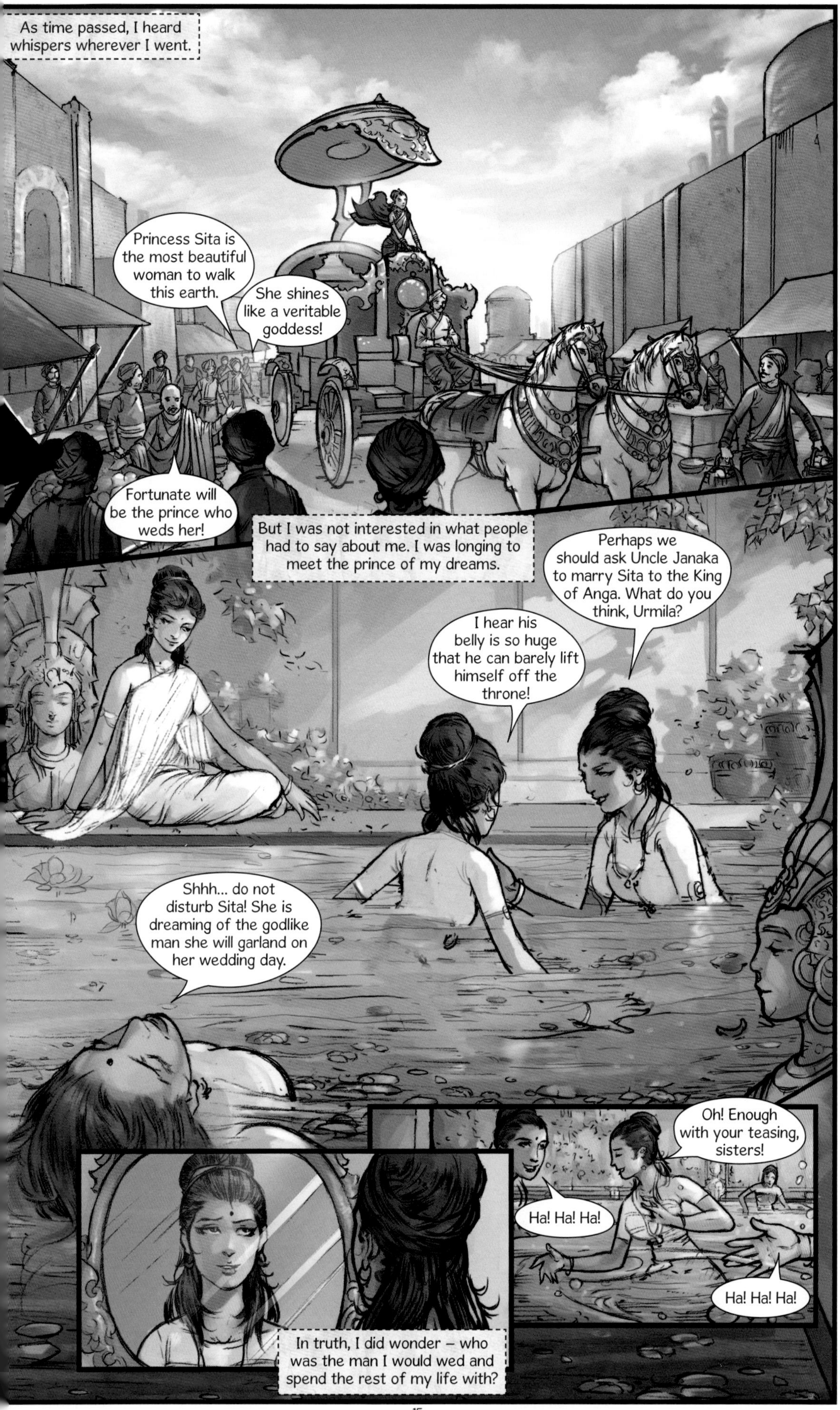
As time passed, I heard whispers wherever I went.
Princess Sita is the most beautiful woman to walk this earth.
She shines like a veritable goddess!
Fortunate will be the prince who weds her!
But I was not interested in what people had to say about me. I was longing to meet the prince of my dreams.
Perhaps we should ask Uncle Janaka to marry Sita to the King of Anga. What do you think, Urmila?
I hear his belly is so huge that he can barely lift himself off the throne!
Shhh... do not disturb Sita! She is dreaming of the godlike man she will garland on her wedding day.
Oh! Enough with your teasing, sisters!
Ha! Ha! Ha!
Ha! Ha! Ha!
In truth, I did wonder – who was the man I would wed and spend the rest of my life with?

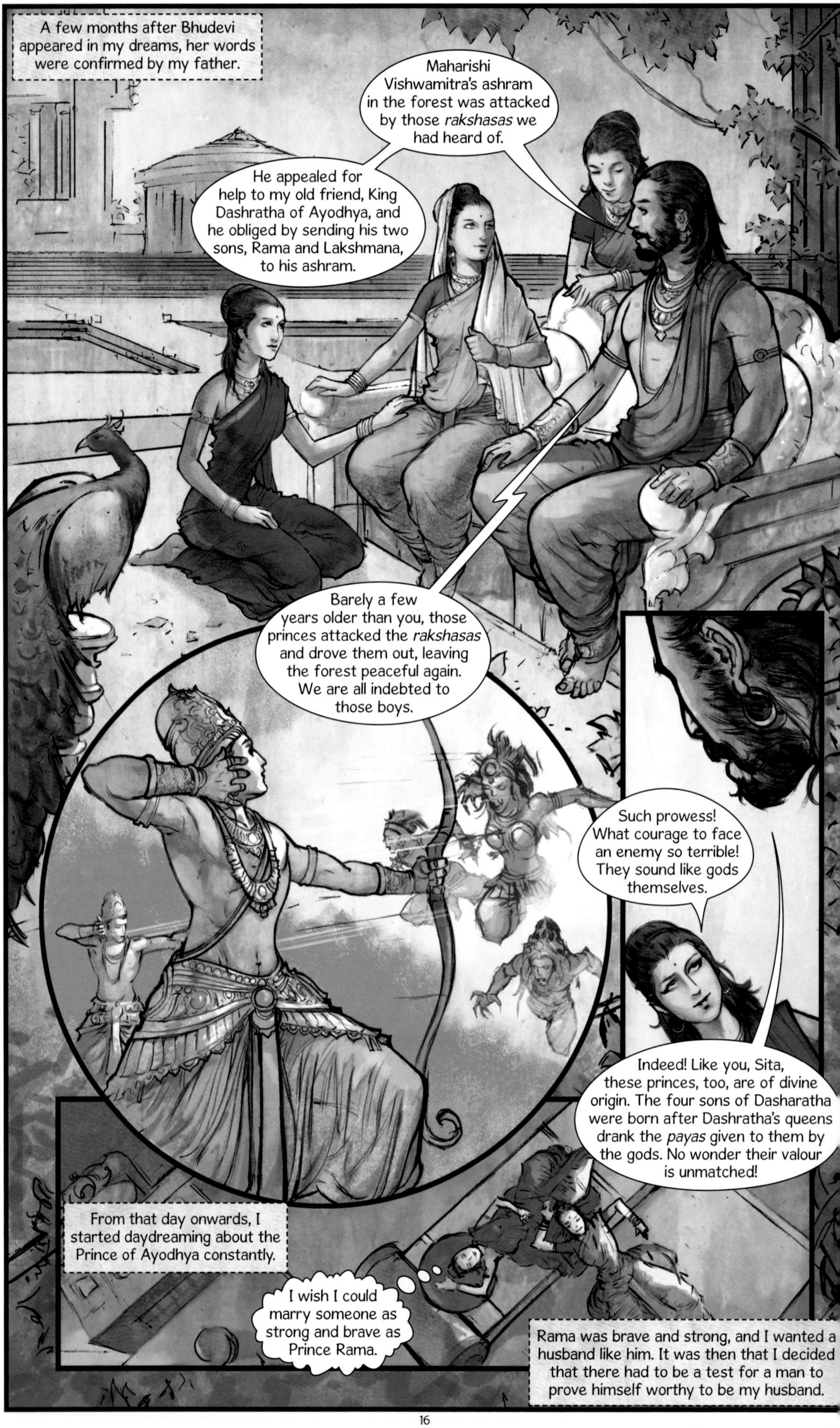
A few months after Bhudevi appeared in my dreams, her words were confirmed by my father.
Maharishi Vishwamitra's ashram in the forest was attacked by those *rakshasas* we had heard of.
He appealed for help to my old friend, King Dashratha of Ayodhya, and he obliged by sending his two sons, Rama and Lakshmana, to his ashram.
Barely a few years older than you, those princes attacked the *rakshasas* and drove them out, leaving the forest peaceful again. We are all indebted to those boys.
Such prowess! What courage to face an enemy so terrible! They sound like gods themselves.
Indeed! Like you, Sita, these princes, too, are of divine origin. The four sons of Dasharatha were born after Dashratha's queens drank the *payas* given to them by the gods. No wonder their valour is unmatched!
From that day onwards, I started daydreaming about the Prince of Ayodhya constantly.
I wish I could marry someone as strong and brave as Prince Rama.
Rama was brave and strong, and I wanted a husband like him. It was then that I decided that there had to be a test for a man to prove himself worthy to be my husband.

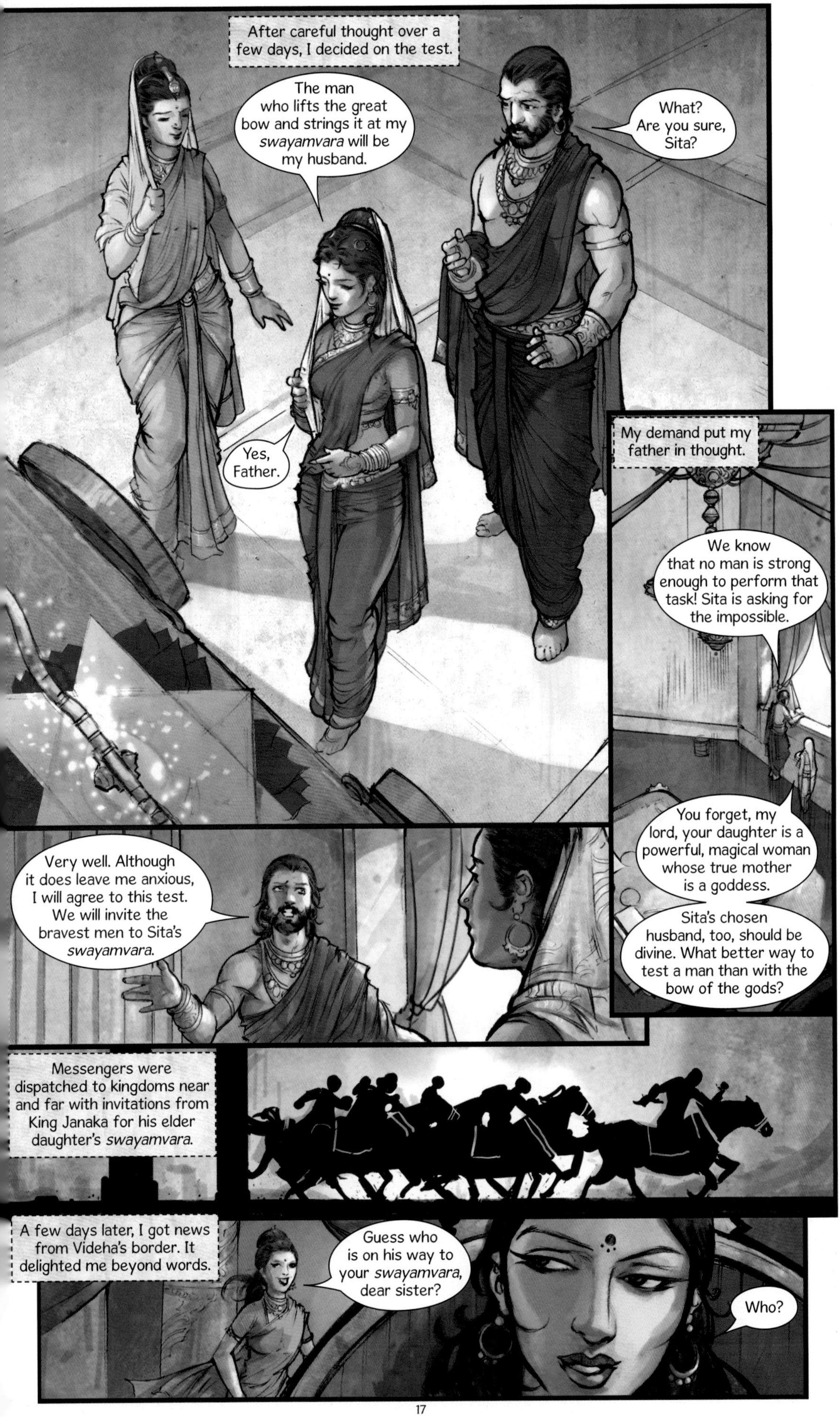
After careful thought over a few days, I decided on the test.
The man who lifts the great bow and strings it at my *swayamvara* will be my husband.
What? Are you sure, Sita?
Yes, Father.
My demand put my father in thought.
We know that no man is strong enough to perform that task! Sita is asking for the impossible.
You forget, my lord, your daughter is a powerful, magical woman whose true mother is a goddess.
Sita's chosen husband, too, should be divine. What better way to test a man than with the bow of the gods?
Very well. Although it does leave me anxious, I will agree to this test. We will invite the bravest men to Sita's *swayamvara*.
Messengers were dispatched to kingdoms near and far with invitations from King Janaka for his elder daughter's *swayamvara*.
A few days later, I got news from Videha's border. It delighted me beyond words.
Guess who is on his way to your *swayamvara*, dear sister?
Who?

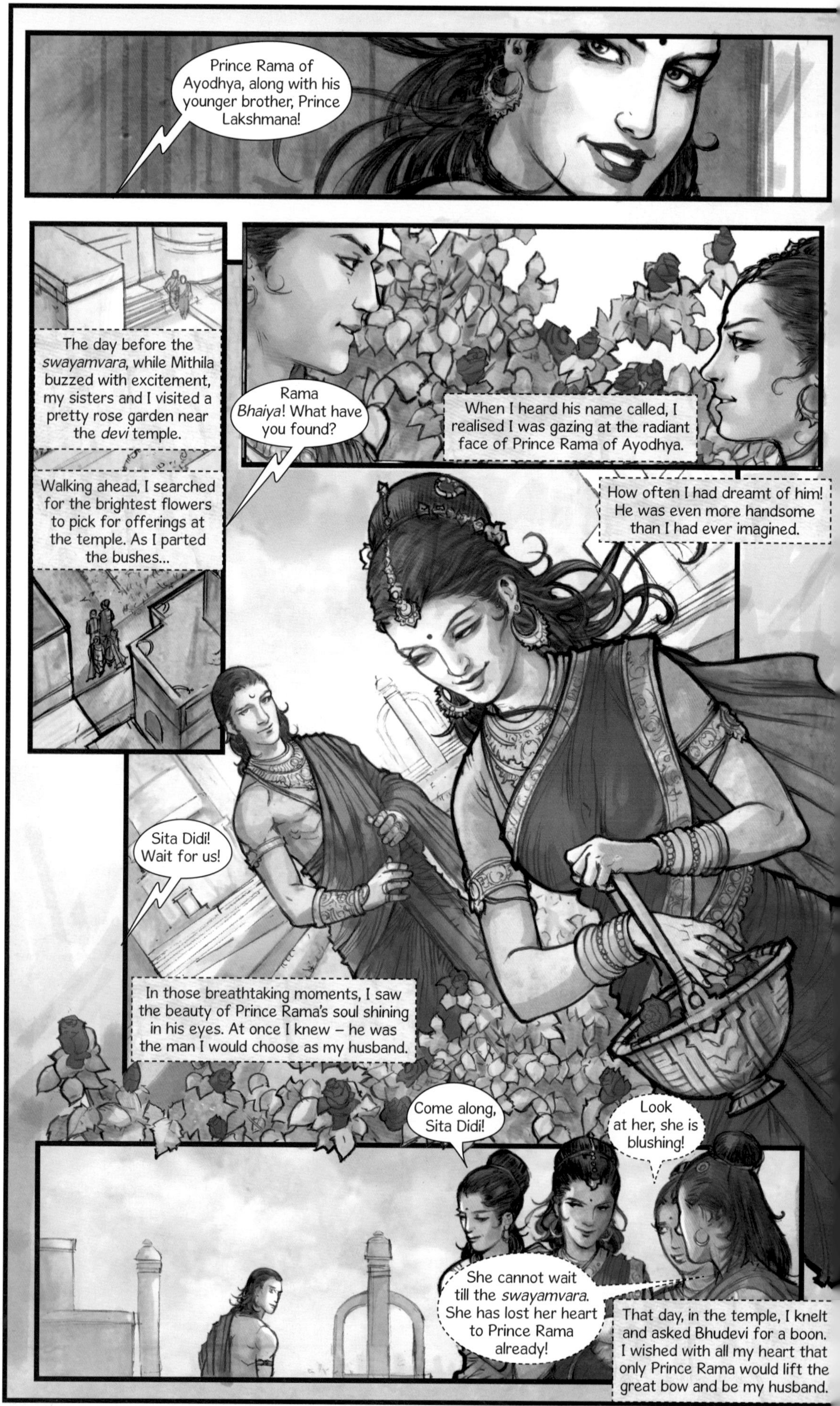
Prince Rama of Ayodhya, along with his younger brother, Prince Lakshmana!
The day before the *swayamvara*, while Mithila buzzed with excitement, my sisters and I visited a pretty rose garden near the *devi* temple.
Rama *Bhaiya*! What have you found?
When I heard his name called, I realised I was gazing at the radiant face of Prince Rama of Ayodhya.
Walking ahead, I searched for the brightest flowers to pick for offerings at the temple. As I parted the bushes...
How often I had dreamt of him! He was even more handsome than I had ever imagined.
Sita Didi! Wait for us!
In those breathtaking moments, I saw the beauty of Prince Rama's soul shining in his eyes. At once I knew – he was the man I would choose as my husband.
Come along, Sita Didi!
Look at her, she is blushing!
She cannot wait till the *swayamvara*. She has lost her heart to Prince Rama already!
That day, in the temple, I knelt and asked Bhudevi for a boon. I wished with all my heart that only Prince Rama would lift the great bow and be my husband.

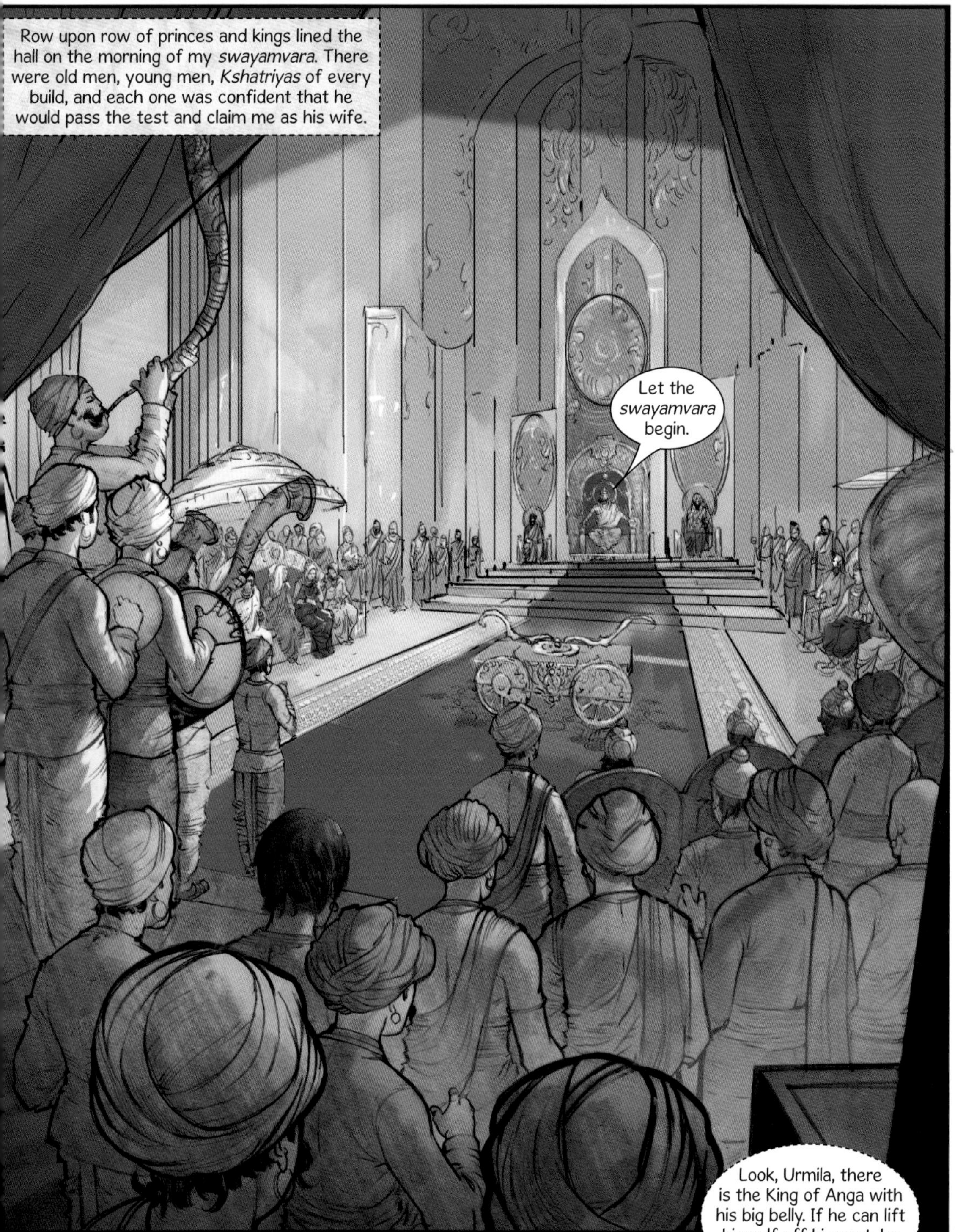
Row upon row of princes and kings lined the hall on the morning of my *swayamvara*. There were old men, young men, *Kshatriyas* of every build, and each one was confident that he would pass the test and claim me as his wife.
Let the *swayamvara* begin.

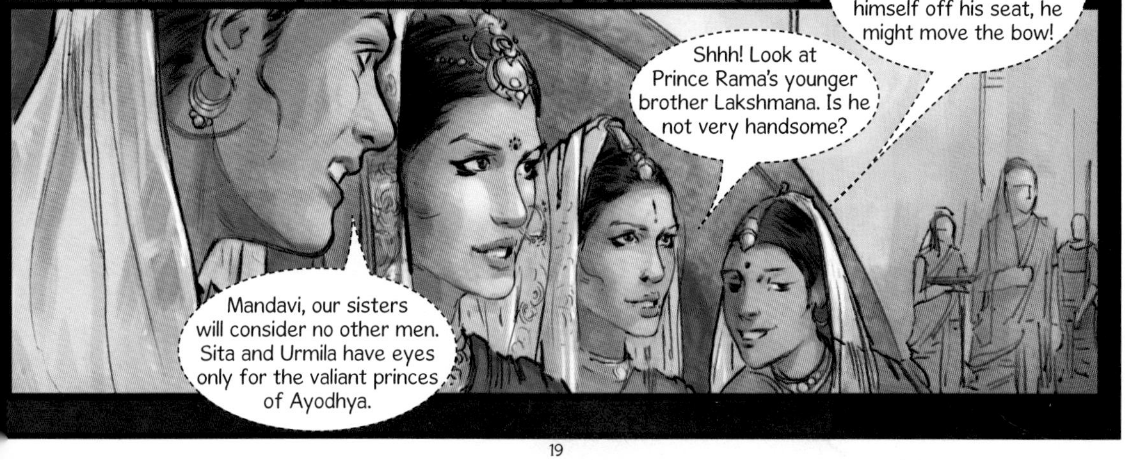
Look, Urmila, there is the King of Anga with his big belly. If he can lift himself off his seat, he might move the bow!
Shhh! Look at Prince Rama's younger brother Lakshmana. Is he not very handsome?
Mandavi, our sisters will consider no other men. Sita and Urmila have eyes only for the valiant princes of Ayodhya.

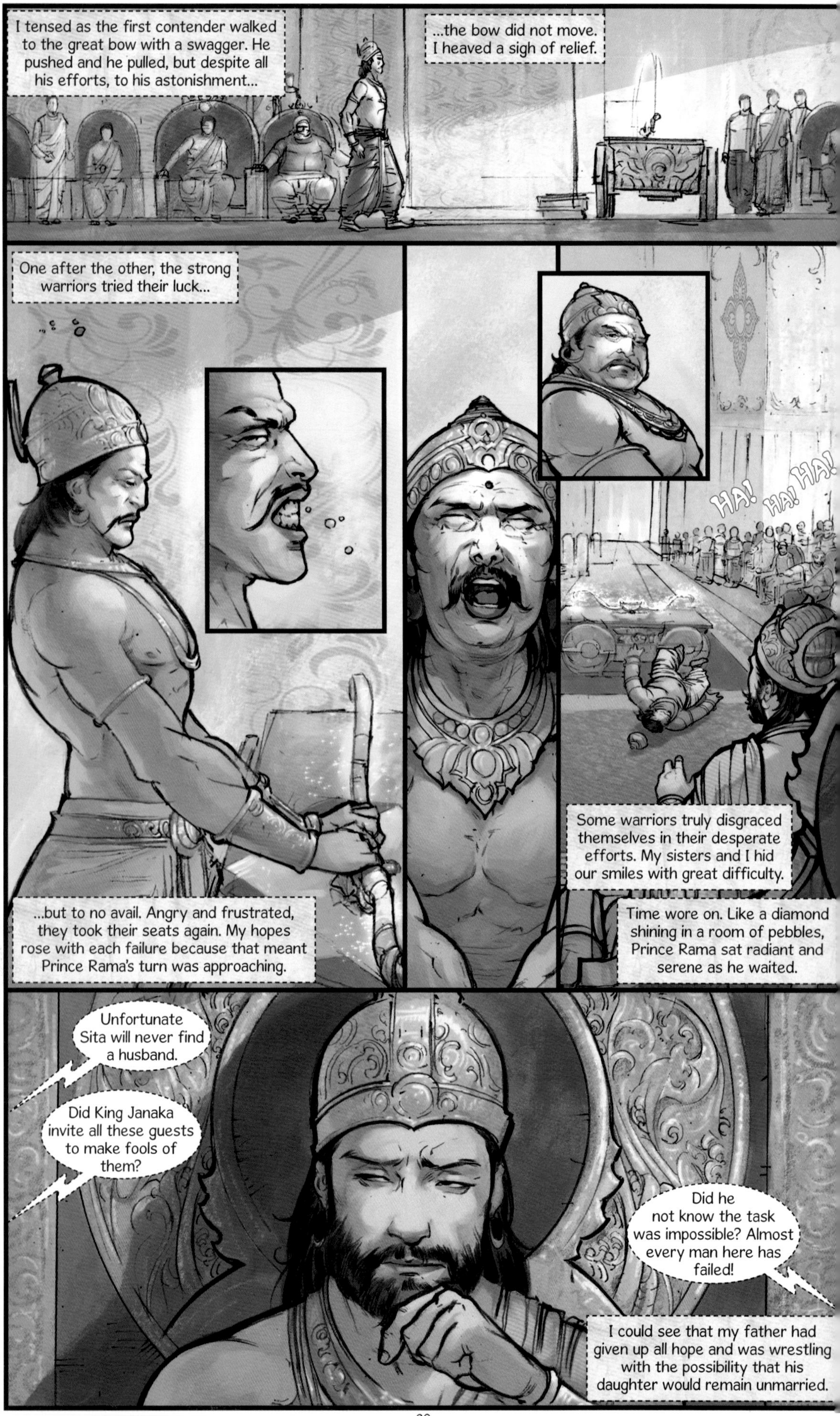

I tensed as the first contender walked to the great bow with a swagger. He pushed and he pulled, but despite all his efforts, to his astonishment...
...the bow did not move. I heaved a sigh of relief.
One after the other, the strong warriors tried their luck...
...but to no avail. Angry and frustrated, they took their seats again. My hopes rose with each failure because that meant Prince Rama's turn was approaching.
HA! HA! HA!
Some warriors truly disgraced themselves in their desperate efforts. My sisters and I hid our smiles with great difficulty.
Time wore on. Like a diamond shining in a room of pebbles, Prince Rama sat radiant and serene as he waited.
Unfortunate Sita will never find a husband.
Did King Janaka invite all these guests to make fools of them?
Did he not know the task was impossible? Almost every man here has failed!
I could see that my father had given up all hope and was wrestling with the possibility that his daughter would remain unmarried.

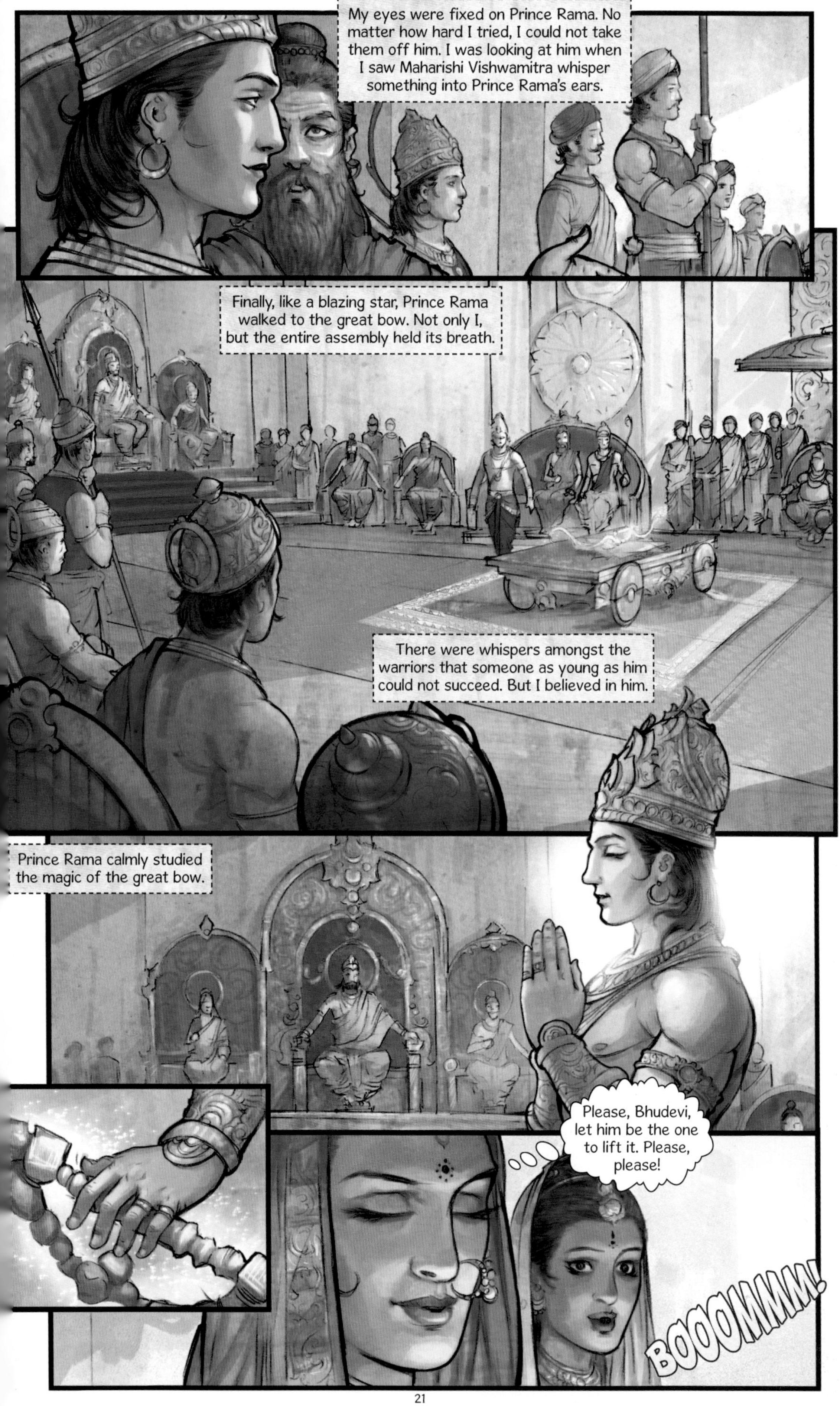
My eyes were fixed on Prince Rama. No matter how hard I tried, I could not take them off him. I was looking at him when I saw Maharishi Vishwamitra whisper something into Prince Rama's ears.
Finally, like a blazing star, Prince Rama walked to the great bow. Not only I, but the entire assembly held its breath.
There were whispers amongst the warriors that someone as young as him could not succeed. But I believed in him.
Prince Rama calmly studied the magic of the great bow.
Please, Bhudevi, let him be the one to lift it. Please, please!
BOOOMMM!

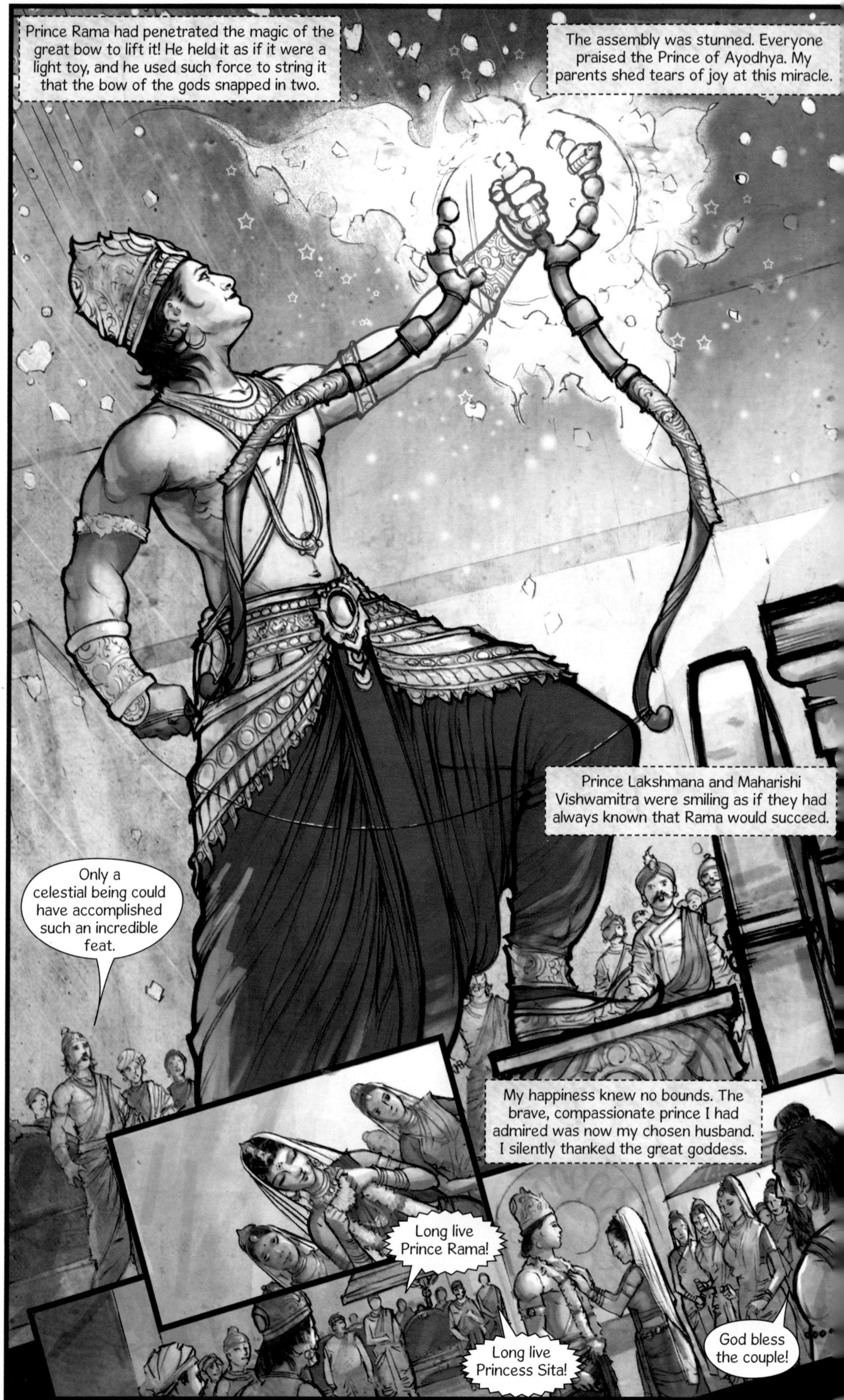
Prince Rama had penetrated the magic of the great bow to lift it! He held it as if it were a light toy, and he used such force to string it that the bow of the gods snapped in two.
The assembly was stunned. Everyone praised the Prince of Ayodhya. My parents shed tears of joy at this miracle.
Prince Lakshmana and Maharishi Vishwamitra were smiling as if they had always known that Rama would succeed.
Only a celestial being could have accomplished such an incredible feat.
My happiness knew no bounds. The brave, compassionate prince I had admired was now my chosen husband. I silently thanked the great goddess.
Long live Prince Rama!
Long live Princess Sita!
God bless the couple!

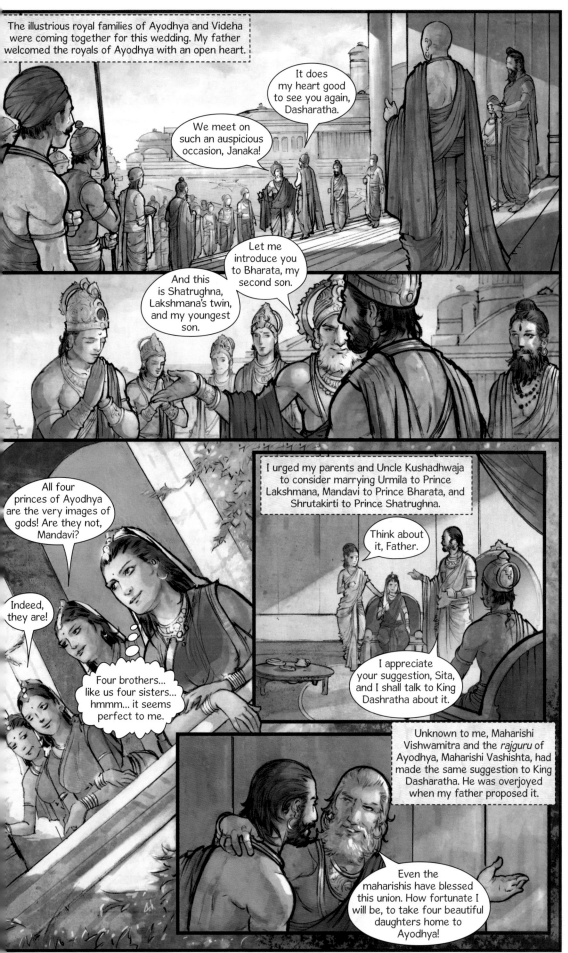

The illustrious royal families of Ayodhya and Videha were coming together for this wedding. My father welcomed the royals of Ayodhya with an open heart.

It does my heart good to see you again, Dasharatha.

We meet on such an auspicious occasion, Janaka!

Let me introduce you to Bharata, my second son.

And this is Shatrughna, Lakshmana's twin, and my youngest son.

All four princes of Ayodhya are the very images of gods! Are they not, Mandavi?

Indeed, they are!

Four brothers... like us four sisters... hmmm... it seems perfect to me.

I urged my parents and Uncle Kushadhwaja to consider marrying Urmila to Prince Lakshmana, Mandavi to Prince Bharata, and Shrutakirti to Prince Shatrughna.

Think about it, Father.

I appreciate your suggestion, Sita, and I shall talk to King Dashratha about it.

Unknown to me, Maharishi Vishwamitra and the *rajguru* of Ayodhya, Maharishi Vashishta, had made the same suggestion to King Dasharatha. He was overjoyed when my father proposed it.

Even the maharishis have blessed this union. How fortunate I will be, to take four beautiful daughters home to Ayodhya!

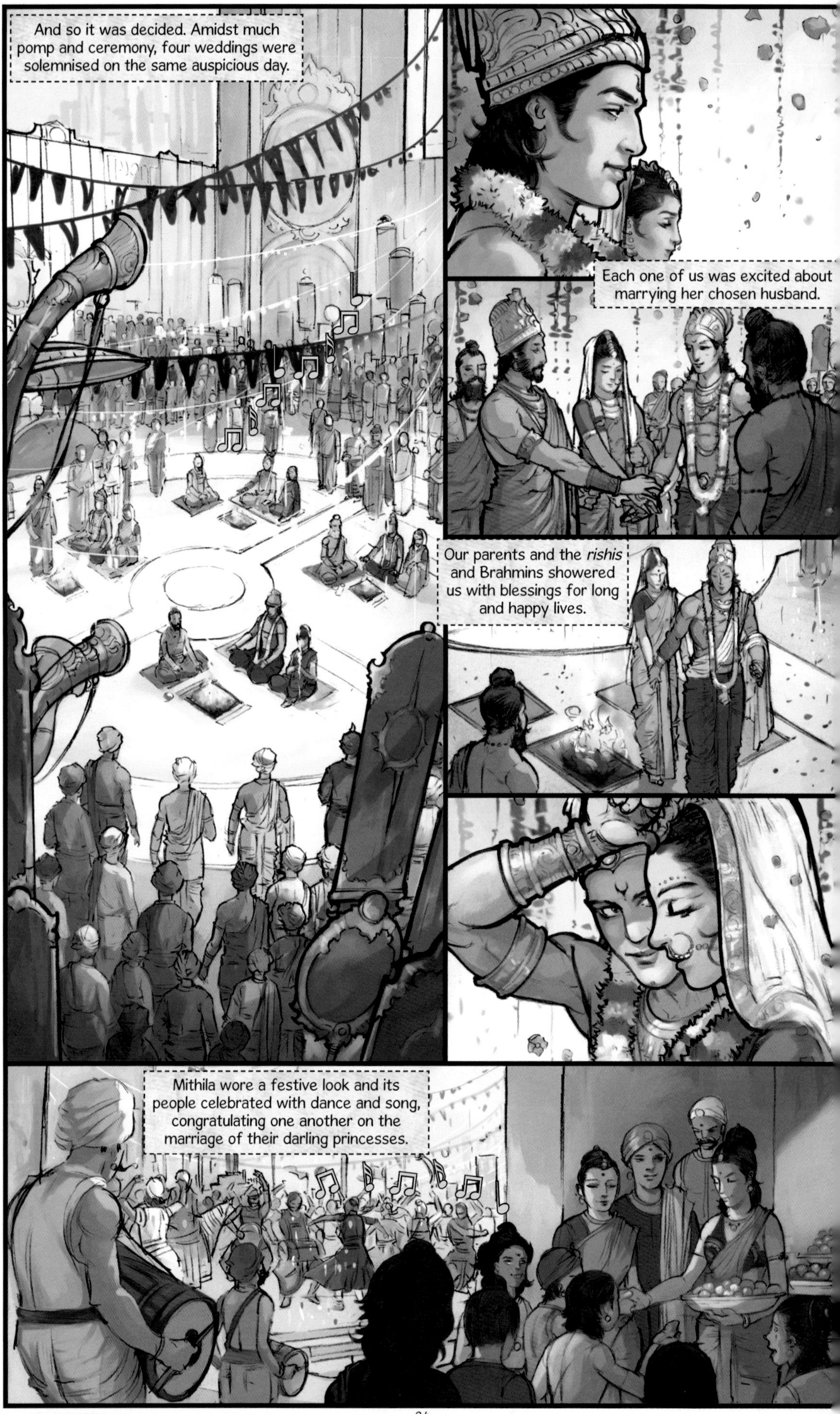
And so it was decided. Amidst much pomp and ceremony, four weddings were solemnised on the same auspicious day.
Each one of us was excited about marrying her chosen husband.
Our parents and the *rishis* and Brahmins showered us with blessings for long and happy lives.
Mithila wore a festive look and its people celebrated with dance and song, congratulating one another on the marriage of their darling princesses.

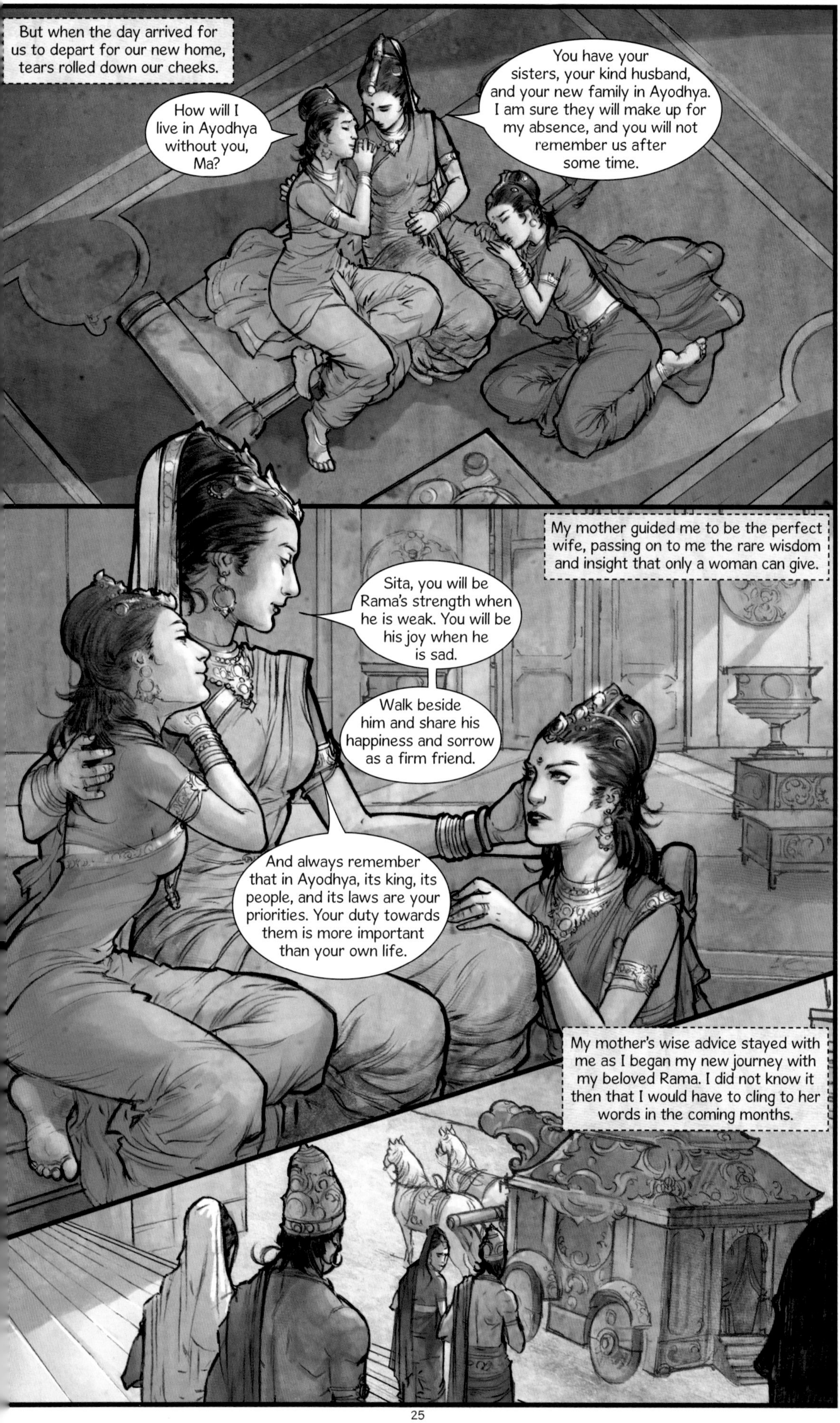
But when the day arrived for us to depart for our new home, tears rolled down our cheeks.
How will I live in Ayodhya without you, Ma?
You have your sisters, your kind husband, and your new family in Ayodhya. I am sure they will make up for my absence, and you will not remember us after some time.
My mother guided me to be the perfect wife, passing on to me the rare wisdom and insight that only a woman can give.
Sita, you will be Rama's strength when he is weak. You will be his joy when he is sad.
Walk beside him and share his happiness and sorrow as a firm friend.
And always remember that in Ayodhya, its king, its people, and its laws are your priorities. Your duty towards them is more important than your own life.
My mother's wise advice stayed with me as I began my new journey with my beloved Rama. I did not know it then that I would have to cling to her words in the coming months.

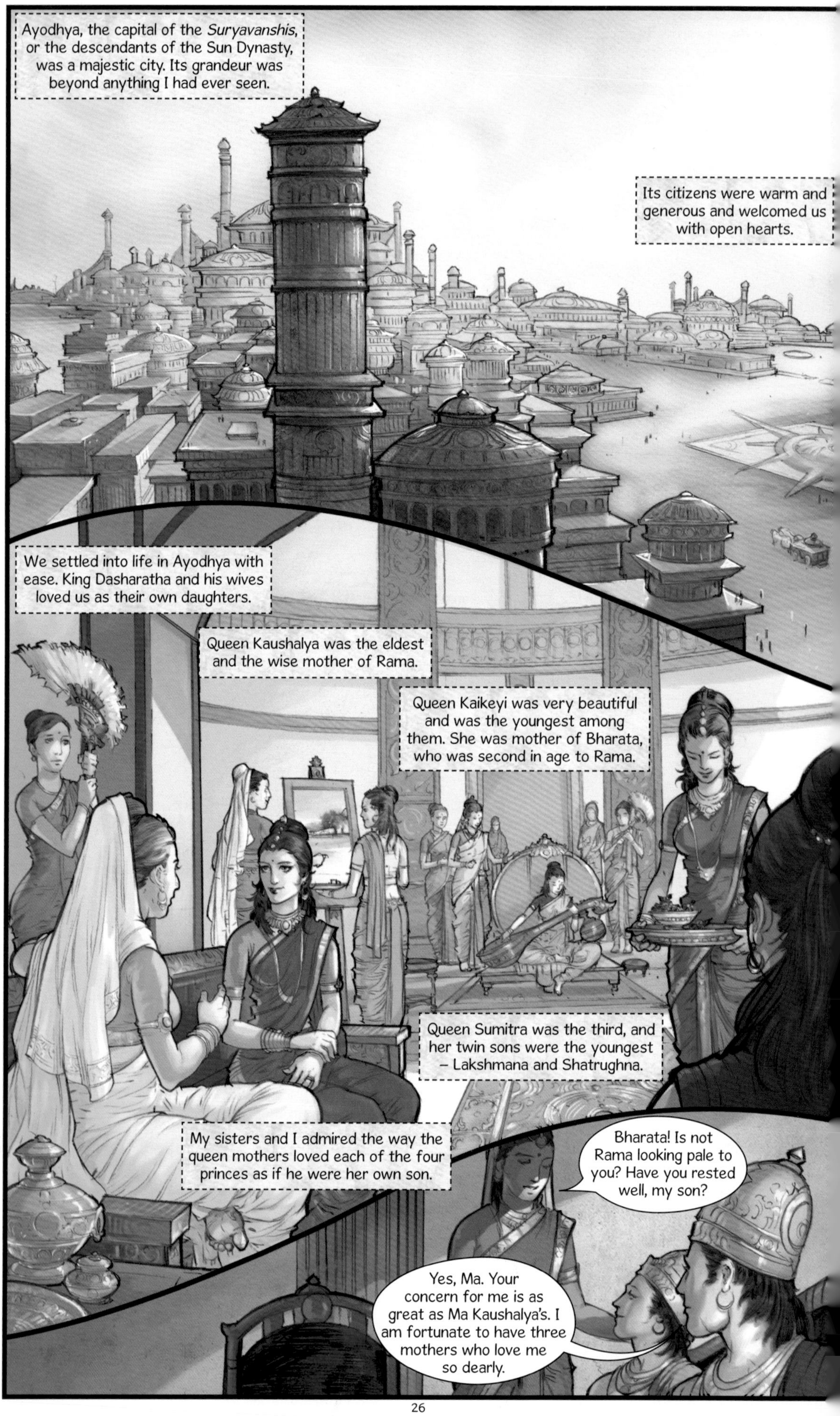
Ayodhya, the capital of the *Suryavanshis*, or the descendants of the Sun Dynasty, was a majestic city. Its grandeur was beyond anything I had ever seen.
Its citizens were warm and generous and welcomed us with open hearts.
We settled into life in Ayodhya with ease. King Dasharatha and his wives loved us as their own daughters.
Queen Kaushalya was the eldest and the wise mother of Rama.
Queen Kaikeyi was very beautiful and was the youngest among them. She was mother of Bharata, who was second in age to Rama.
Queen Sumitra was the third, and her twin sons were the youngest – Lakshmana and Shatrughna.
My sisters and I admired the way the queen mothers loved each of the four princes as if he were her own son.
Bharata! Is not Rama looking pale to you? Have you rested well, my son?
Yes, Ma. Your concern for me is as great as Ma Kaushalya's. I am fortunate to have three mothers who love me so dearly.

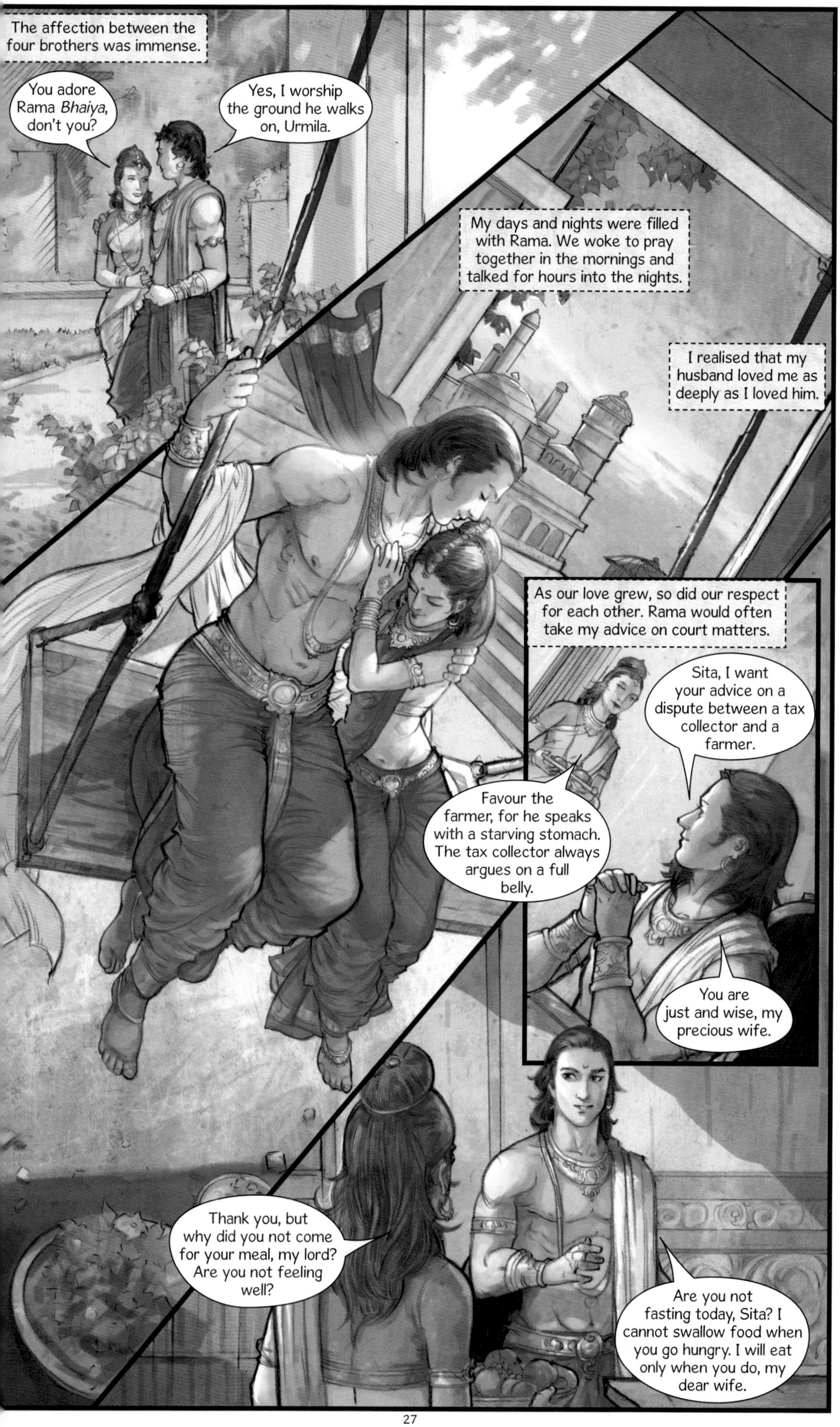
The affection between the four brothers was immense.
You adore Rama *Bhaiya*, don't you?
Yes, I worship the ground he walks on, Urmila.
My days and nights were filled with Rama. We woke to pray together in the mornings and talked for hours into the nights.
I realised that my husband loved me as deeply as I loved him.
As our love grew, so did our respect for each other. Rama would often take my advice on court matters.
Sita, I want your advice on a dispute between a tax collector and a farmer.
Favour the farmer, for he speaks with a starving stomach. The tax collector always argues on a full belly.
You are just and wise, my precious wife.
Thank you, but why did you not come for your meal, my lord? Are you not feeling well?
Are you not fasting today, Sita? I cannot swallow food when you go hungry. I will eat only when you do, my dear wife.

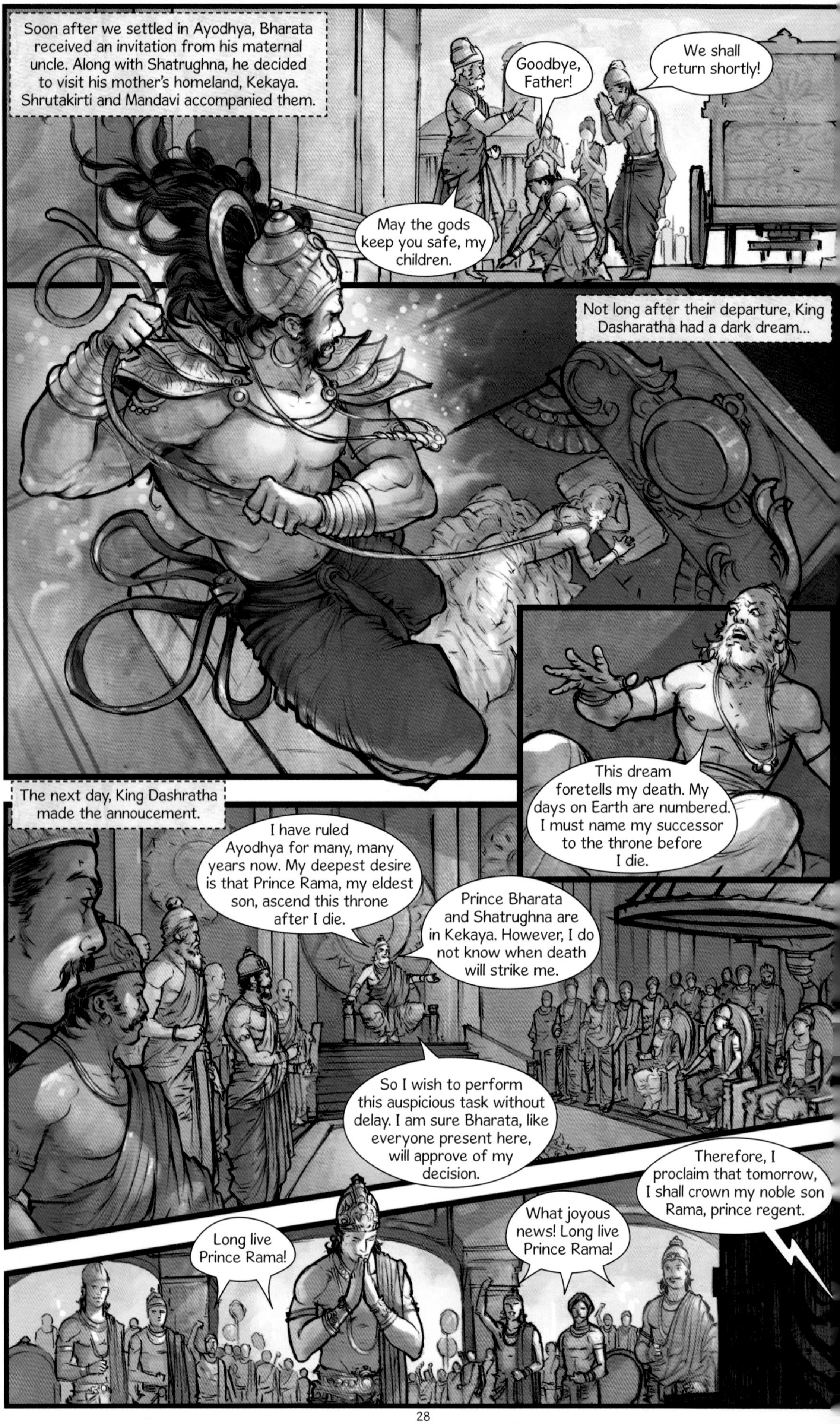

Soon after we settled in Ayodhya, Bharata received an invitation from his maternal uncle. Along with Shatrughna, he decided to visit his mother's homeland, Kekaya. Shrutakirti and Mandavi accompanied them.
Goodbye, Father!
We shall return shortly!
May the gods keep you safe, my children.
Not long after their departure, King Dasharatha had a dark dream...
This dream foretells my death. My days on Earth are numbered. I must name my successor to the throne before I die.
The next day, King Dashratha made the annoucement.
I have ruled Ayodhya for many, many years now. My deepest desire is that Prince Rama, my eldest son, ascend this throne after I die.
Prince Bharata and Shatrughna are in Kekaya. However, I do not know when death will strike me.
So I wish to perform this auspicious task without delay. I am sure Bharata, like everyone present here, will approve of my decision.
Therefore, I proclaim that tomorrow, I shall crown my noble son Rama, prince regent.
Long live Prince Rama!
What joyous news! Long live Prince Rama!

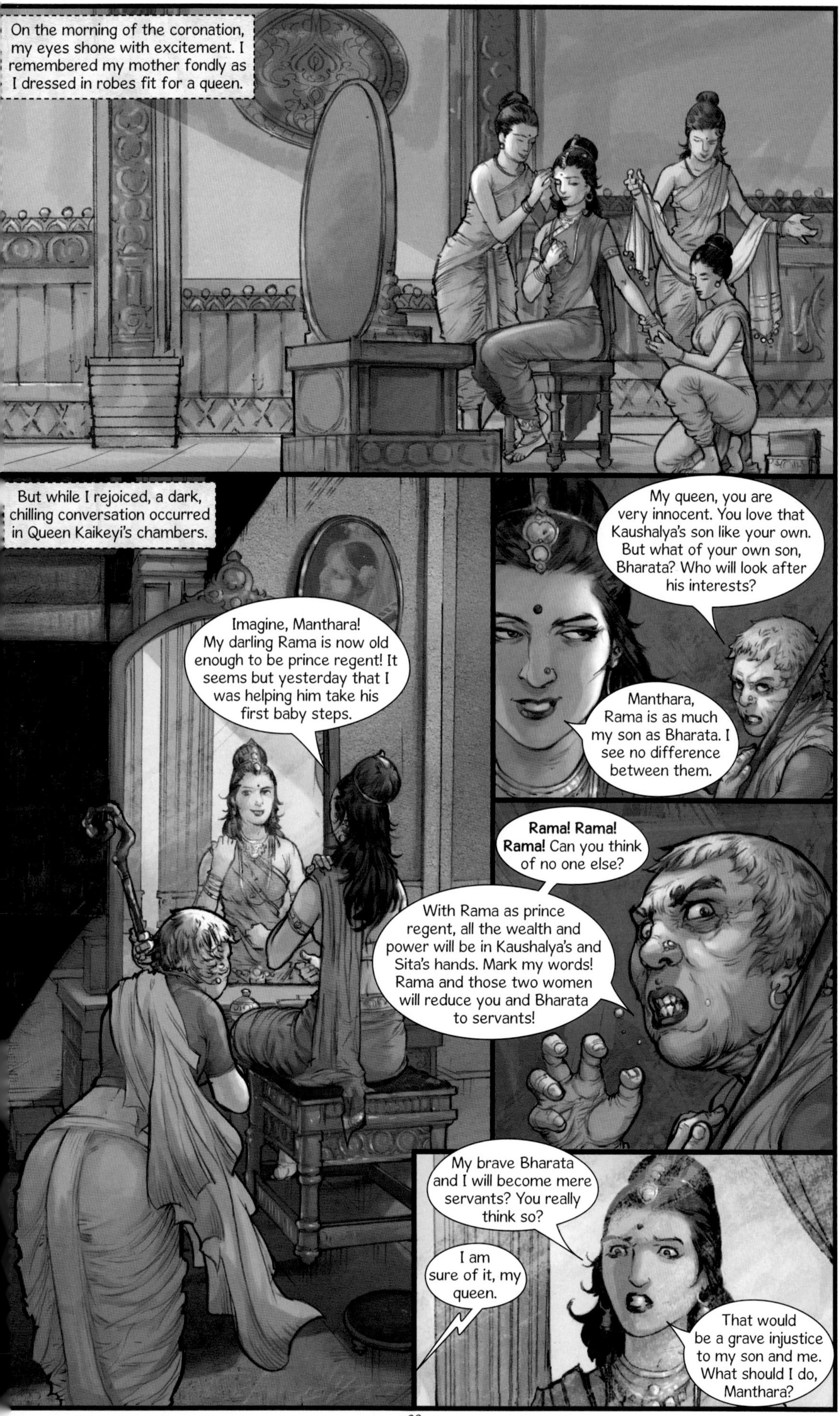
On the morning of the coronation, my eyes shone with excitement. I remembered my mother fondly as I dressed in robes fit for a queen.
But while I rejoiced, a dark, chilling conversation occurred in Queen Kaikeyi's chambers.
Imagine, Manthara! My darling Rama is now old enough to be prince regent! It seems but yesterday that I was helping him take his first baby steps.
My queen, you are very innocent. You love that Kaushalya's son like your own. But what of your own son, Bharata? Who will look after his interests?
Manthara, Rama is as much my son as Bharata. I see no difference between them.
Rama! Rama! Rama! Can you think of no one else?
With Rama as prince regent, all the wealth and power will be in Kaushalya's and Sita's hands. Mark my words! Rama and those two women will reduce you and Bharata to servants!
My brave Bharata and I will become mere servants? You really think so?
I am sure of it, my queen.
That would be a grave injustice to my son and me. What should I do, Manthara?

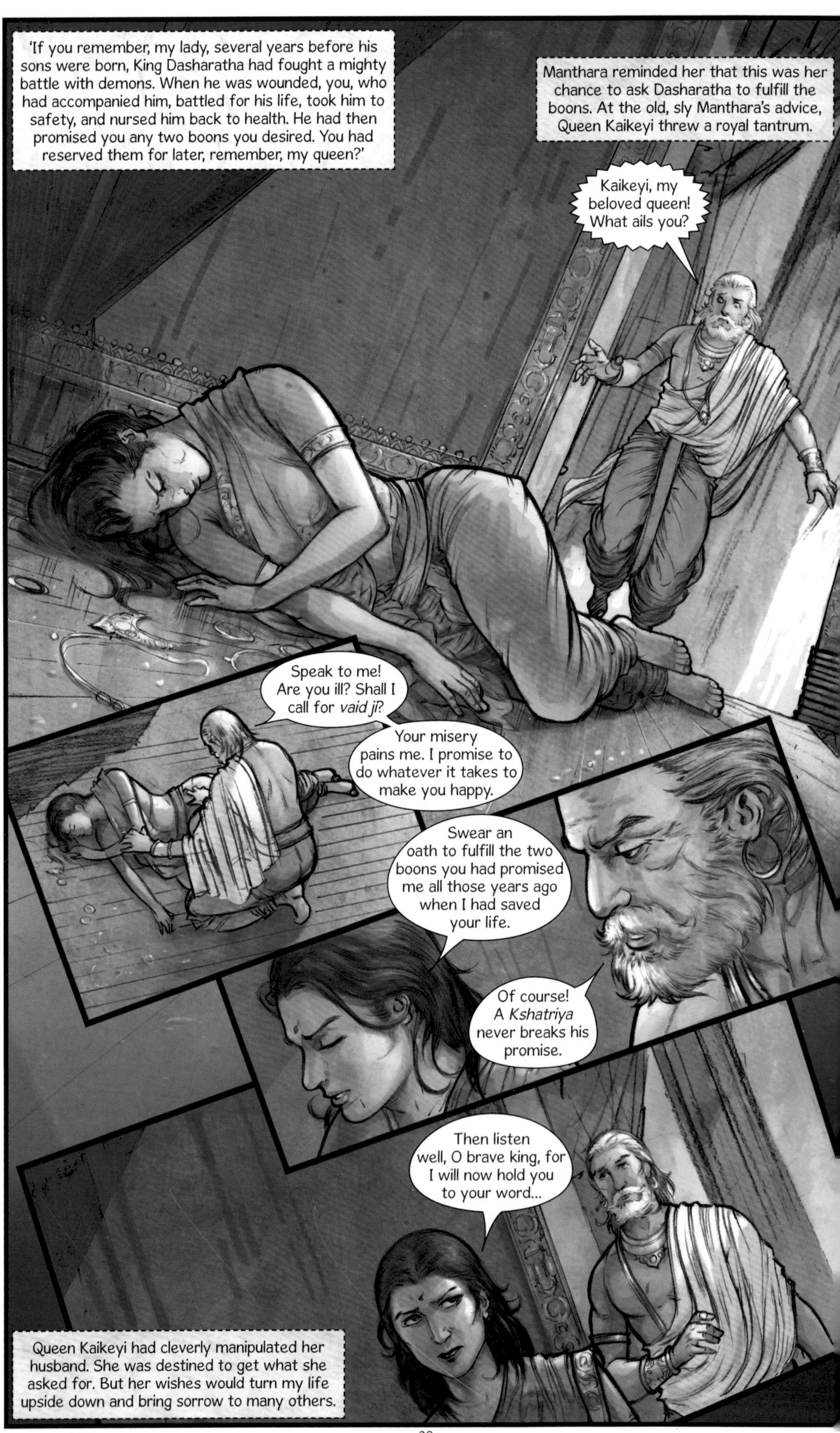

'If you remember, my lady, several years before his sons were born, King Dasharatha had fought a mighty battle with demons. When he was wounded, you, who had accompanied him, battled for his life, took him to safety, and nursed him back to health. He had then promised you any two boons you desired. You had reserved them for later, remember, my queen?'
Manthara reminded her that this was her chance to ask Dasharatha to fulfill the boons. At the old, sly Manthara's advice, Queen Kaikeyi threw a royal tantrum.
Kaikeyi, my beloved queen! What ails you?
Speak to me! Are you ill? Shall I call for *vaid ji*?
Your misery pains me. I promise to do whatever it takes to make you happy.
Swear an oath to fulfill the two boons you had promised me all those years ago when I had saved your life.
Of course! A *Kshatriya* never breaks his promise.
Then listen well, O brave king, for I will now hold you to your word...
Queen Kaikeyi had cleverly manipulated her husband. She was destined to get what she asked for. But her wishes would turn my life upside down and bring sorrow to many others.

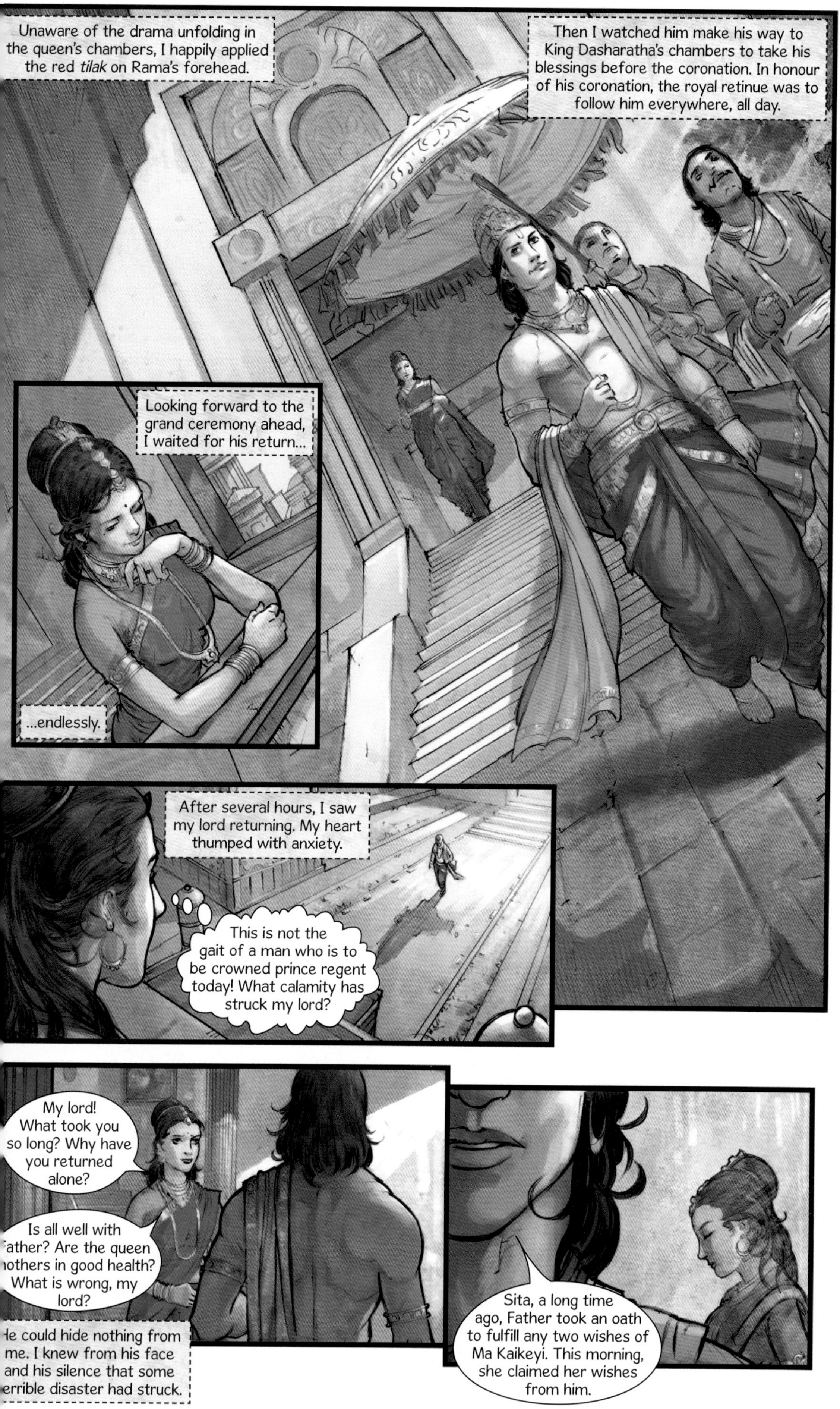

Unaware of the drama unfolding in the queen's chambers, I happily applied the red *tilak* on Rama's forehead.
Then I watched him make his way to King Dasharatha's chambers to take his blessings before the coronation. In honour of his coronation, the royal retinue was to follow him everywhere, all day.
Looking forward to the grand ceremony ahead, I waited for his return...
...endlessly.
After several hours, I saw my lord returning. My heart thumped with anxiety.
This is not the gait of a man who is to be crowned prince regent today! What calamity has struck my lord?
My lord! What took you so long? Why have you returned alone?
Is all well with Father? Are the queen mothers in good health? What is wrong, my lord?
He could hide nothing from me. I knew from his face and his silence that some terrible disaster had struck.
Sita, a long time ago, Father took an oath to fulfill any two wishes of Ma Kaikeyi. This morning, she claimed her wishes from him.

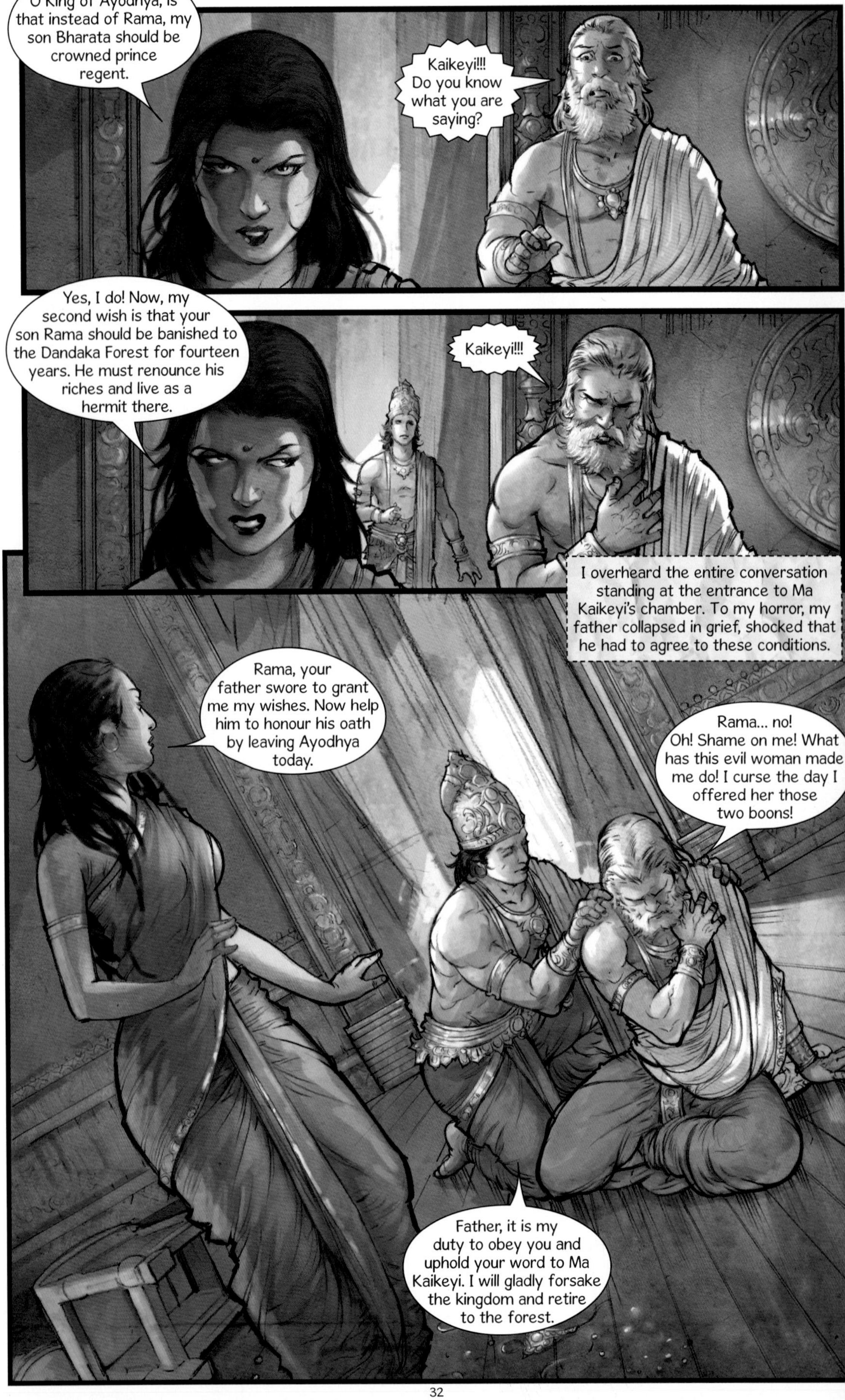

My first wish, O King of Ayodhya, is that instead of Rama, my son Bharata should be crowned prince regent.
Kaikeyi!!! Do you know what you are saying?
Yes, I do! Now, my second wish is that your son Rama should be banished to the Dandaka Forest for fourteen years. He must renounce his riches and live as a hermit there.
Kaikeyi!!!
I overheard the entire conversation standing at the entrance to Ma Kaikeyi's chamber. To my horror, my father collapsed in grief, shocked that he had to agree to these conditions.
Rama, your father swore to grant me my wishes. Now help him to honour his oath by leaving Ayodhya today.
Rama... no! Oh! Shame on me! What has this evil woman made me do! I curse the day I offered her those two boons!
Father, it is my duty to obey you and uphold your word to Ma Kaikeyi. I will gladly forsake the kingdom and retire to the forest.

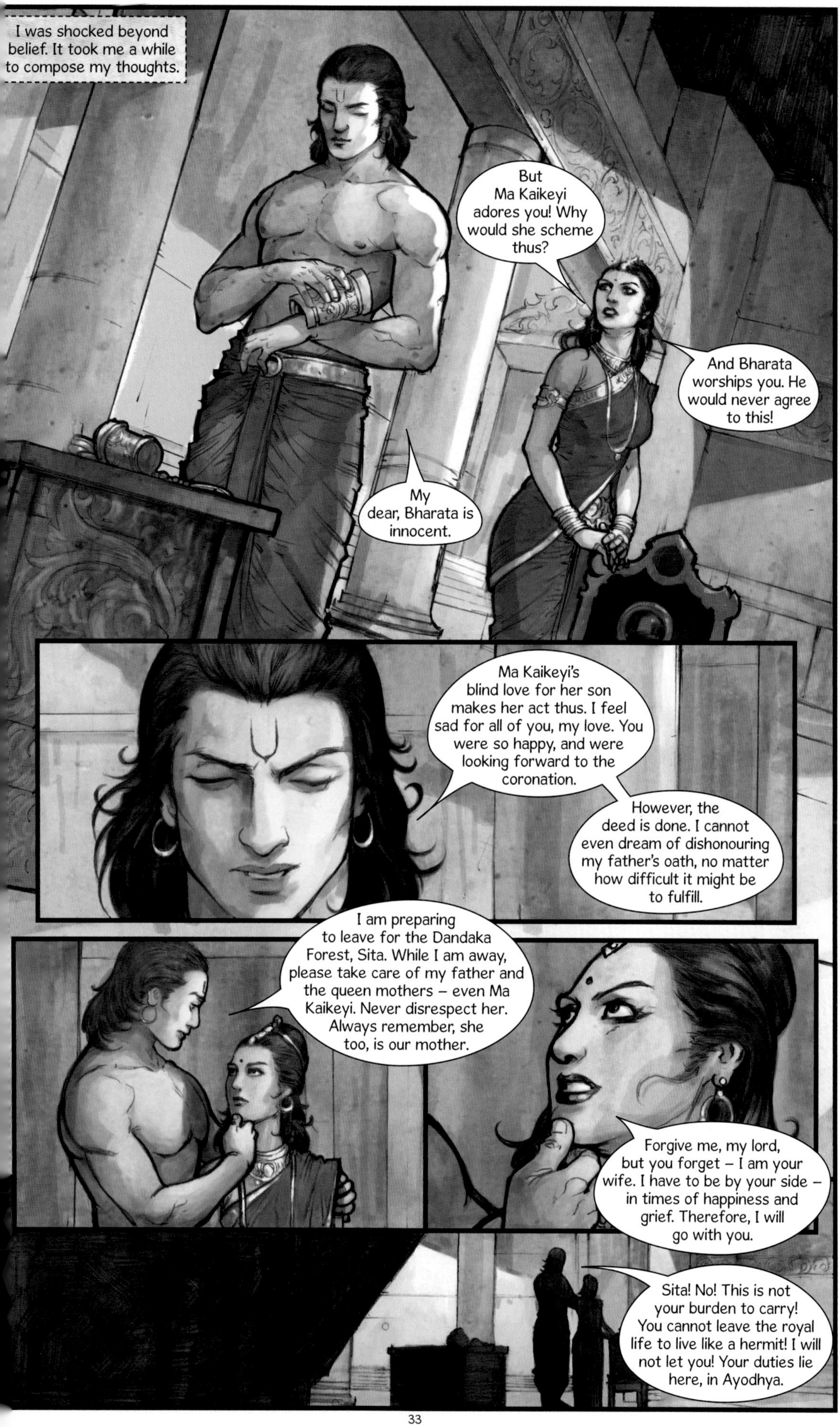
I was shocked beyond belief. It took me a while to compose my thoughts.
But Ma Kaikeyi adores you! Why would she scheme thus?
And Bharata worships you. He would never agree to this!
My dear, Bharata is innocent.
Ma Kaikeyi's blind love for her son makes her act thus. I feel sad for all of you, my love. You were so happy, and were looking forward to the coronation.
However, the deed is done. I cannot even dream of dishonouring my father's oath, no matter how difficult it might be to fulfill.
I am preparing to leave for the Dandaka Forest, Sita. While I am away, please take care of my father and the queen mothers – even Ma Kaikeyi. Never disrespect her. Always remember, she too, is our mother.
Forgive me, my lord, but you forget – I am your wife. I have to be by your side – in times of happiness and grief. Therefore, I will go with you.
Sita! No! This is not your burden to carry! You cannot leave the royal life to live like a hermit! I will not let you! Your duties lie here, in Ayodhya.

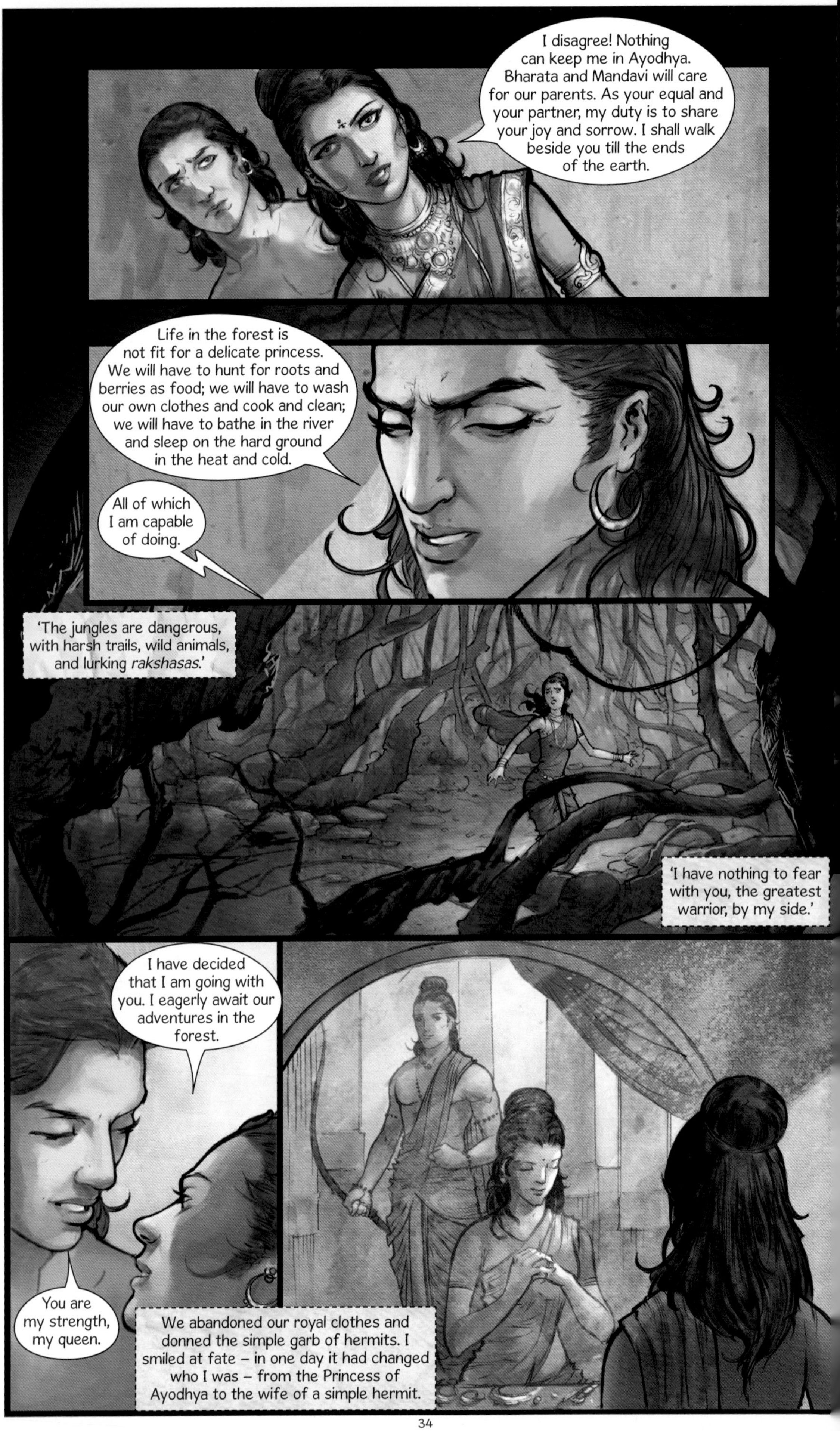
I disagree! Nothing can keep me in Ayodhya. Bharata and Mandavi will care for our parents. As your equal and your partner, my duty is to share your joy and sorrow. I shall walk beside you till the ends of the earth.
Life in the forest is not fit for a delicate princess. We will have to hunt for roots and berries as food; we will have to wash our own clothes and cook and clean; we will have to bathe in the river and sleep on the hard ground in the heat and cold.
All of which I am capable of doing.
'The jungles are dangerous, with harsh trails, wild animals, and lurking *rakshasas*.'
'I have nothing to fear with you, the greatest warrior, by my side.'
I have decided that I am going with you. I eagerly await our adventures in the forest.
You are my strength, my queen.
We abandoned our royal clothes and donned the simple garb of hermits. I smiled at fate – in one day it had changed who I was – from the Princess of Ayodhya to the wife of a simple hermit.

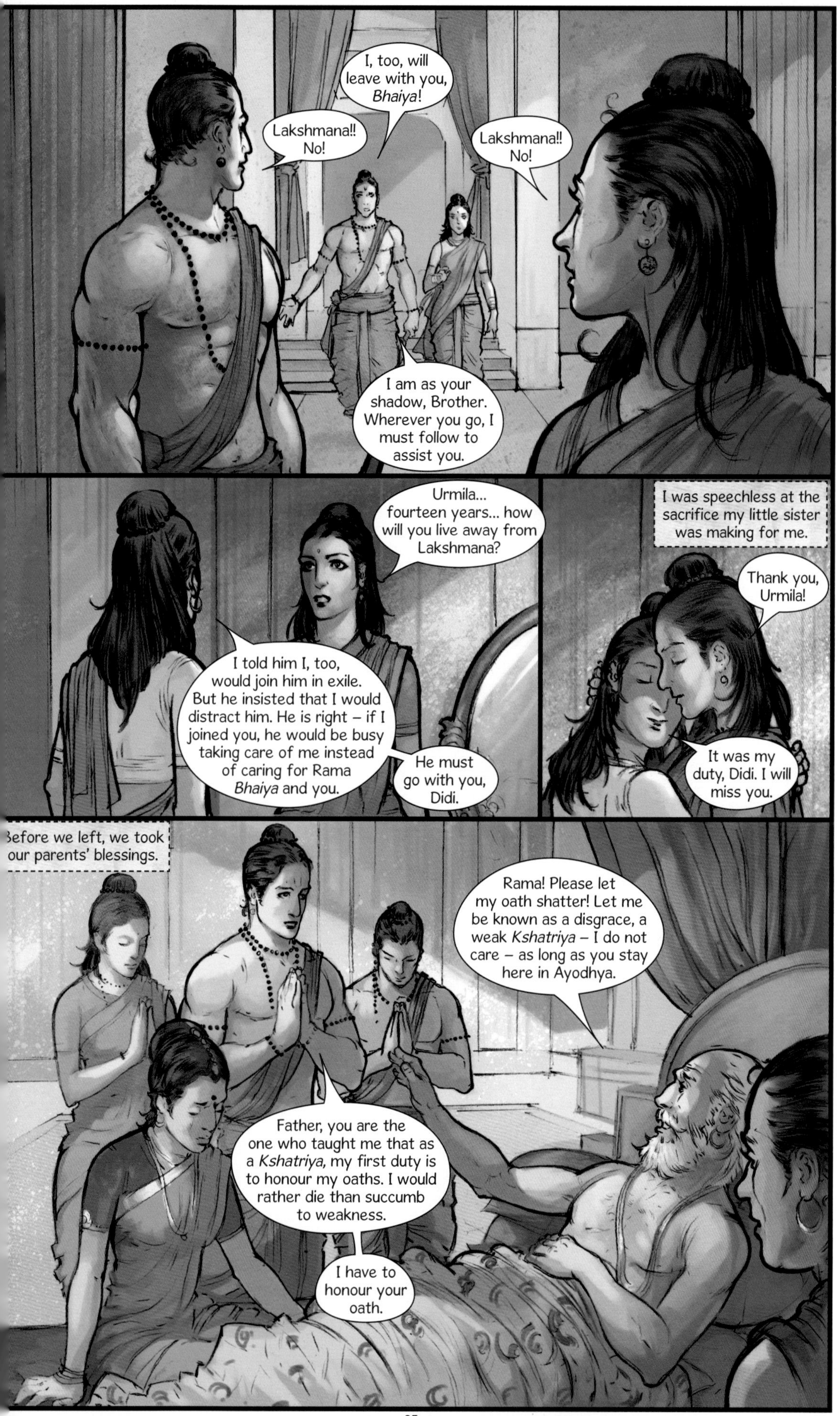
I, too, will leave with you, *Bhaiya*!
Lakshmana!! No!
Lakshmana!! No!
I am as your shadow, Brother. Wherever you go, I must follow to assist you.
Urmila... fourteen years... how will you live away from Lakshmana?
I told him I, too, would join him in exile. But he insisted that I would distract him. He is right – if I joined you, he would be busy taking care of me instead of caring for Rama *Bhaiya* and you.
He must go with you, Didi.
I was speechless at the sacrifice my little sister was making for me.
Thank you, Urmila!
It was my duty, Didi. I will miss you.
Before we left, we took our parents' blessings.
Rama! Please let my oath shatter! Let me be known as a disgrace, a weak *Kshatriya* – I do not care – as long as you stay here in Ayodhya.
Father, you are the one who taught me that as a *Kshatriya,* my first duty is to honour my oaths. I would rather die than succumb to weakness.
I have to honour your oath.

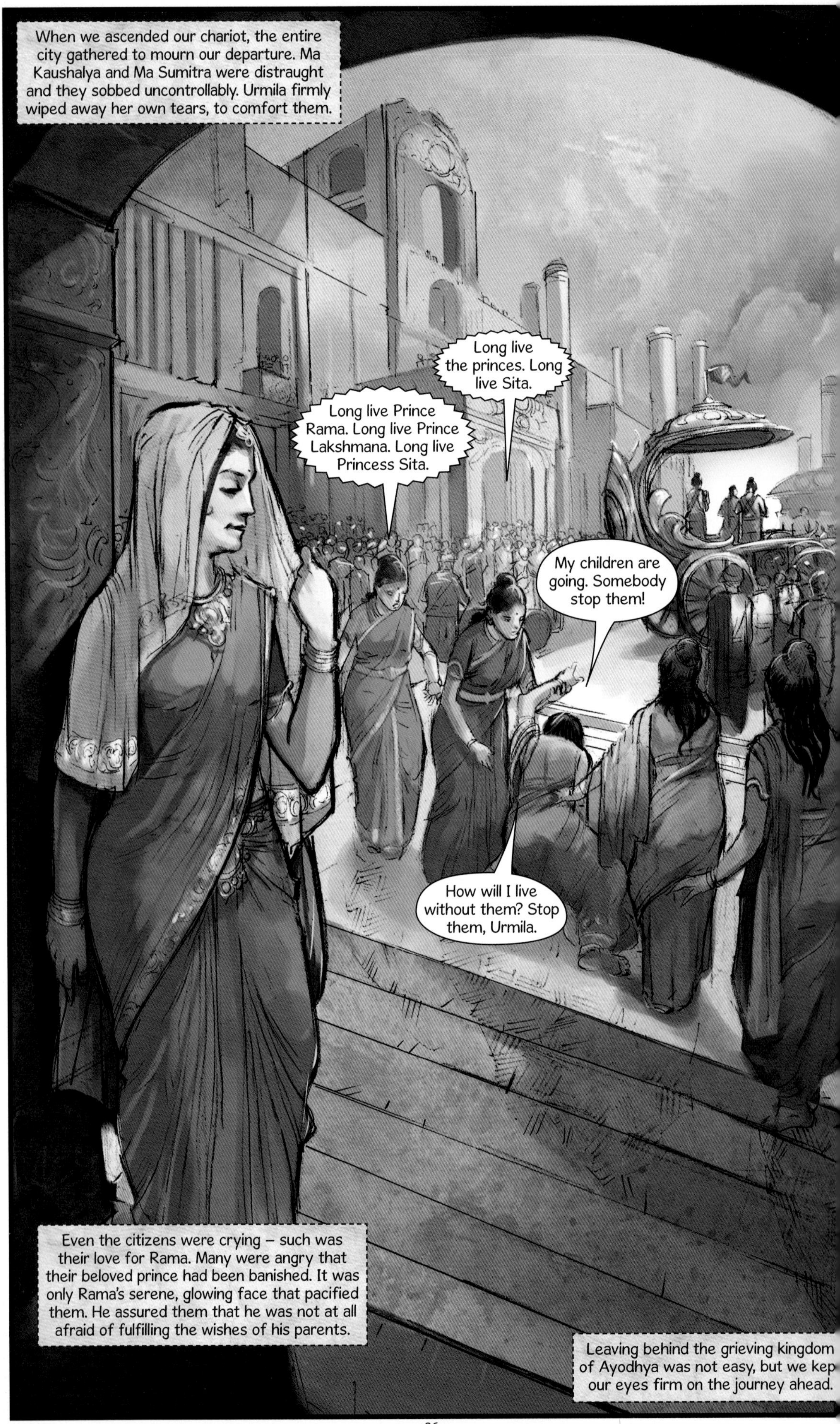
When we ascended our chariot, the entire city gathered to mourn our departure. Ma Kaushalya and Ma Sumitra were distraught and they sobbed uncontrollably. Urmila firmly wiped away her own tears, to comfort them.
Long live the princes. Long live Sita.
Long live Prince Rama. Long live Prince Lakshmana. Long live Princess Sita.
My children are going. Somebody stop them!
How will I live without them? Stop them, Urmila.
Even the citizens were crying – such was their love for Rama. Many were angry that their beloved prince had been banished. It was only Rama's serene, glowing face that pacified them. He assured them that he was not at all afraid of fulfilling the wishes of his parents.
Leaving behind the grieving kingdom of Ayodhya was not easy, but we kep our eyes firm on the journey ahead.

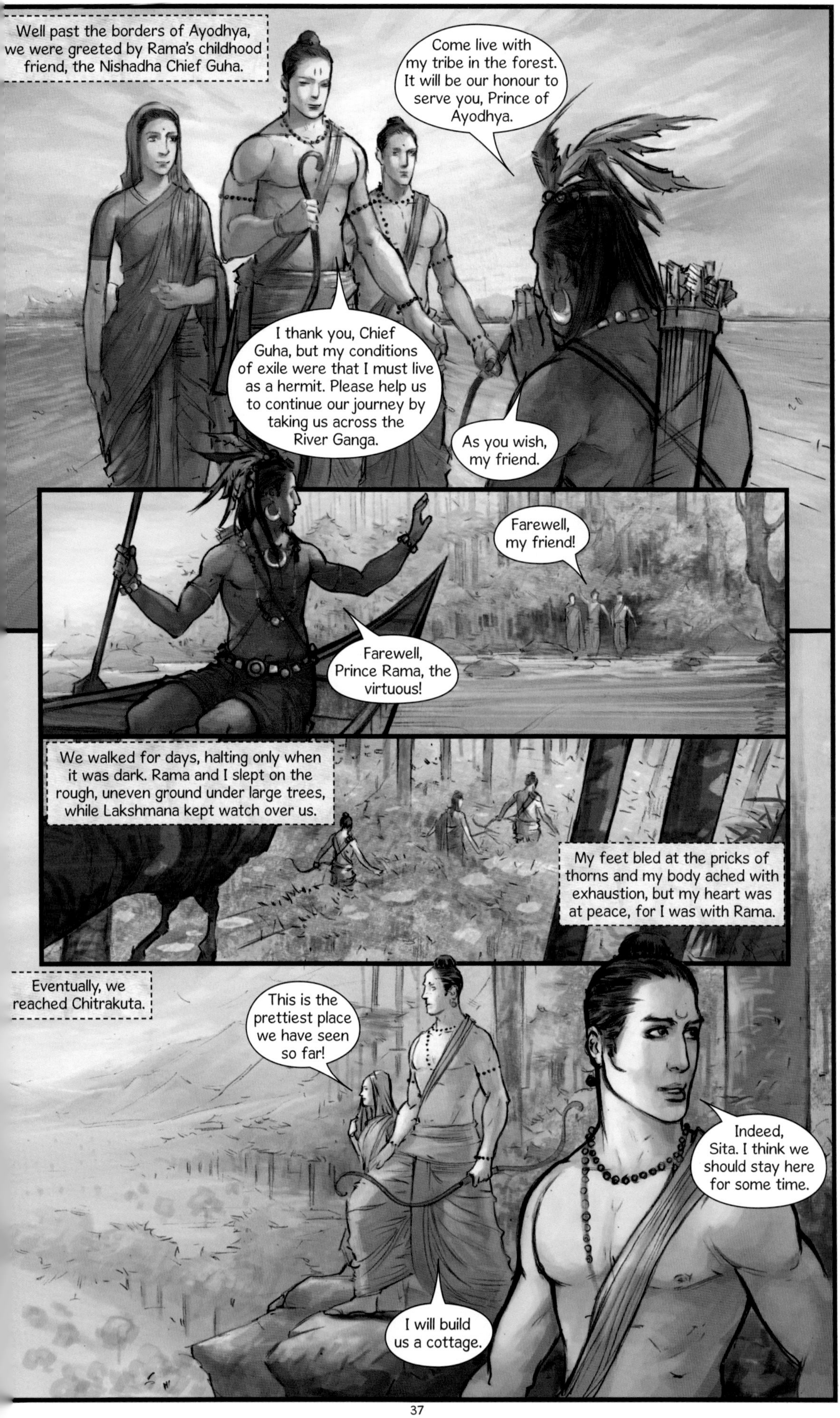

Well past the borders of Ayodhya, we were greeted by Rama's childhood friend, the Nishadha Chief Guha.
Come live with my tribe in the forest. It will be our honour to serve you, Prince of Ayodhya.
I thank you, Chief Guha, but my conditions of exile were that I must live as a hermit. Please help us to continue our journey by taking us across the River Ganga.
As you wish, my friend.
Farewell, my friend!
Farewell, Prince Rama, the virtuous!
We walked for days, halting only when it was dark. Rama and I slept on the rough, uneven ground under large trees, while Lakshmana kept watch over us.
My feet bled at the pricks of thorns and my body ached with exhaustion, but my heart was at peace, for I was with Rama.
Eventually, we reached Chitrakuta.
This is the prettiest place we have seen so far!
Indeed, Sita. I think we should stay here for some time.
I will build us a cottage.

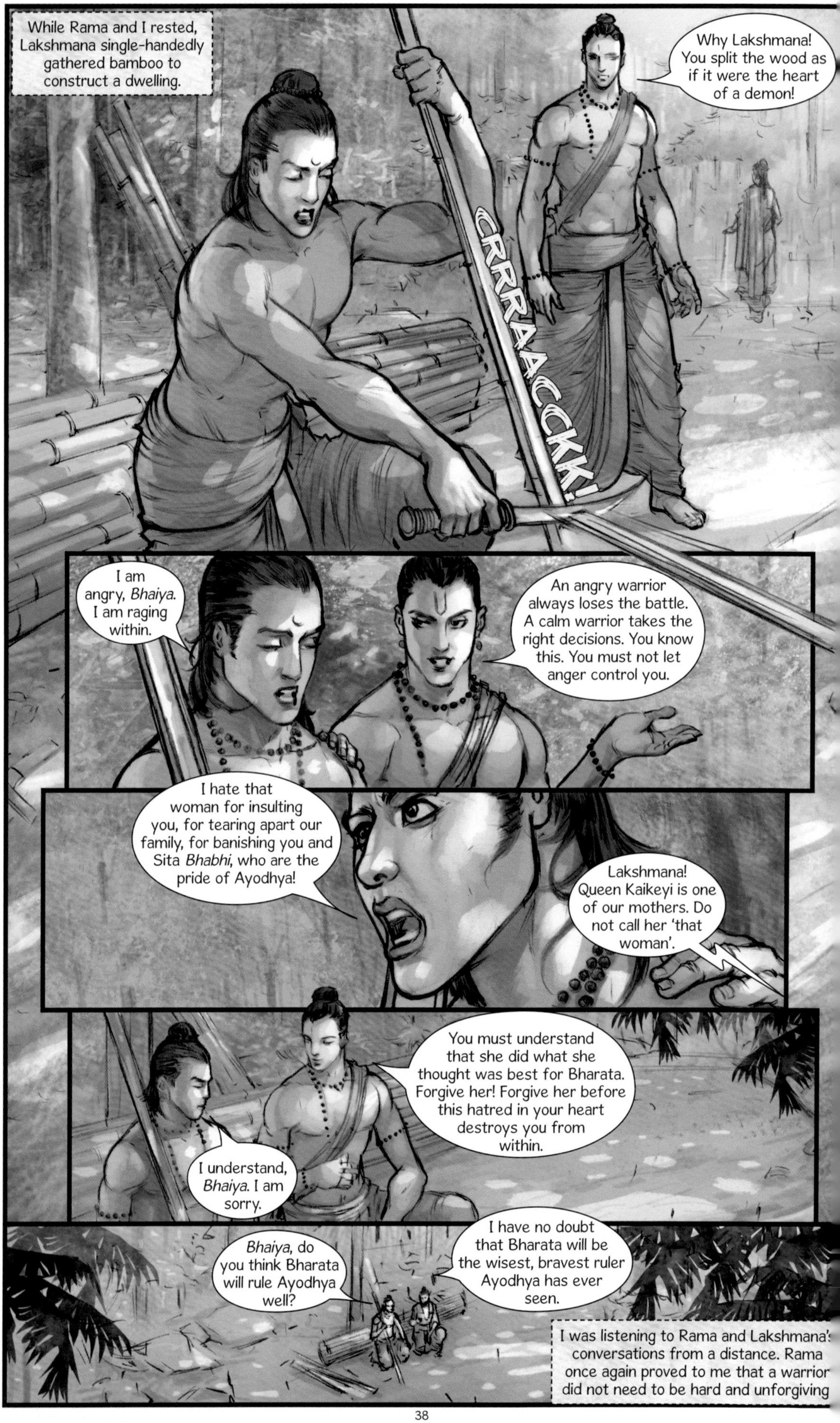

While Rama and I rested, Lakshmana single-handedly gathered bamboo to construct a dwelling.
Why Lakshmana! You split the wood as if it were the heart of a demon!
CRRRAACCKK!
I am angry, *Bhaiya*. I am raging within.
An angry warrior always loses the battle. A calm warrior takes the right decisions. You know this. You must not let anger control you.
I hate that woman for insulting you, for tearing apart our family, for banishing you and Sita *Bhabhi*, who are the pride of Ayodhya!
Lakshmana! Queen Kaikeyi is one of our mothers. Do not call her 'that woman'.
You must understand that she did what she thought was best for Bharata. Forgive her! Forgive her before this hatred in your heart destroys you from within.
I understand, *Bhaiya*. I am sorry.
Bhaiya, do you think Bharata will rule Ayodhya well?
I have no doubt that Bharata will be the wisest, bravest ruler Ayodhya has ever seen.
I was listening to Rama and Lakshmana's conversations from a distance. Rama once again proved to me that a warrior did not need to be hard and unforgiving

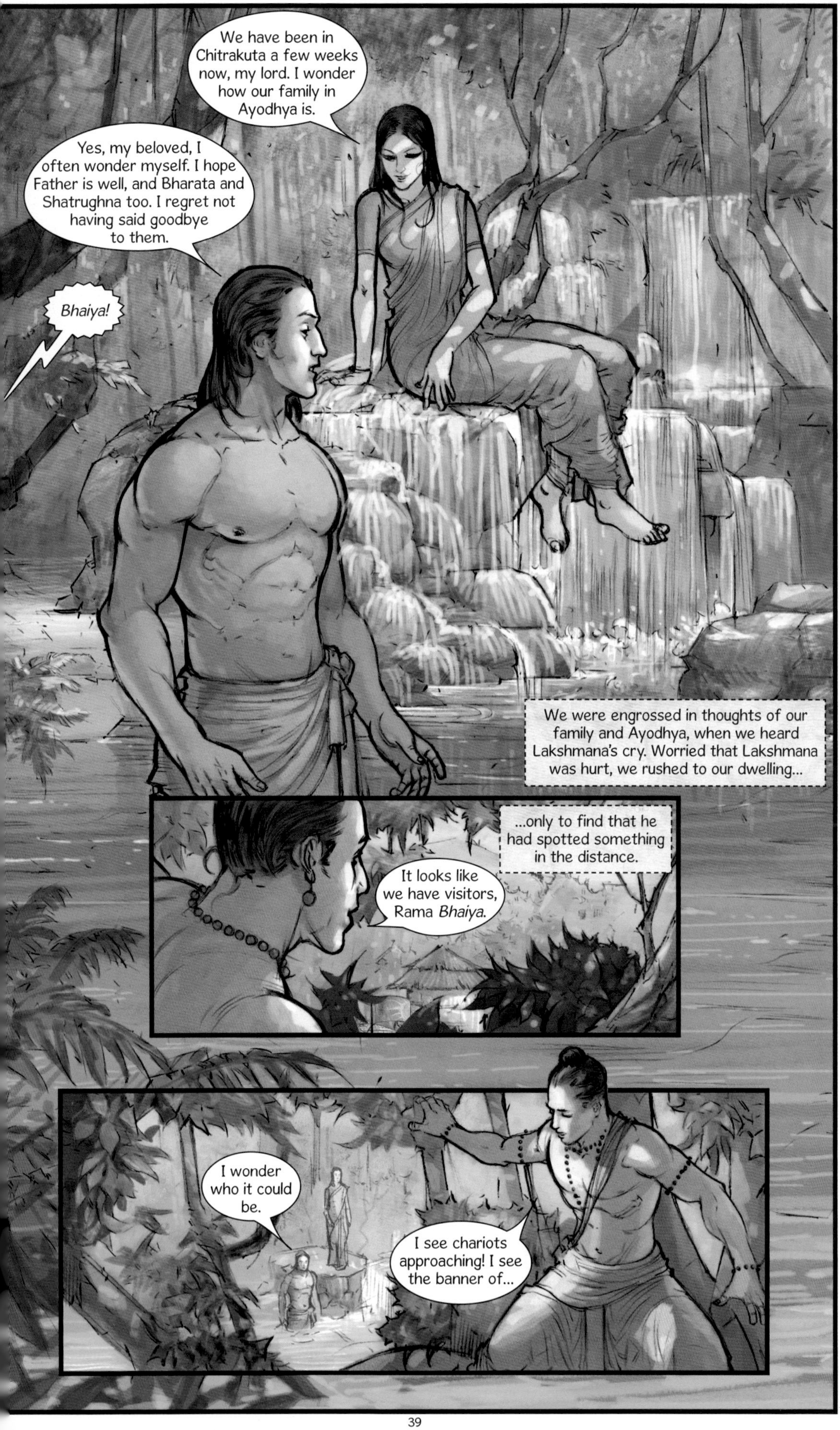

We have been in Chitrakuta a few weeks now, my lord. I wonder how our family in Ayodhya is.
Yes, my beloved, I often wonder myself. I hope Father is well, and Bharata and Shatrughna too. I regret not having said goodbye to them.
Bhaiya!
We were engrossed in thoughts of our family and Ayodhya, when we heard Lakshmana's cry. Worried that Lakshmana was hurt, we rushed to our dwelling...
...only to find that he had spotted something in the distance.
It looks like we have visitors, Rama *Bhaiya*.
I wonder who it could be.
I see chariots approaching! I see the banner of...

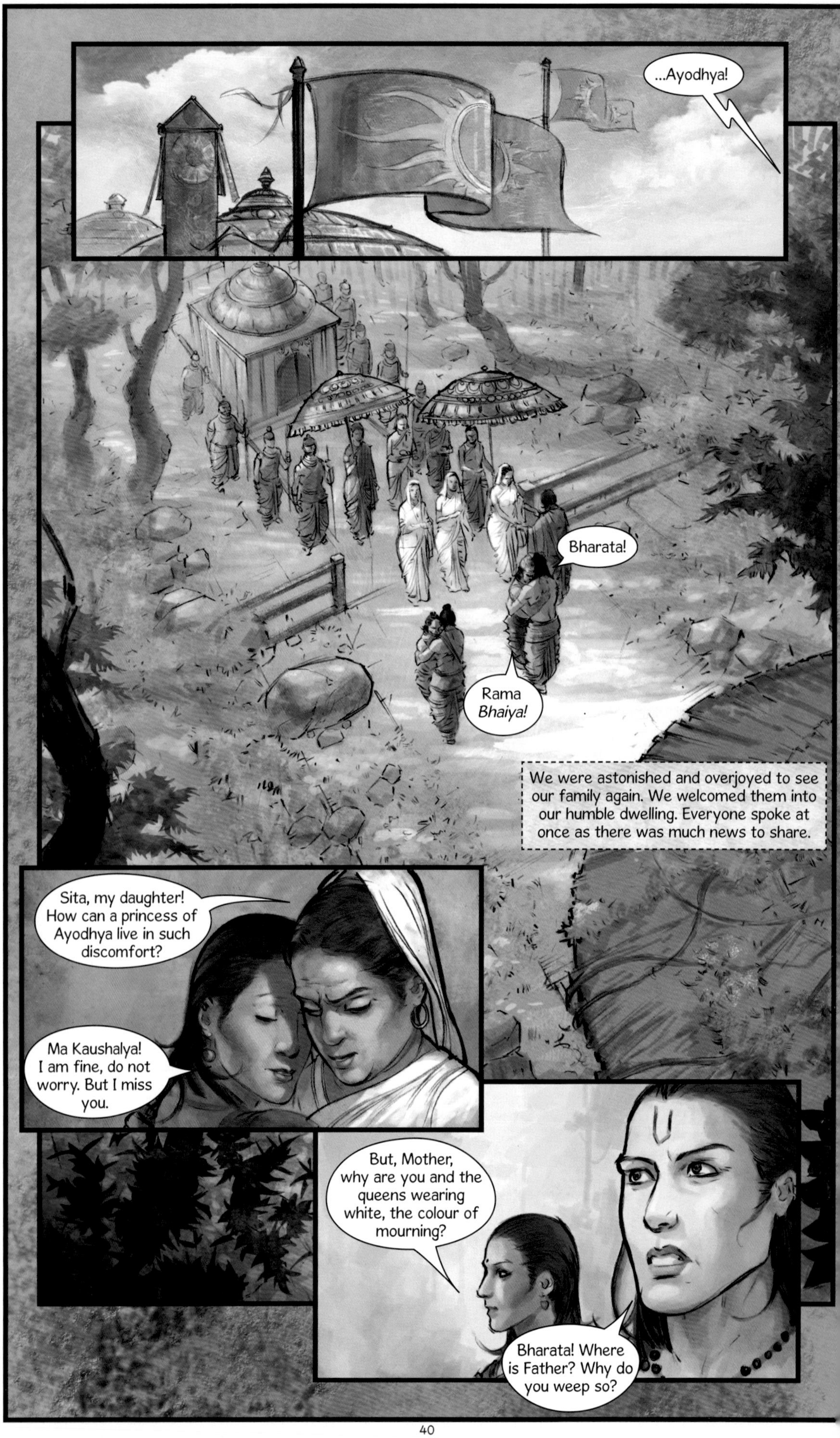

...Ayodhya!
Bharata!
Rama *Bhaiya!*
We were astonished and overjoyed to see our family again. We welcomed them into our humble dwelling. Everyone spoke at once as there was much news to share.
Sita, my daughter! How can a princess of Ayodhya live in such discomfort?
Ma Kaushalya! I am fine, do not worry. But I miss you.
But, Mother, why are you and the queens wearing white, the colour of mourning?
Bharata! Where is Father? Why do you weep so?

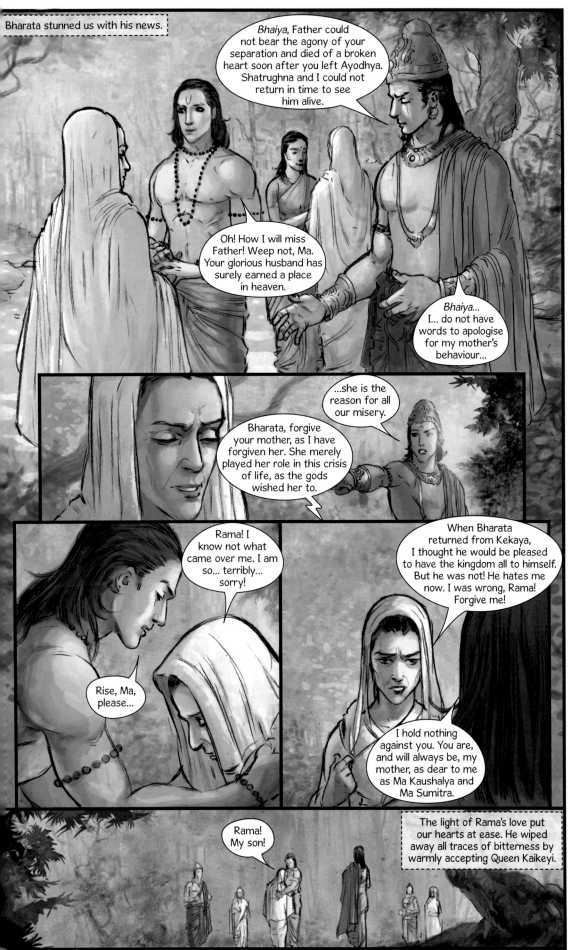

Bharata stunned us with his news.

Bhaiya, Father could not bear the agony of your separation and died of a broken heart soon after you left Ayodhya. Shatrughna and I could not return in time to see him alive.

Oh! How I will miss Father! Weep not, Ma. Your glorious husband has surely earned a place in heaven.

Bhaiya... I... do not have words to apologise for my mother's behaviour...

...she is the reason for all our misery.

Bharata, forgive your mother, as I have forgiven her. She merely played her role in this crisis of life, as the gods wished her to.

Rama! I know not what came over me. I am so... terribly... sorry!

Rise, Ma, please...

When Bharata returned from Kekaya, I thought he would be pleased to have the kingdom all to himself. But he was not! He hates me now. I was wrong, Rama! Forgive me!

I hold nothing against you. You are, and will always be, my mother, as dear to me as Ma Kaushalya and Ma Sumitra.

Rama! My son!

The light of Rama's love put our hearts at ease. He wiped away all traces of bitterness by warmly accepting Queen Kaikeyi.

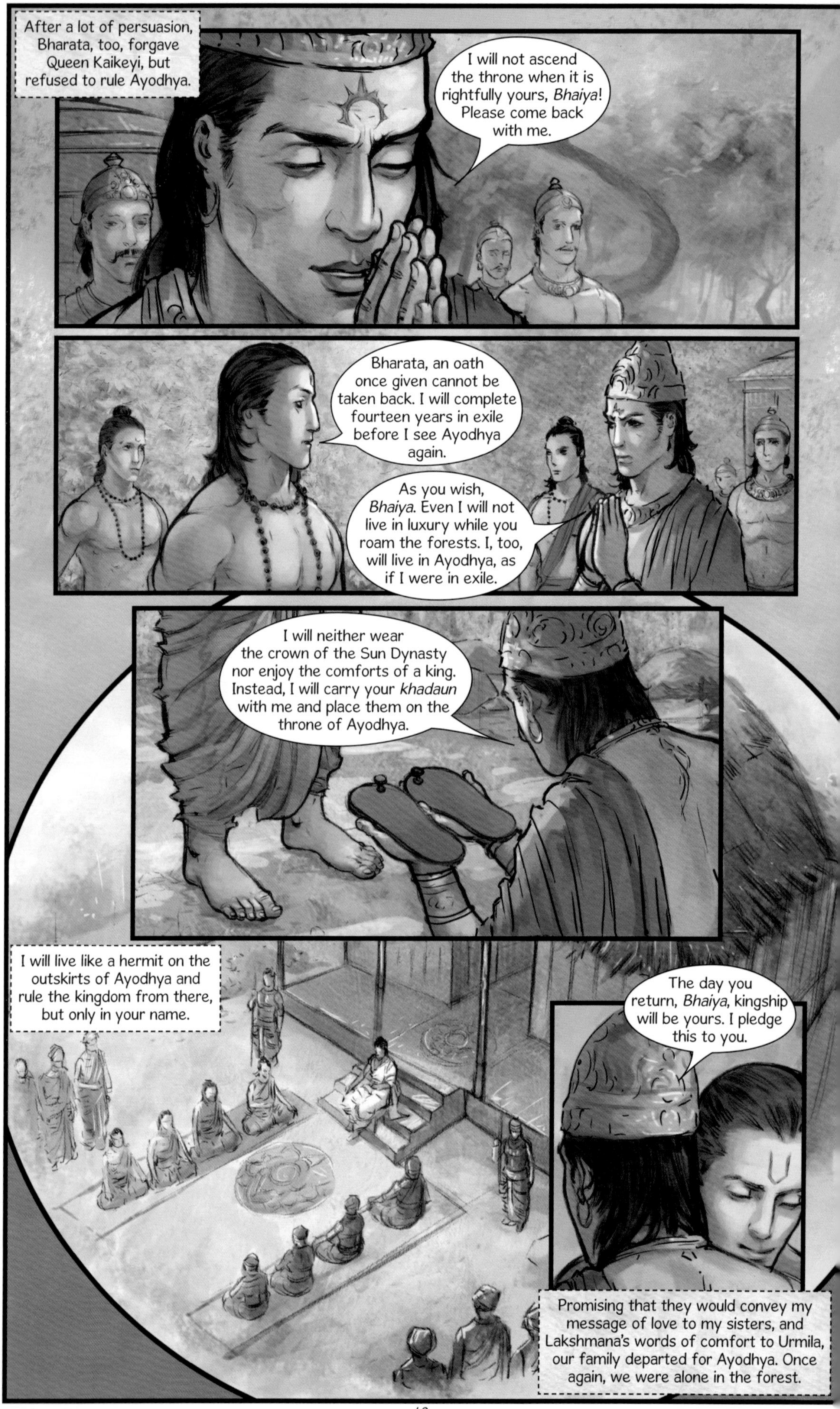

After a lot of persuasion, Bharata, too, forgave Queen Kaikeyi, but refused to rule Ayodhya.
I will not ascend the throne when it is rightfully yours, *Bhaiya*! Please come back with me.
Bharata, an oath once given cannot be taken back. I will complete fourteen years in exile before I see Ayodhya again.
As you wish, *Bhaiya*. Even I will not live in luxury while you roam the forests. I, too, will live in Ayodhya, as if I were in exile.
I will neither wear the crown of the Sun Dynasty nor enjoy the comforts of a king. Instead, I will carry your *khadaun* with me and place them on the throne of Ayodhya.
I will live like a hermit on the outskirts of Ayodhya and rule the kingdom from there, but only in your name.
The day you return, *Bhaiya*, kingship will be yours. I pledge this to you.
Promising that they would convey my message of love to my sisters, and Lakshmana's words of comfort to Urmila, our family departed for Ayodhya. Once again, we were alone in the forest.

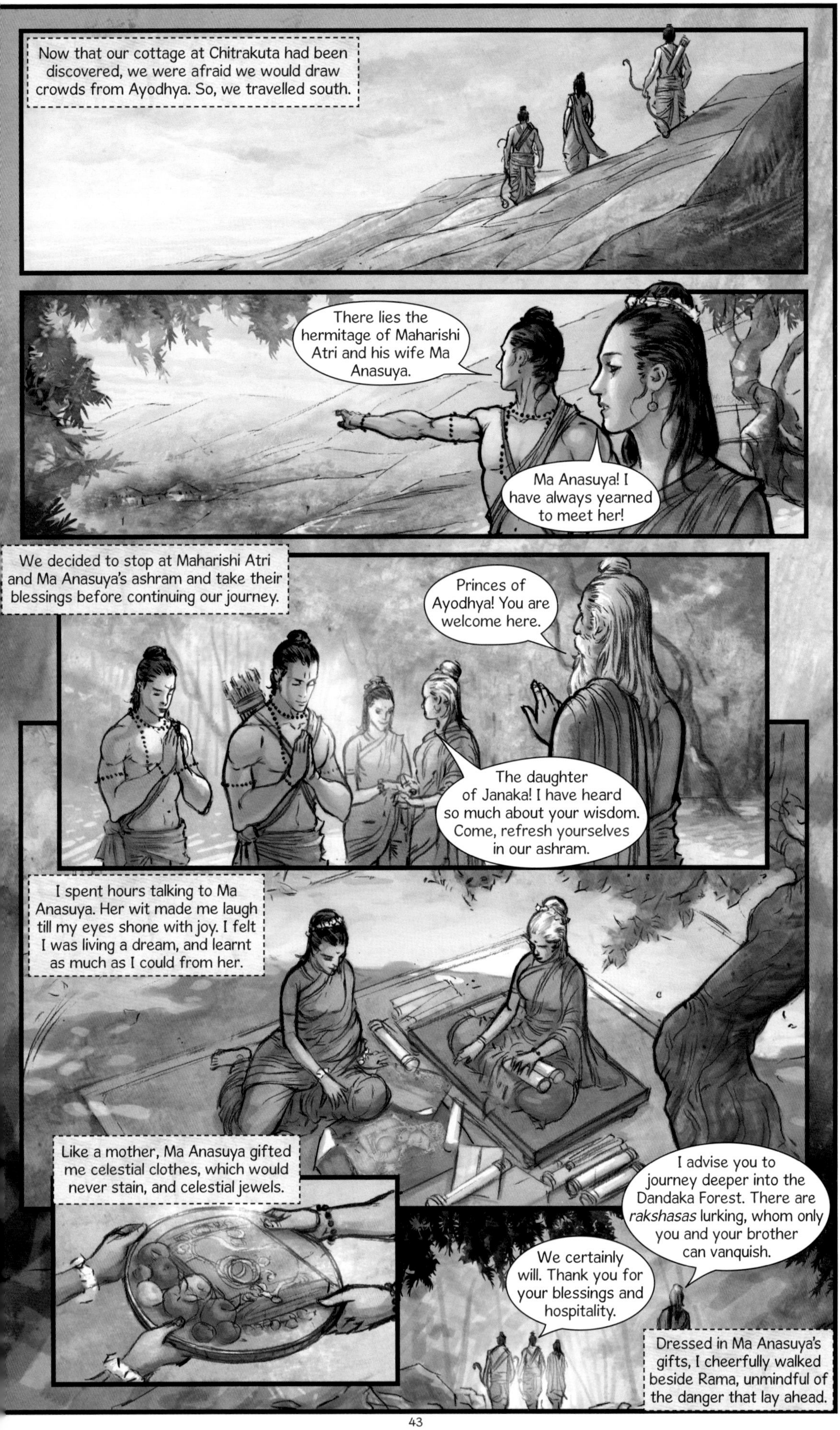
Now that our cottage at Chitrakuta had been discovered, we were afraid we would draw crowds from Ayodhya. So, we travelled south.
There lies the hermitage of Maharishi Atri and his wife Ma Anasuya.
Ma Anasuya! I have always yearned to meet her!
We decided to stop at Maharishi Atri and Ma Anasuya's ashram and take their blessings before continuing our journey.
Princes of Ayodhya! You are welcome here.
The daughter of Janaka! I have heard so much about your wisdom. Come, refresh yourselves in our ashram.
I spent hours talking to Ma Anasuya. Her wit made me laugh till my eyes shone with joy. I felt I was living a dream, and learnt as much as I could from her.
Like a mother, Ma Anasuya gifted me celestial clothes, which would never stain, and celestial jewels.
I advise you to journey deeper into the Dandaka Forest. There are *rakshasas* lurking, whom only you and your brother can vanquish.
We certainly will. Thank you for your blessings and hospitality.
Dressed in Ma Anasuya's gifts, I cheerfully walked beside Rama, unmindful of the danger that lay ahead.

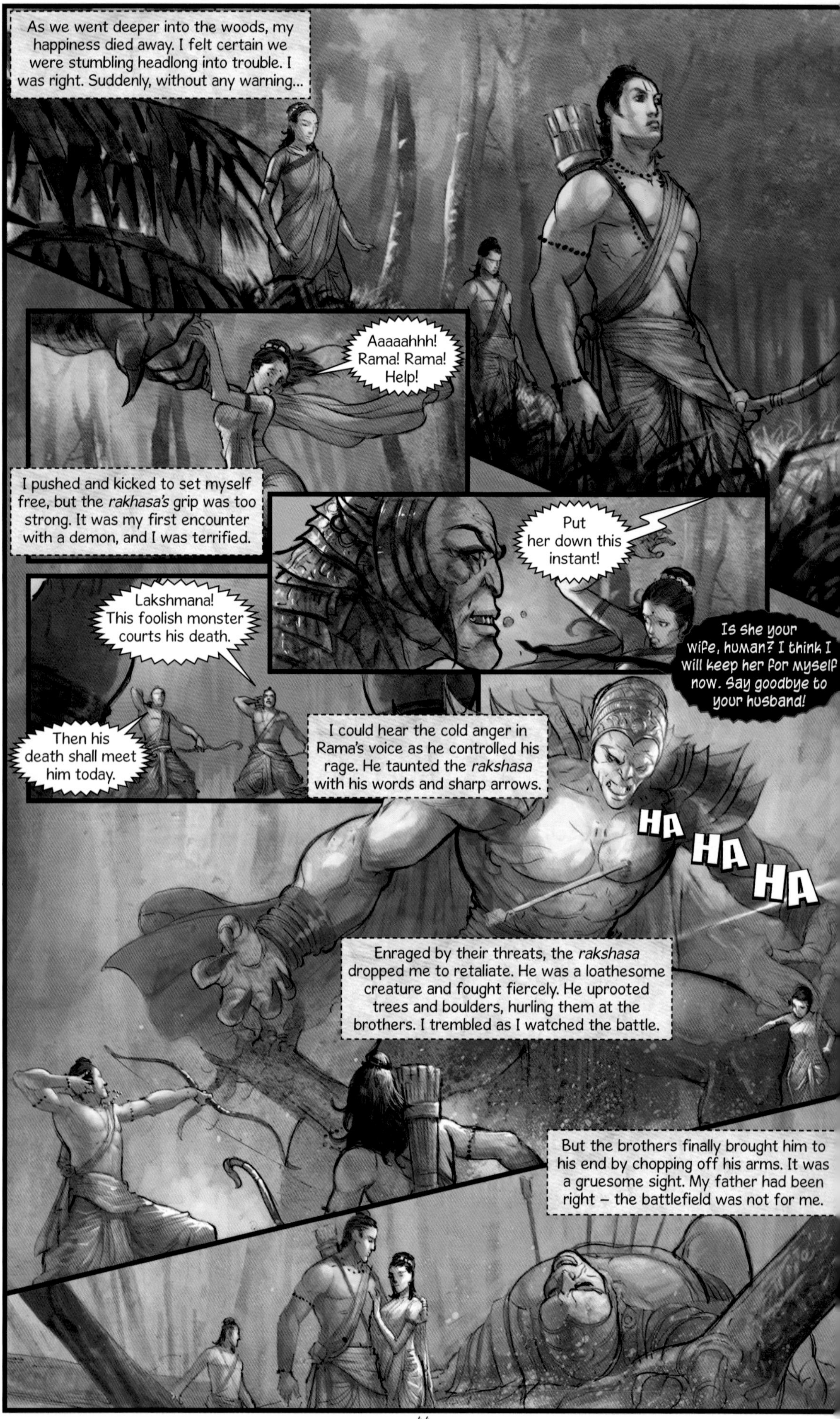

As we went deeper into the woods, my happiness died away. I felt certain we were stumbling headlong into trouble. I was right. Suddenly, without any warning...
Aaaaahhh! Rama! Rama! Help!
I pushed and kicked to set myself free, but the *rakhasa's* grip was too strong. It was my first encounter with a demon, and I was terrified.
Put her down this instant!
Lakshmana! This foolish monster courts his death.
Then his death shall meet him today.
Is she your wife, human? I think I will keep her for myself now. Say goodbye to your husband!
I could hear the cold anger in Rama's voice as he controlled his rage. He taunted the *rakshasa* with his words and sharp arrows.
HA HA HA
Enraged by their threats, the *rakshasa* dropped me to retaliate. He was a loathesome creature and fought fiercely. He uprooted trees and boulders, hurling them at the brothers. I trembled as I watched the battle.
But the brothers finally brought him to his end by chopping off his arms. It was a gruesome sight. My father had been right – the battlefield was not for me.

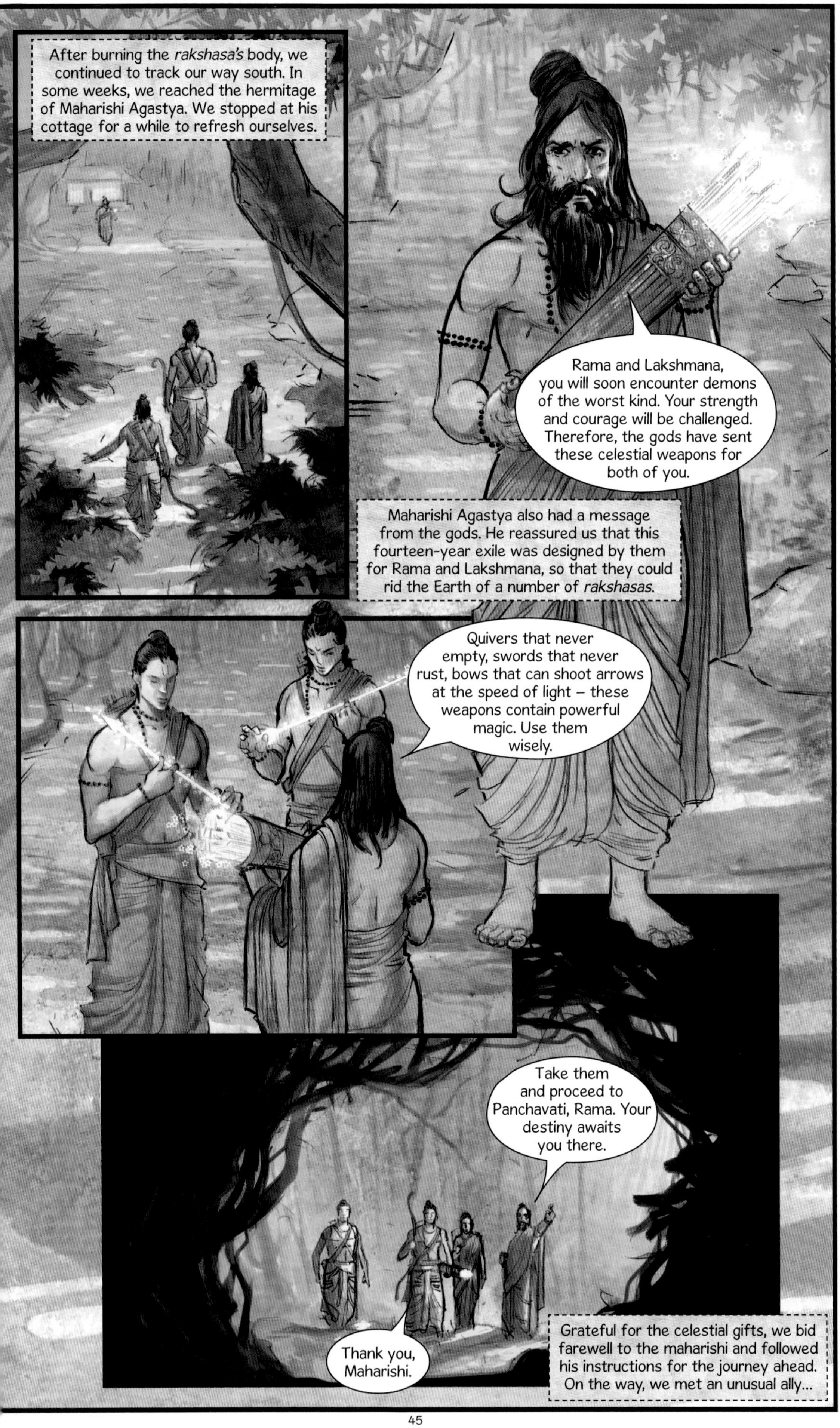

After burning the *rakshasa's* body, we continued to track our way south. In some weeks, we reached the hermitage of Maharishi Agastya. We stopped at his cottage for a while to refresh ourselves.
Rama and Lakshmana, you will soon encounter demons of the worst kind. Your strength and courage will be challenged. Therefore, the gods have sent these celestial weapons for both of you.
Maharishi Agastya also had a message from the gods. He reassured us that this fourteen-year exile was designed by them for Rama and Lakshmana, so that they could rid the Earth of a number of *rakshasas*.
Quivers that never empty, swords that never rust, bows that can shoot arrows at the speed of light – these weapons contain powerful magic. Use them wisely.
Take them and proceed to Panchavati, Rama. Your destiny awaits you there.
Thank you, Maharishi.
Grateful for the celestial gifts, we bid farewell to the maharishi and followed his instructions for the journey ahead. On the way, we met an unusual ally...

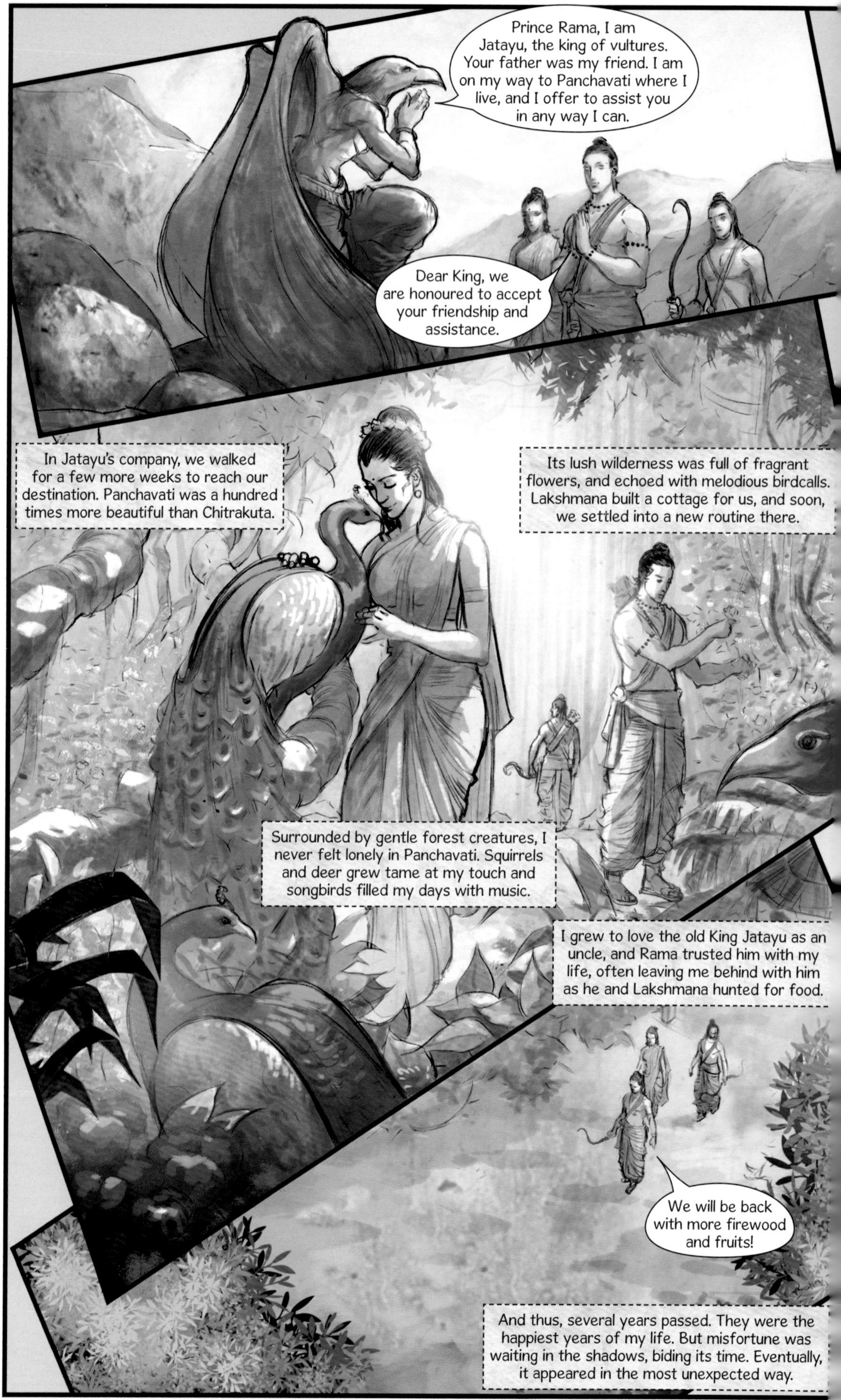

Prince Rama, I am Jatayu, the king of vultures. Your father was my friend. I am on my way to Panchavati where I live, and I offer to assist you in any way I can.
Dear King, we are honoured to accept your friendship and assistance.
In Jatayu's company, we walked for a few more weeks to reach our destination. Panchavati was a hundred times more beautiful than Chitrakuta.
Its lush wilderness was full of fragrant flowers, and echoed with melodious birdcalls. Lakshmana built a cottage for us, and soon, we settled into a new routine there.
Surrounded by gentle forest creatures, I never felt lonely in Panchavati. Squirrels and deer grew tame at my touch and songbirds filled my days with music.
I grew to love the old King Jatayu as an uncle, and Rama trusted him with my life, often leaving me behind with him as he and Lakshmana hunted for food.
We will be back with more firewood and fruits!
And thus, several years passed. They were the happiest years of my life. But misfortune was waiting in the shadows, biding its time. Eventually, it appeared in the most unexpected way.

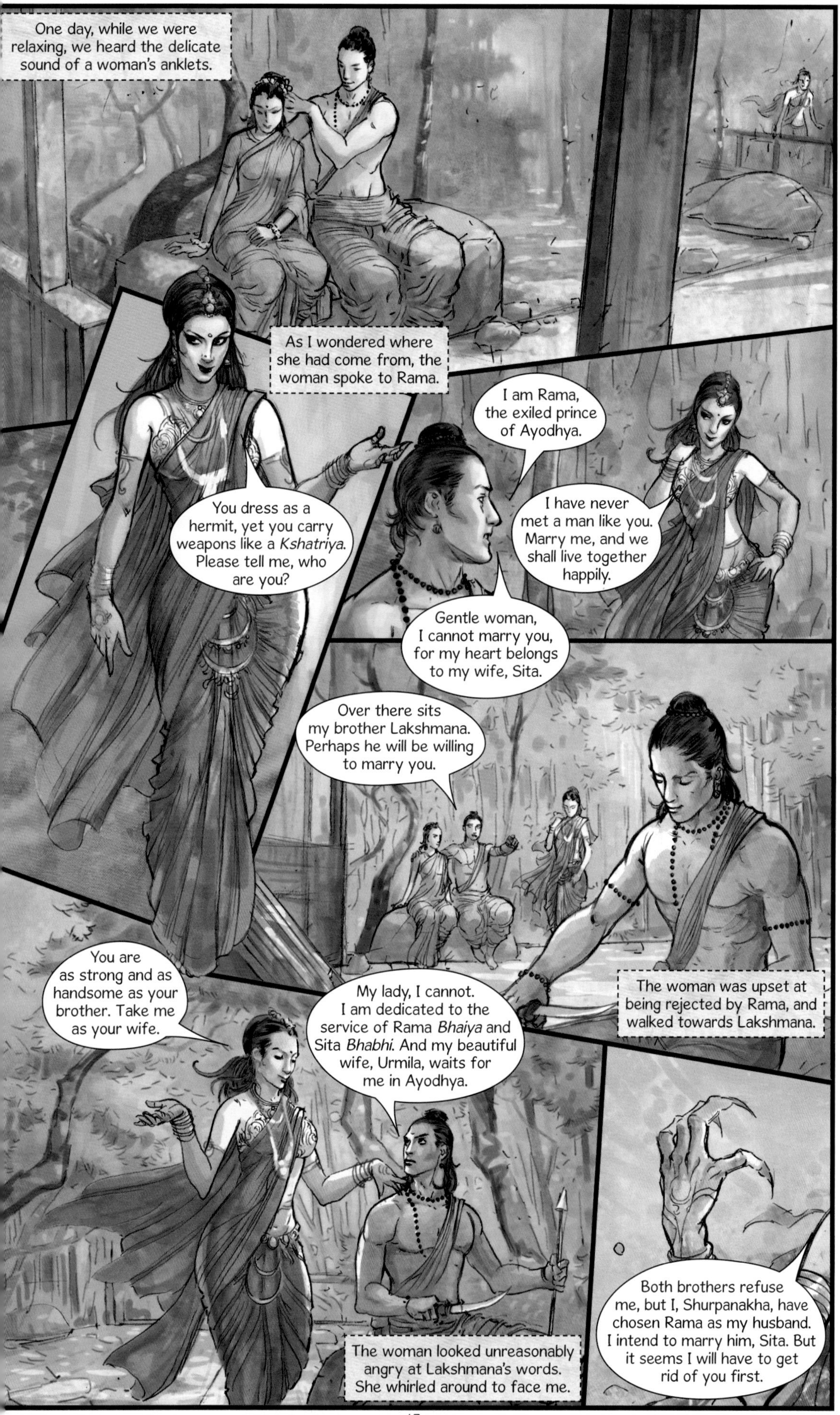
One day, while we were relaxing, we heard the delicate sound of a woman's anklets.
As I wondered where she had come from, the woman spoke to Rama.
You dress as a hermit, yet you carry weapons like a *Kshatriya*. Please tell me, who are you?
I am Rama, the exiled prince of Ayodhya.
I have never met a man like you. Marry me, and we shall live together happily.
Gentle woman, I cannot marry you, for my heart belongs to my wife, Sita.
Over there sits my brother Lakshmana. Perhaps he will be willing to marry you.
The woman was upset at being rejected by Rama, and walked towards Lakshmana.
You are as strong and as handsome as your brother. Take me as your wife.
My lady, I cannot. I am dedicated to the service of Rama *Bhaiya* and Sita *Bhabhi*. And my beautiful wife, Urmila, waits for me in Ayodhya.
The woman looked unreasonably angry at Lakshmana's words. She whirled around to face me.
Both brothers refuse me, but I, Shurpanakha, have chosen Rama as my husband. I intend to marry him, Sita. But it seems I will have to get rid of you first.

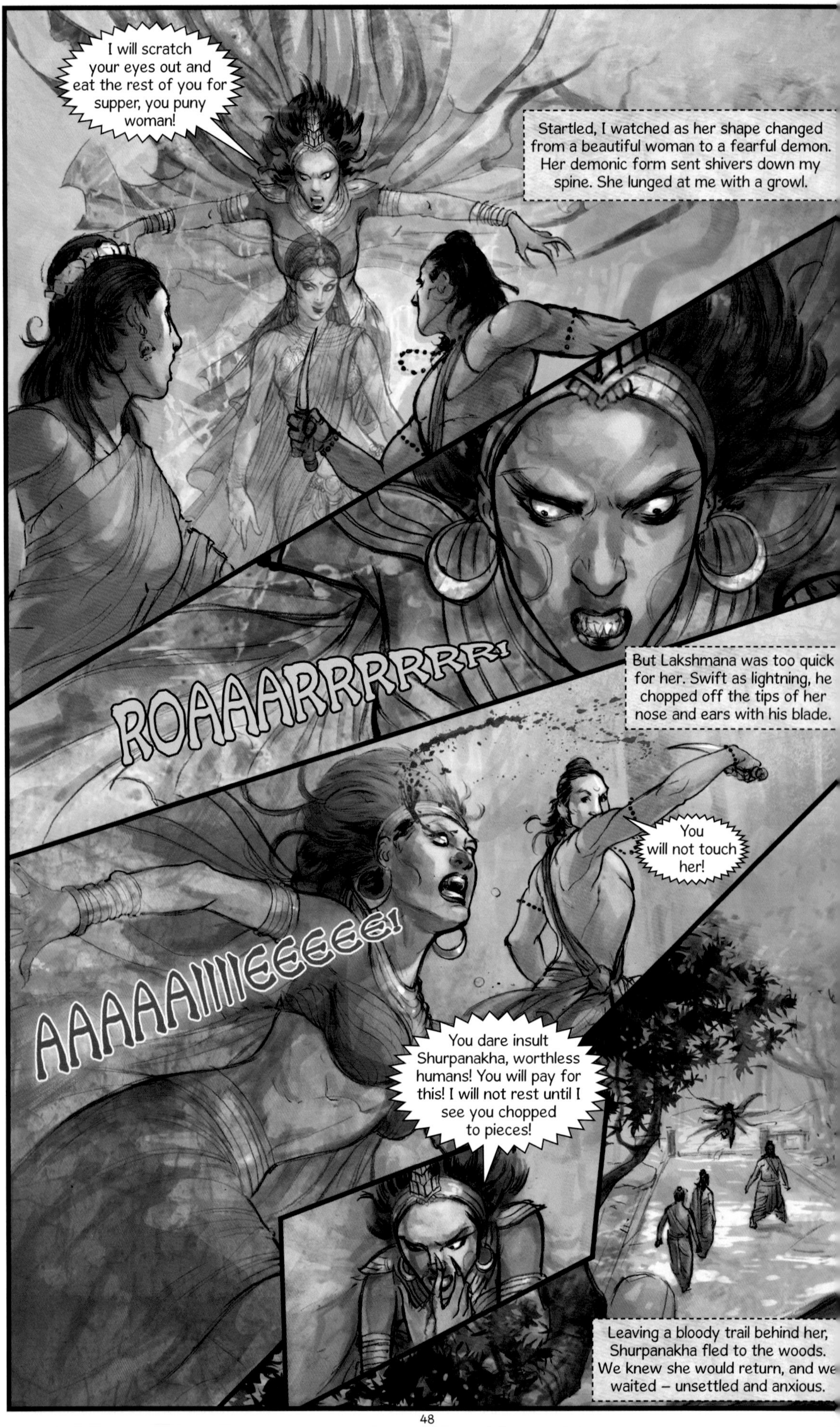
I will scratch your eyes out and eat the rest of you for supper, you puny woman!
Startled, I watched as her shape changed from a beautiful woman to a fearful demon. Her demonic form sent shivers down my spine. She lunged at me with a growl.
ROAAARRRRRR!
But Lakshmana was too quick for her. Swift as lightning, he chopped off the tips of her nose and ears with his blade.
You will not touch her!
AAAAAIIIIEEEEEE!
You dare insult Shurpanakha, worthless humans! You will pay for this! I will not rest until I see you chopped to pieces!
Leaving a bloody trail behind her, Shurpanakha fled to the woods. We knew she would return, and we waited – unsettled and anxious.

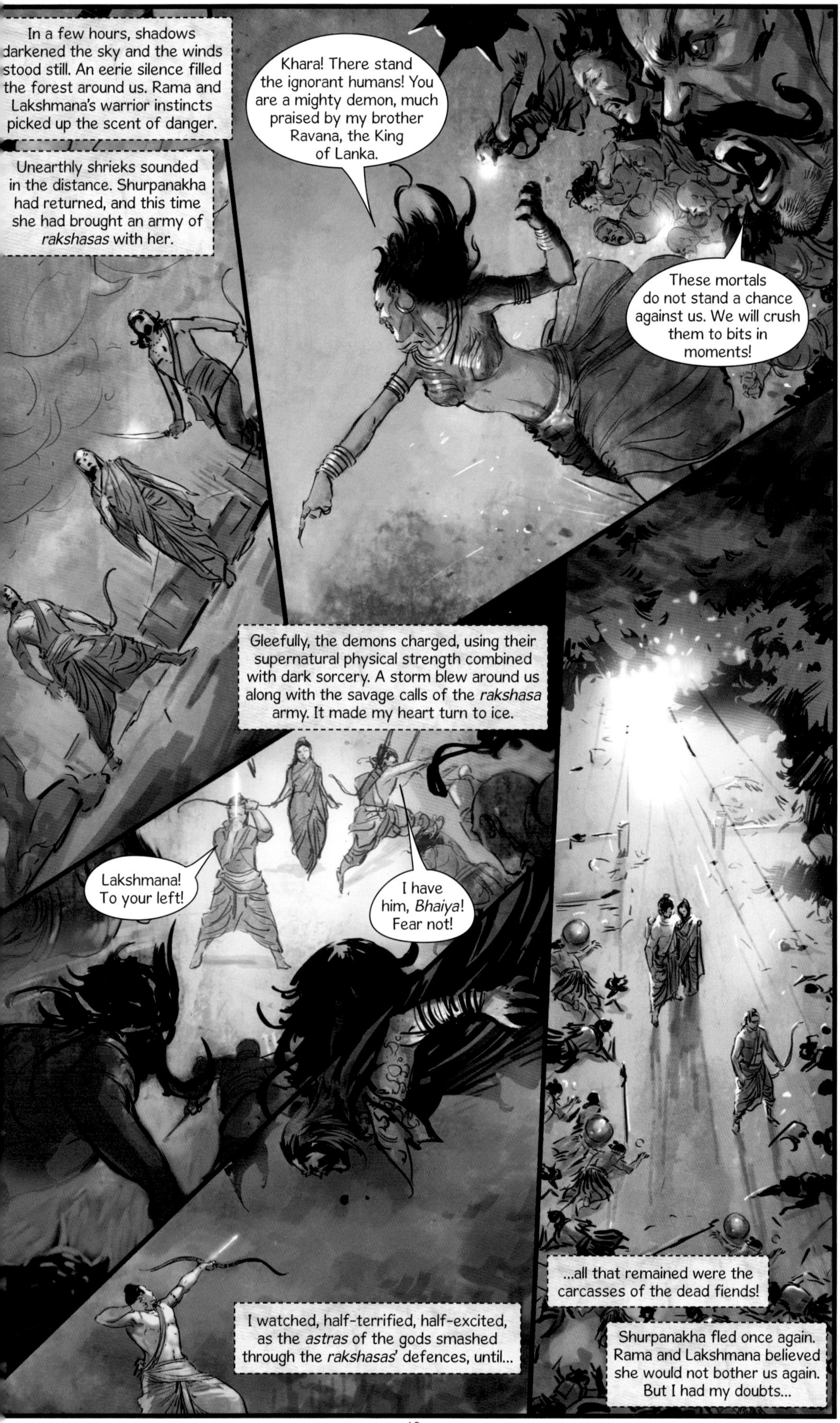
In a few hours, shadows darkened the sky and the winds stood still. An eerie silence filled the forest around us. Rama and Lakshmana's warrior instincts picked up the scent of danger.
Unearthly shrieks sounded in the distance. Shurpanakha had returned, and this time she had brought an army of *rakshasas* with her.
Khara! There stand the ignorant humans! You are a mighty demon, much praised by my brother Ravana, the King of Lanka.
These mortals do not stand a chance against us. We will crush them to bits in moments!
Gleefully, the demons charged, using their supernatural physical strength combined with dark sorcery. A storm blew around us along with the savage calls of the *rakshasa* army. It made my heart turn to ice.
Lakshmana! To your left!
I have him, *Bhaiya*! Fear not!
I watched, half-terrified, half-excited, as the *astras* of the gods smashed through the *rakshasas*' defences, until...
...all that remained were the carcasses of the dead fiends!
Shurpanakha fled once again. Rama and Lakshmana believed she would not bother us again. But I had my doubts...

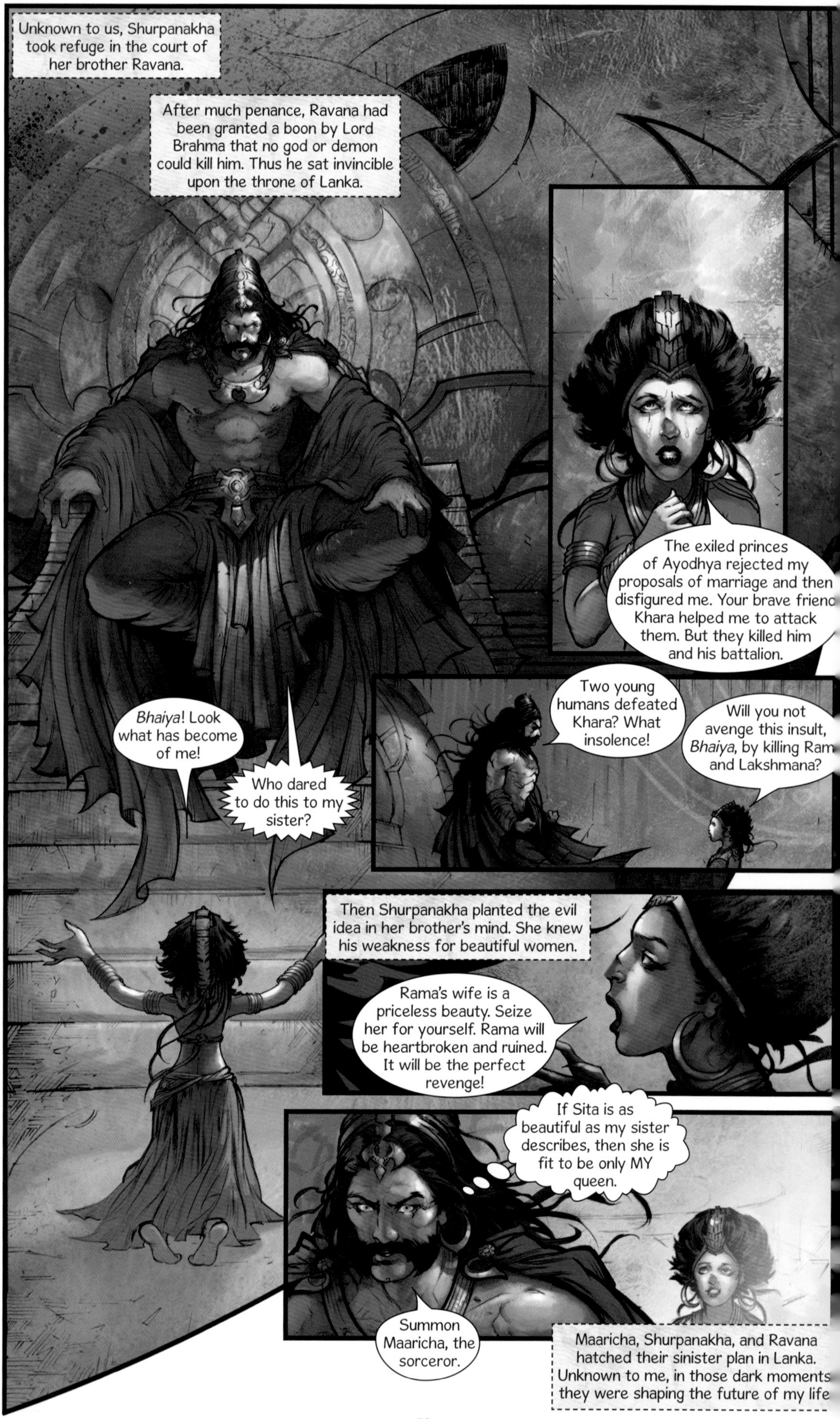
Unknown to us, Shurpanakha took refuge in the court of her brother Ravana.
After much penance, Ravana had been granted a boon by Lord Brahma that no god or demon could kill him. Thus he sat invincible upon the throne of Lanka.
The exiled princes of Ayodhya rejected my proposals of marriage and then disfigured me. Your brave friend Khara helped me to attack them. But they killed him and his battalion.
Bhaiya! Look what has become of me!
Who dared to do this to my sister?
Two young humans defeated Khara? What insolence!
Will you not avenge this insult, *Bhaiya*, by killing Ram and Lakshmana?
Then Shurpanakha planted the evil idea in her brother's mind. She knew his weakness for beautiful women.
Rama's wife is a priceless beauty. Seize her for yourself. Rama will be heartbroken and ruined. It will be the perfect revenge!
If Sita is as beautiful as my sister describes, then she is fit to be only MY queen.
Summon Maaricha, the sorceror.
Maaricha, Shurpanakha, and Ravana hatched their sinister plan in Lanka. Unknown to me, in those dark moments they were shaping the future of my life

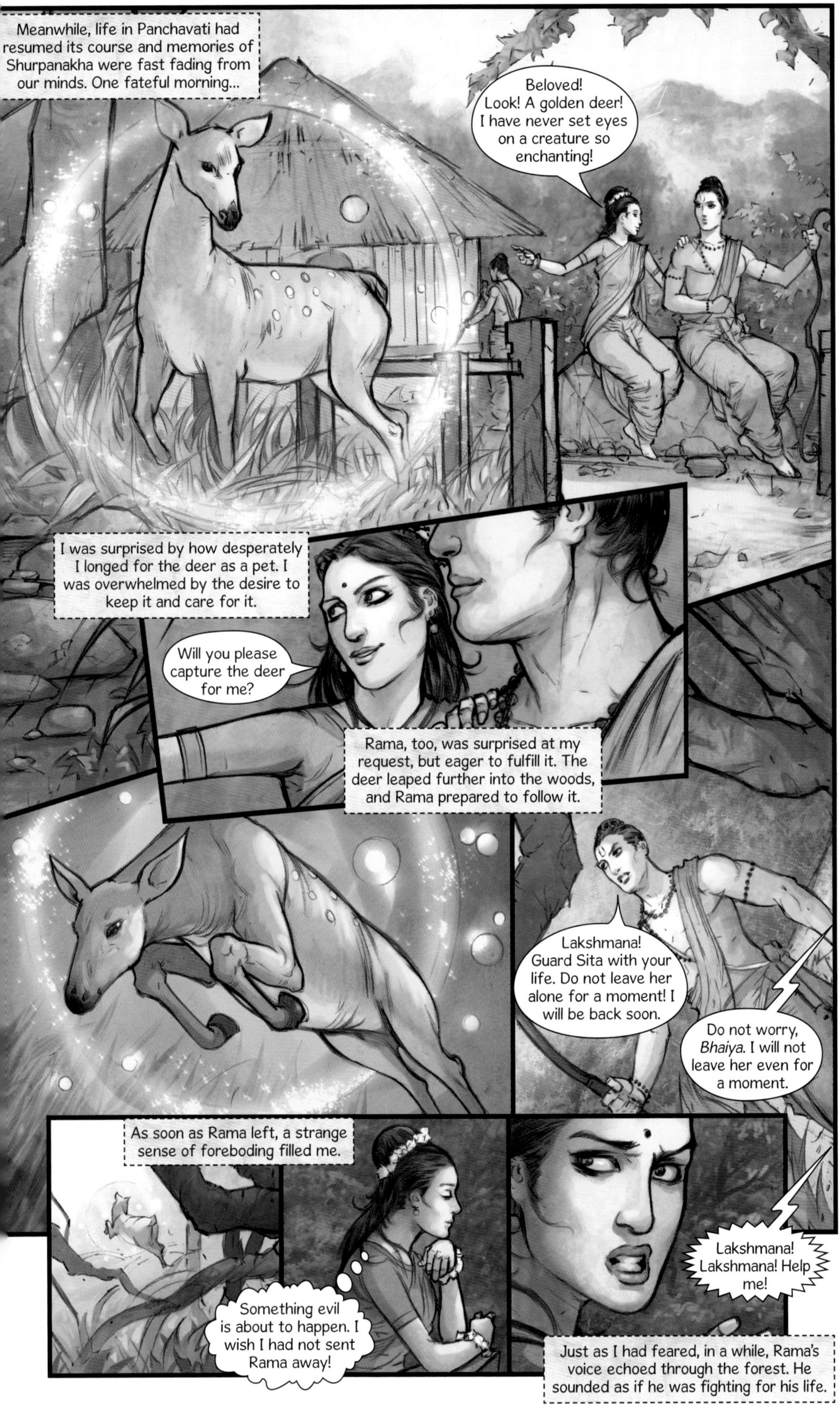

Meanwhile, life in Panchavati had resumed its course and memories of Shurpanakha were fast fading from our minds. One fateful morning...
Beloved! Look! A golden deer! I have never set eyes on a creature so enchanting!
I was surprised by how desperately I longed for the deer as a pet. I was overwhelmed by the desire to keep it and care for it.
Will you please capture the deer for me?
Rama, too, was surprised at my request, but eager to fulfill it. The deer leaped further into the woods, and Rama prepared to follow it.
Lakshmana! Guard Sita with your life. Do not leave her alone for a moment! I will be back soon.
Do not worry, *Bhaiya*. I will not leave her even for a moment.
As soon as Rama left, a strange sense of foreboding filled me.
Something evil is about to happen. I wish I had not sent Rama away!
Lakshmana! Lakshmana! Help me!
Just as I had feared, in a while, Rama's voice echoed through the forest. He sounded as if he was fighting for his life.

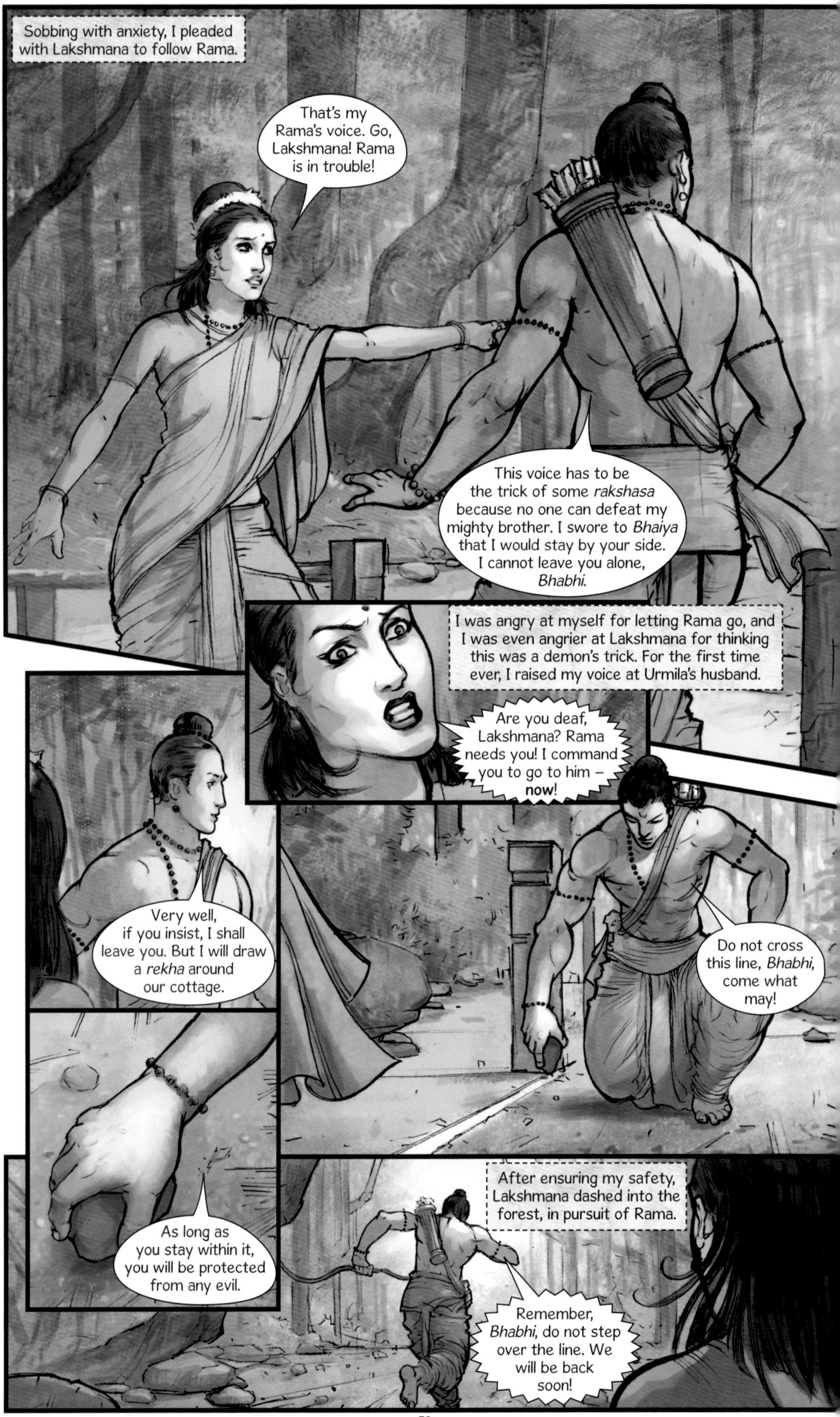
Sobbing with anxiety, I pleaded with Lakshmana to follow Rama.
That's my Rama's voice. Go, Lakshmana! Rama is in trouble!
This voice has to be the trick of some *rakshasa* because no one can defeat my mighty brother. I swore to *Bhaiya* that I would stay by your side. I cannot leave you alone, *Bhabhi*.
I was angry at myself for letting Rama go, and I was even angrier at Lakshmana for thinking this was a demon's trick. For the first time ever, I raised my voice at Urmila's husband.
Are you deaf, Lakshmana? Rama needs you! I command you to go to him – **now**!
Very well, if you insist, I shall leave you. But I will draw a *rekha* around our cottage.
Do not cross this line, *Bhabhi*, come what may!
As long as you stay within it, you will be protected from any evil.
After ensuring my safety, Lakshmana dashed into the forest, in pursuit of Rama.
Remember, *Bhabhi*, do not step over the line. We will be back soon!

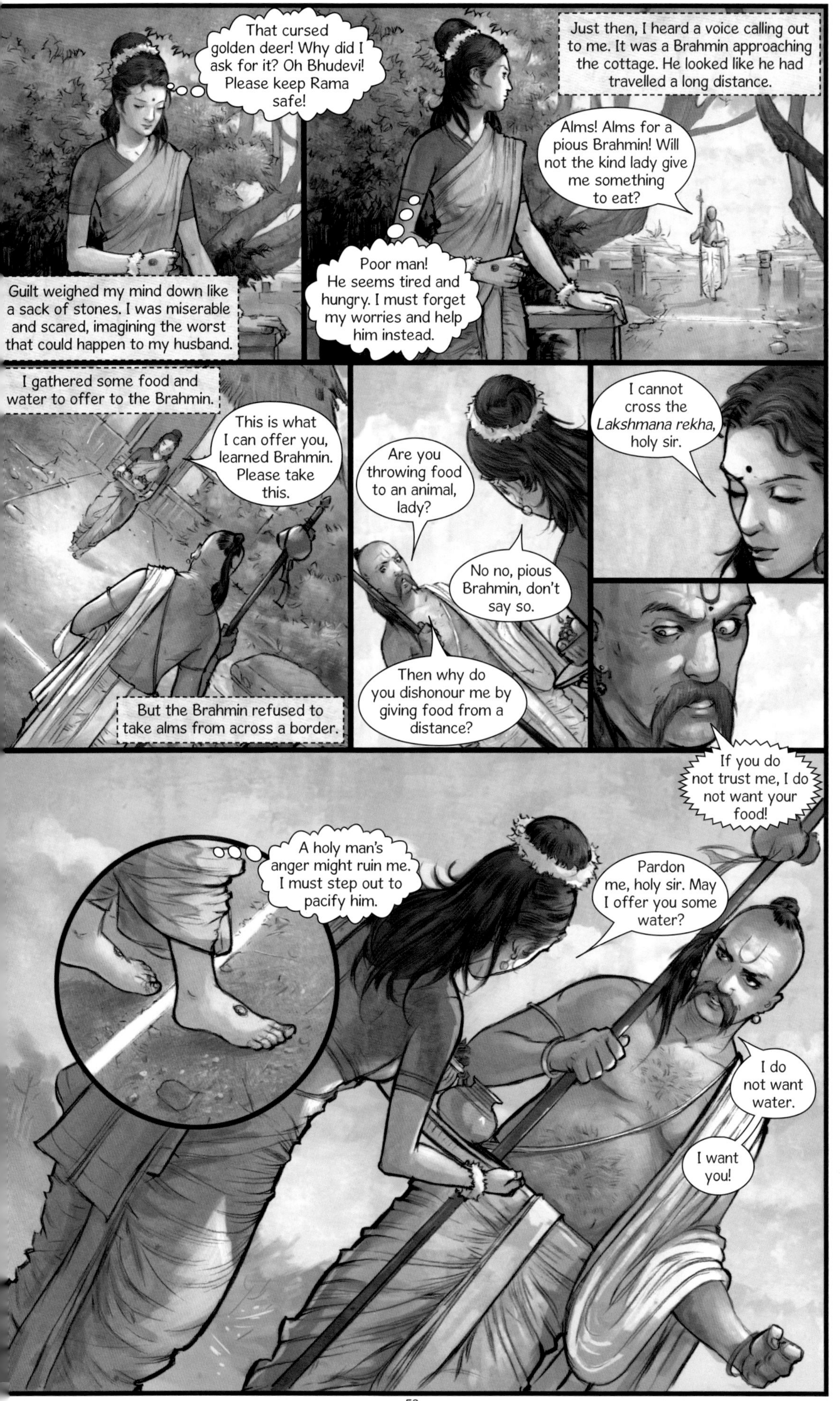
That cursed golden deer! Why did I ask for it? Oh Bhudevi! Please keep Rama safe!
Guilt weighed my mind down like a sack of stones. I was miserable and scared, imagining the worst that could happen to my husband.
Just then, I heard a voice calling out to me. It was a Brahmin approaching the cottage. He looked like he had travelled a long distance.
Alms! Alms for a pious Brahmin! Will not the kind lady give me something to eat?
Poor man! He seems tired and hungry. I must forget my worries and help him instead.
I gathered some food and water to offer to the Brahmin.
This is what I can offer you, learned Brahmin. Please take this.
But the Brahmin refused to take alms from across a border.
Are you throwing food to an animal, lady?
No no, pious Brahmin, don't say so.
Then why do you dishonour me by giving food from a distance?
I cannot cross the *Lakshmana rekha*, holy sir.
If you do not trust me, I do not want your food!
A holy man's anger might ruin me. I must step out to pacify him.
Pardon me, holy sir. May I offer you some water?
I do not want water.
I want you!

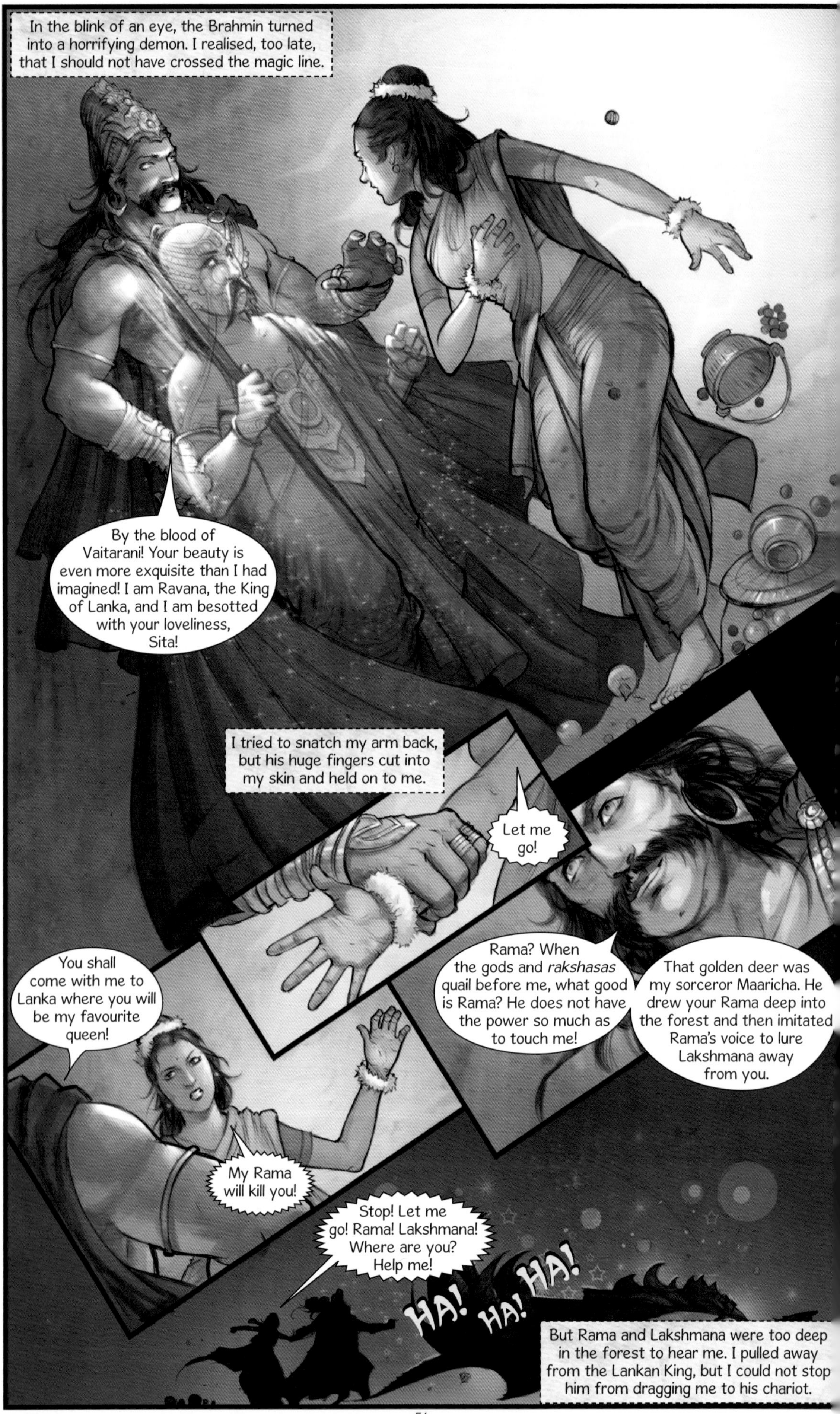

In the blink of an eye, the Brahmin turned into a horrifying demon. I realised, too late, that I should not have crossed the magic line.
By the blood of Vaitarani! Your beauty is even more exquisite than I had imagined! I am Ravana, the King of Lanka, and I am besotted with your loveliness, Sita!
I tried to snatch my arm back, but his huge fingers cut into my skin and held on to me.
Let me go!
Rama? When the gods and *rakshasas* quail before me, what good is Rama? He does not have the power so much as to touch me!
That golden deer was my sorceror Maaricha. He drew your Rama deep into the forest and then imitated Rama's voice to lure Lakshmana away from you.
You shall come with me to Lanka where you will be my favourite queen!
My Rama will kill you!
Stop! Let me go! Rama! Lakshmana! Where are you? Help me!
HA! HA! HA!
But Rama and Lakshmana were too deep in the forest to hear me. I pulled away from the Lankan King, but I could not stop him from dragging me to his chariot.

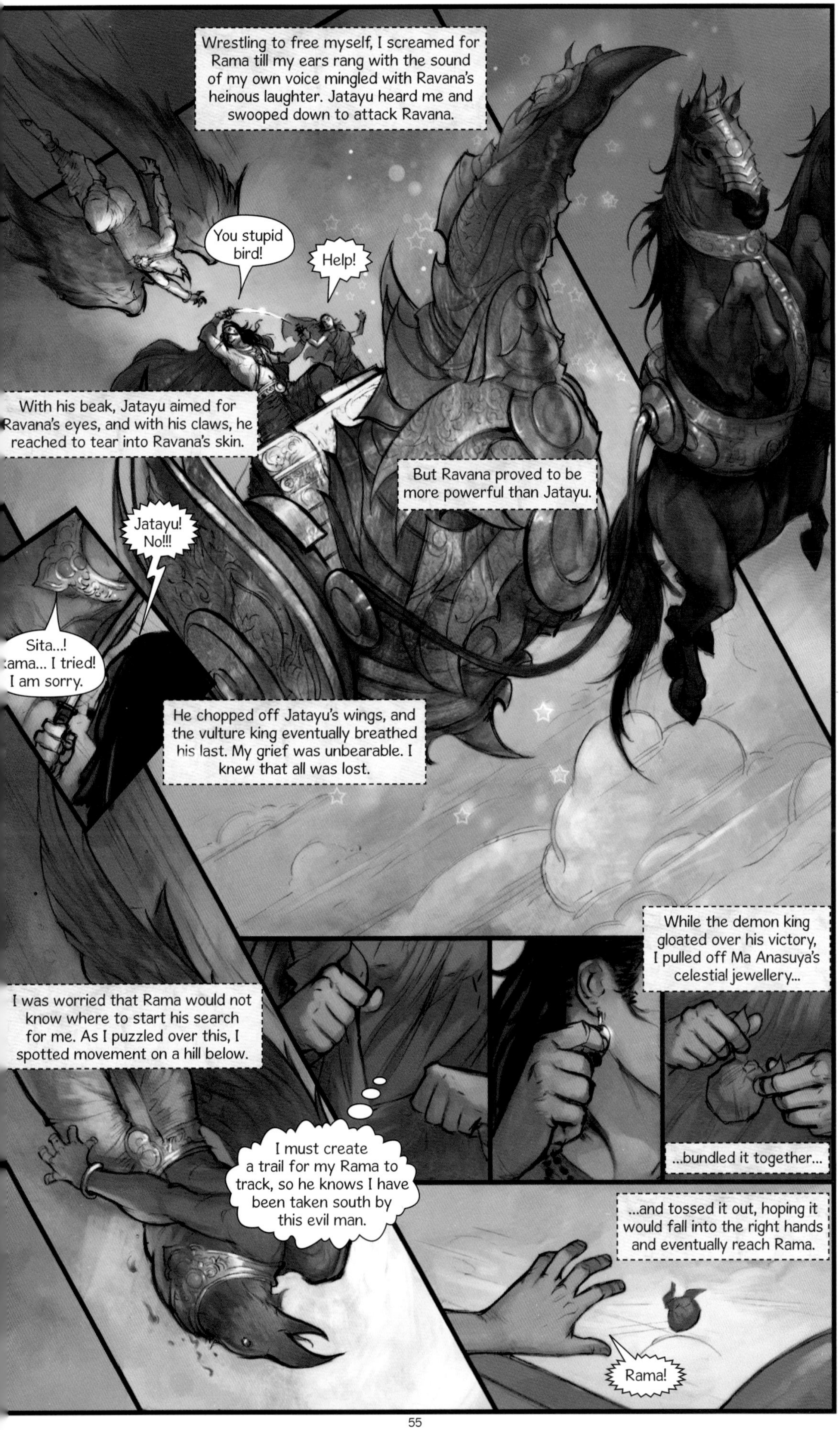

Wrestling to free myself, I screamed for Rama till my ears rang with the sound of my own voice mingled with Ravana's heinous laughter. Jatayu heard me and swooped down to attack Ravana.
You stupid bird!
Help!
With his beak, Jatayu aimed for Ravana's eyes, and with his claws, he reached to tear into Ravana's skin.
But Ravana proved to be more powerful than Jatayu.
Jatayu! No!!!
Sita...! Rama... I tried! I am sorry.
He chopped off Jatayu's wings, and the vulture king eventually breathed his last. My grief was unbearable. I knew that all was lost.
I was worried that Rama would not know where to start his search for me. As I puzzled over this, I spotted movement on a hill below.
I must create a trail for my Rama to track, so he knows I have been taken south by this evil man.
While the demon king gloated over his victory, I pulled off Ma Anasuya's celestial jewellery...
...bundled it together...
...and tossed it out, hoping it would fall into the right hands and eventually reach Rama.
Rama!

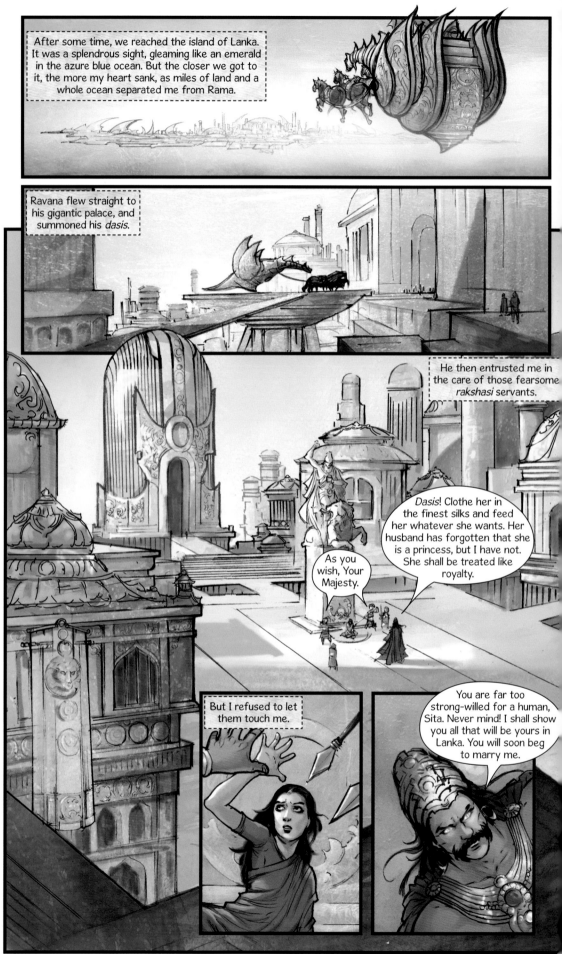

After some time, we reached the island of Lanka. It was a splendrous sight, gleaming like an emerald in the azure blue ocean. But the closer we got to it, the more my heart sank, as miles of land and a whole ocean separated me from Rama.

Ravana flew straight to his gigantic palace, and summoned his *dasis*.

He then entrusted me in the care of those fearsome *rakshasi* servants.

Dasis! Clothe her in the finest silks and feed her whatever she wants. Her husband has forgotten that she is a princess, but I have not. She shall be treated like royalty.

As you wish, Your Majesty.

But I refused to let them touch me.

You are far too strong-willed for a human, Sita. Never mind! I shall show you all that will be yours in Lanka. You will soon beg to marry me.

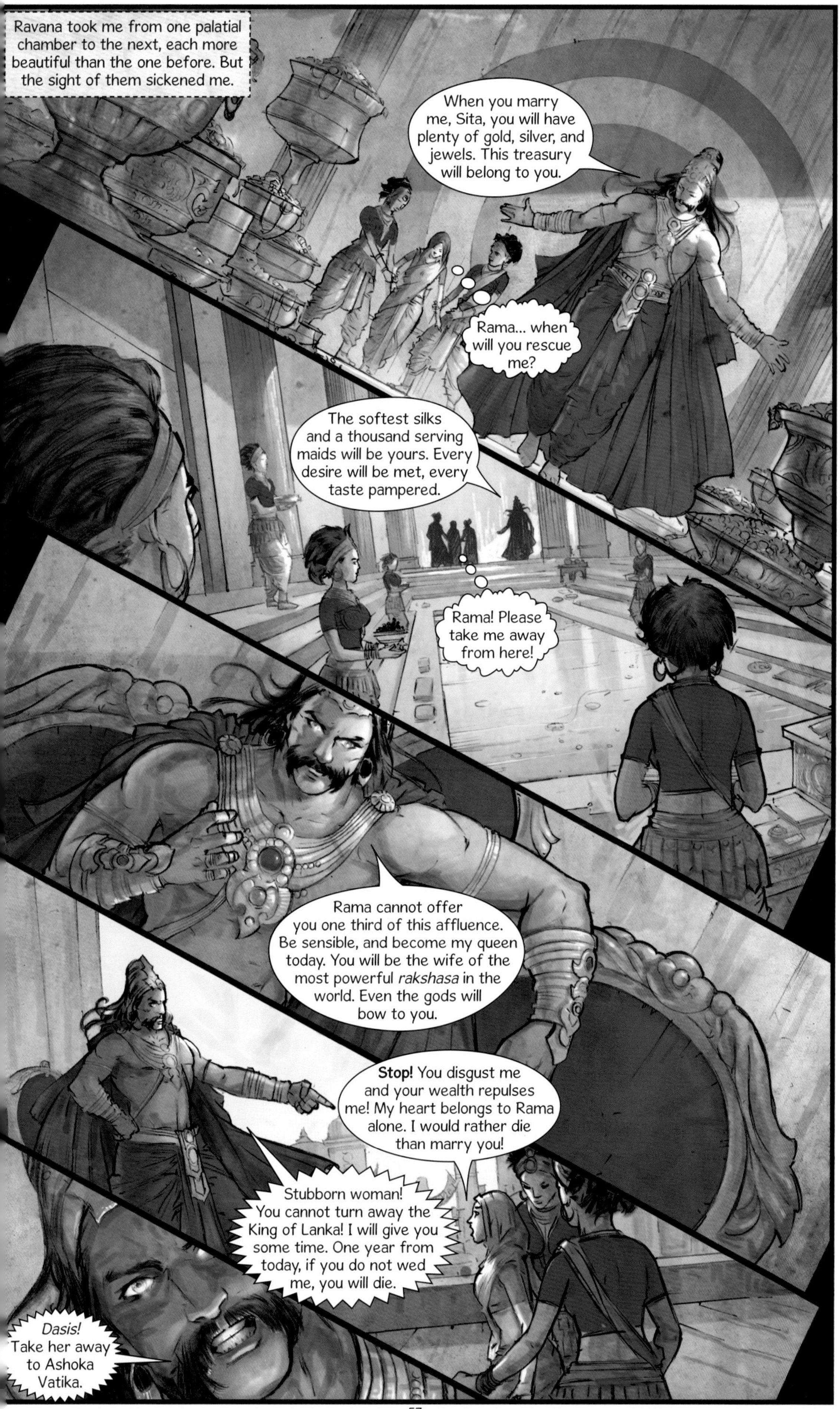
Ravana took me from one palatial chamber to the next, each more beautiful than the one before. But the sight of them sickened me.
When you marry me, Sita, you will have plenty of gold, silver, and jewels. This treasury will belong to you.
Rama... when will you rescue me?
The softest silks and a thousand serving maids will be yours. Every desire will be met, every taste pampered.
Rama! Please take me away from here!
Rama cannot offer you one third of this affluence. Be sensible, and become my queen today. You will be the wife of the most powerful *rakshasa* in the world. Even the gods will bow to you.
Stop! You disgust me and your wealth repulses me! My heart belongs to Rama alone. I would rather die than marry you!
Stubborn woman! You cannot turn away the King of Lanka! I will give you some time. One year from today, if you do not wed me, you will die.
Dasis! Take her away to Ashoka Vatika.

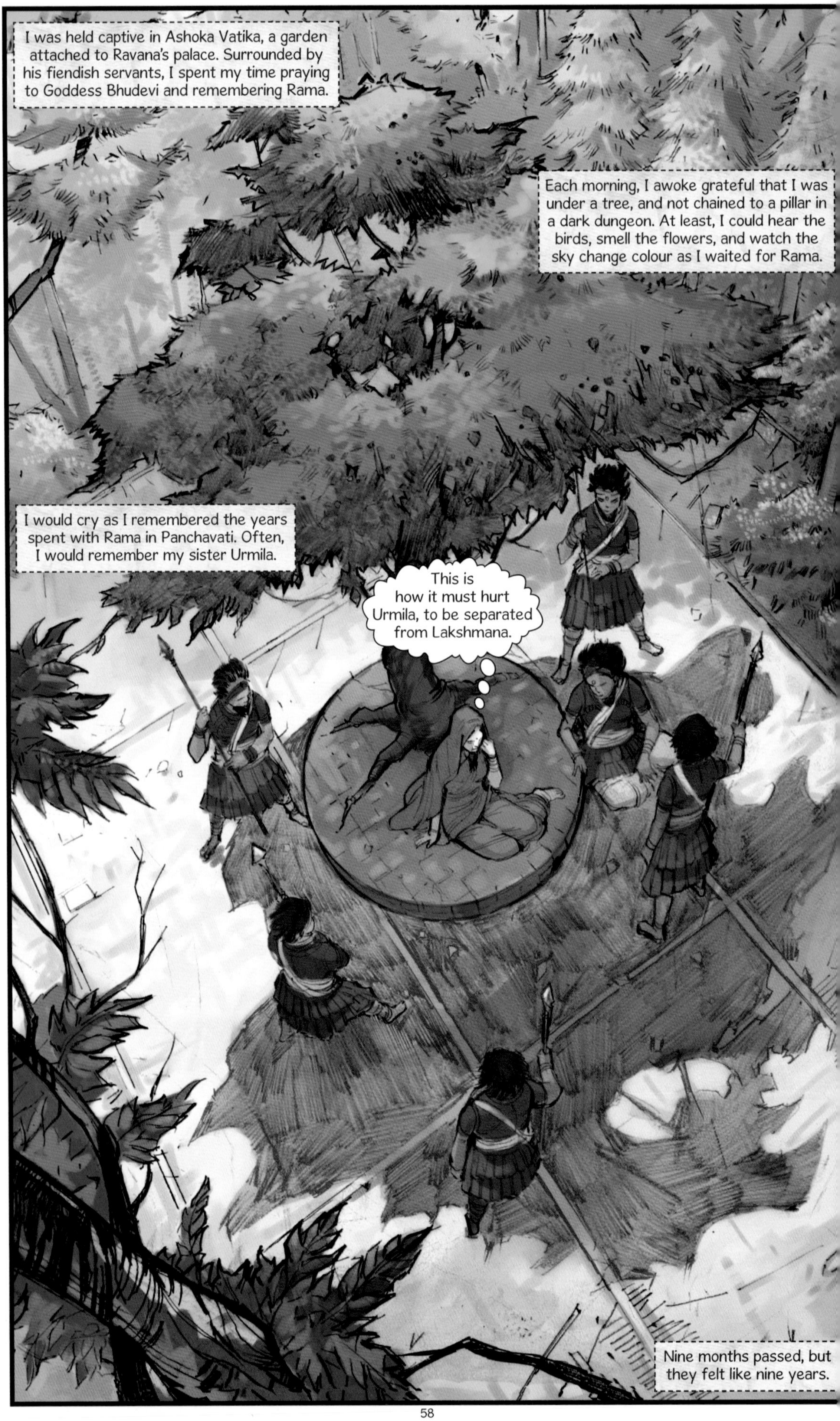
I was held captive in Ashoka Vatika, a garden attached to Ravana's palace. Surrounded by his fiendish servants, I spent my time praying to Goddess Bhudevi and remembering Rama.
Each morning, I awoke grateful that I was under a tree, and not chained to a pillar in a dark dungeon. At least, I could hear the birds, smell the flowers, and watch the sky change colour as I waited for Rama.
I would cry as I remembered the years spent with Rama in Panchavati. Often, I would remember my sister Urmila.
This is how it must hurt Urmila, to be separated from Lakshmana.
Nine months passed, but they felt like nine years.

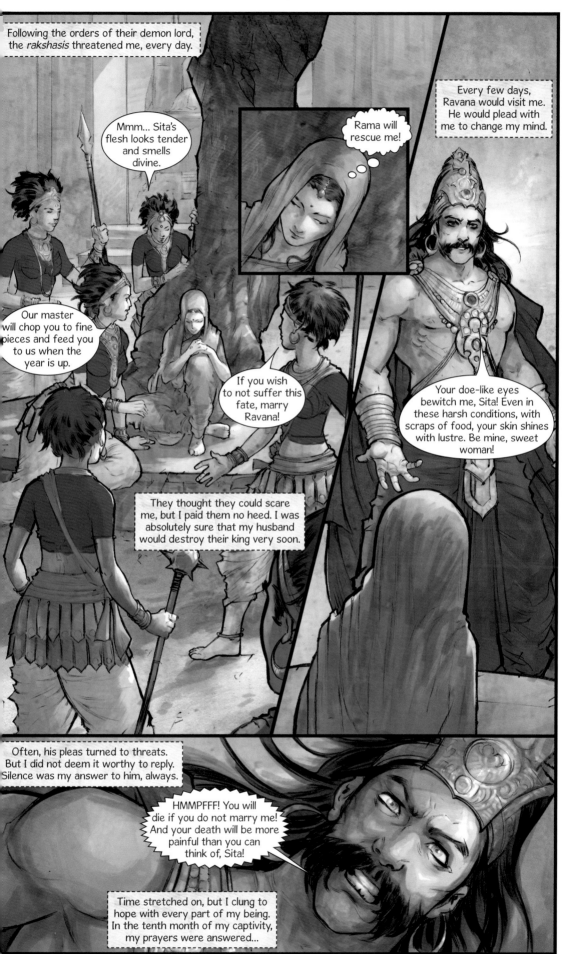

Following the orders of their demon lord, the *rakshasis* threatened me, every day.

Mmm... Sita's flesh looks tender and smells divine.

Rama will rescue me!

Every few days, Ravana would visit me. He would plead with me to change my mind.

Our master will chop you to fine pieces and feed you to us when the year is up.

If you wish to not suffer this fate, marry Ravana!

Your doe-like eyes bewitch me, Sita! Even in these harsh conditions, with scraps of food, your skin shines with lustre. Be mine, sweet woman!

They thought they could scare me, but I paid them no heed. I was absolutely sure that my husband would destroy their king very soon.

Often, his pleas turned to threats. But I did not deem it worthy to reply. Silence was my answer to him, always.

HMMPFFF! You will die if you do not marry me! And your death will be more painful than you can think of, Sita!

Time stretched on, but I clung to hope with every part of my being. In the tenth month of my captivity, my prayers were answered...

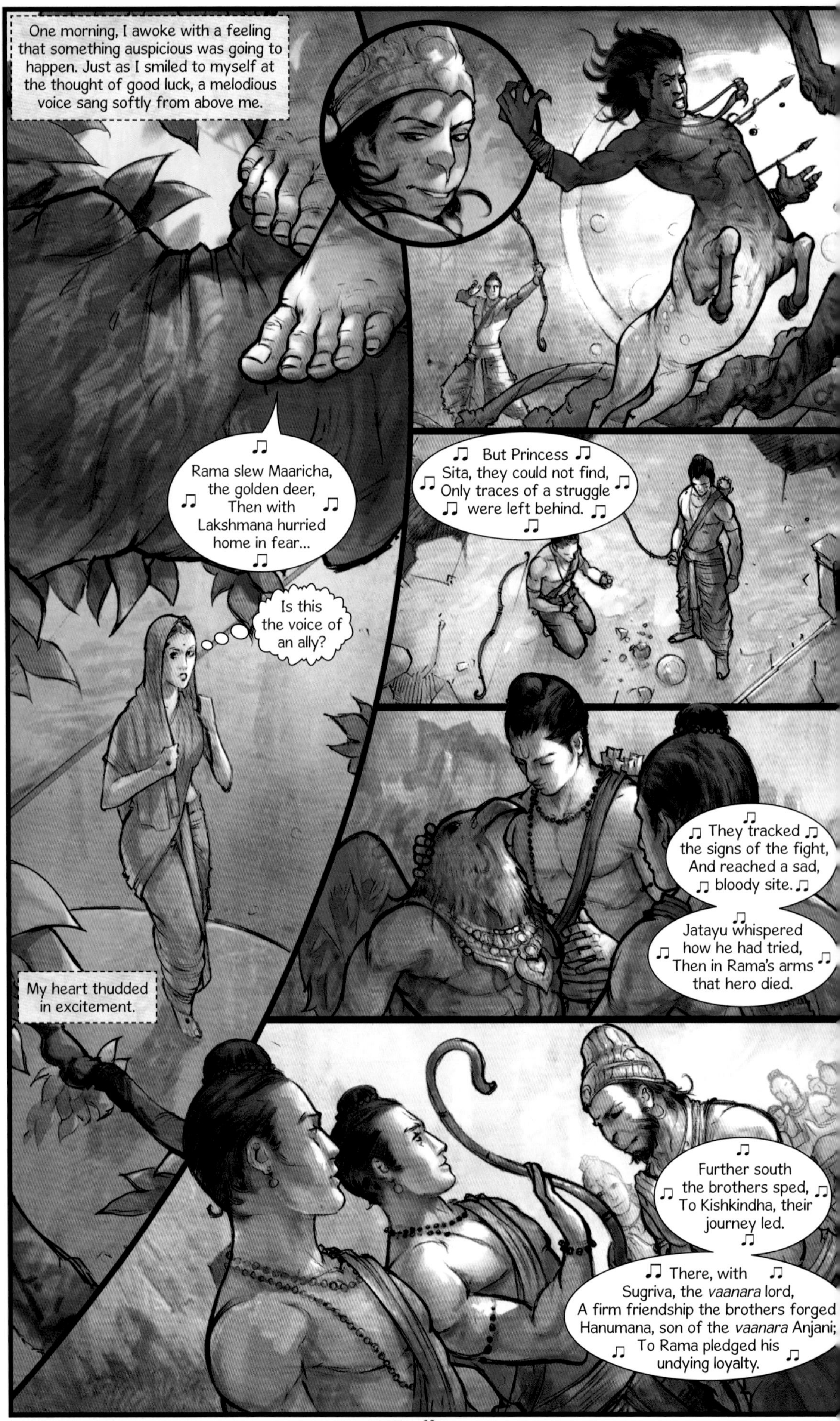
One morning, I awoke with a feeling that something auspicious was going to happen. Just as I smiled to myself at the thought of good luck, a melodious voice sang softly from above me.
♫ Rama slew Maaricha, the golden deer, ♫ Then with ♫ Lakshmana hurried home in fear... ♫
Is this the voice of an ally?
♫ But Princess ♫ Sita, they could not find, ♫ Only traces of a struggle ♫ ♫ were left behind. ♫ ♫
My heart thudded in excitement.
♫ ♫ They tracked ♫ the signs of the fight, And reached a sad, ♫ bloody site. ♫
♫ Jatayu whispered ♫ how he had tried, Then in Rama's arms ♫ that hero died.
♫ Further south ♫ the brothers sped, ♫ To Kishkindha, their journey led. ♫
♫ There, with ♫ Sugriva, the *vaanara* lord, A firm friendship the brothers forged Hanumana, son of the *vaanara* Anjani; ♫ To Rama pledged his ♫ undying loyalty.

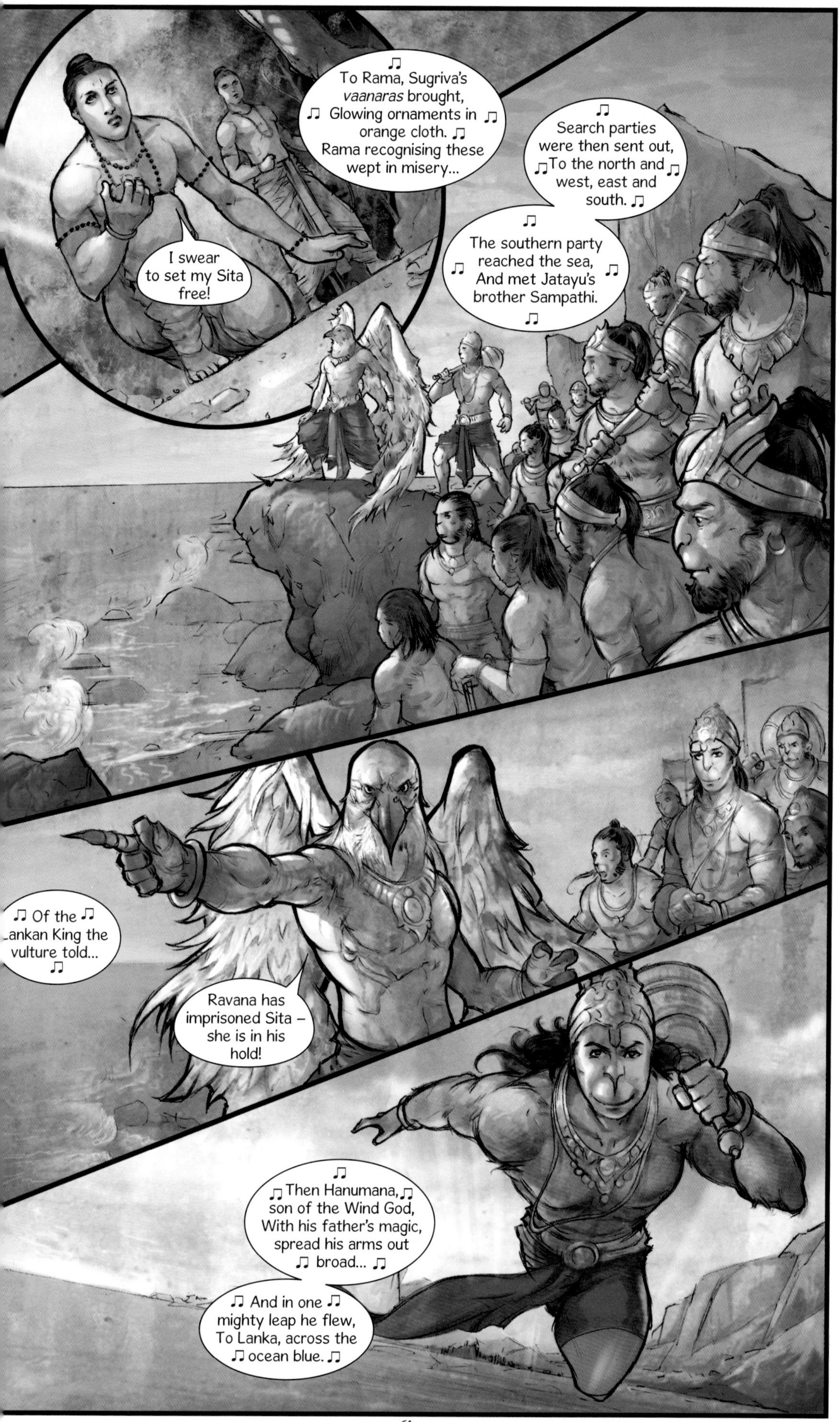
♫ To Rama, Sugriva's *vaanaras* brought, ♫ Glowing ornaments in ♫ orange cloth. ♫ Rama recognising these wept in misery...
I swear to set my Sita free!
♫ Search parties were then sent out, ♫ To the north and ♫ west, east and south. ♫
♫ The southern party reached the sea, ♫ And met Jatayu's ♫ brother Sampathi. ♫
♫ Of the ♫ Lankan King the vulture told... ♫
Ravana has imprisoned Sita – she is in his hold!
♫ ♫ Then Hanumana, ♫ son of the Wind God, With his father's magic, spread his arms out ♫ broad... ♫
♫ And in one ♫ mighty leap he flew, To Lanka, across the ♫ ocean blue. ♫

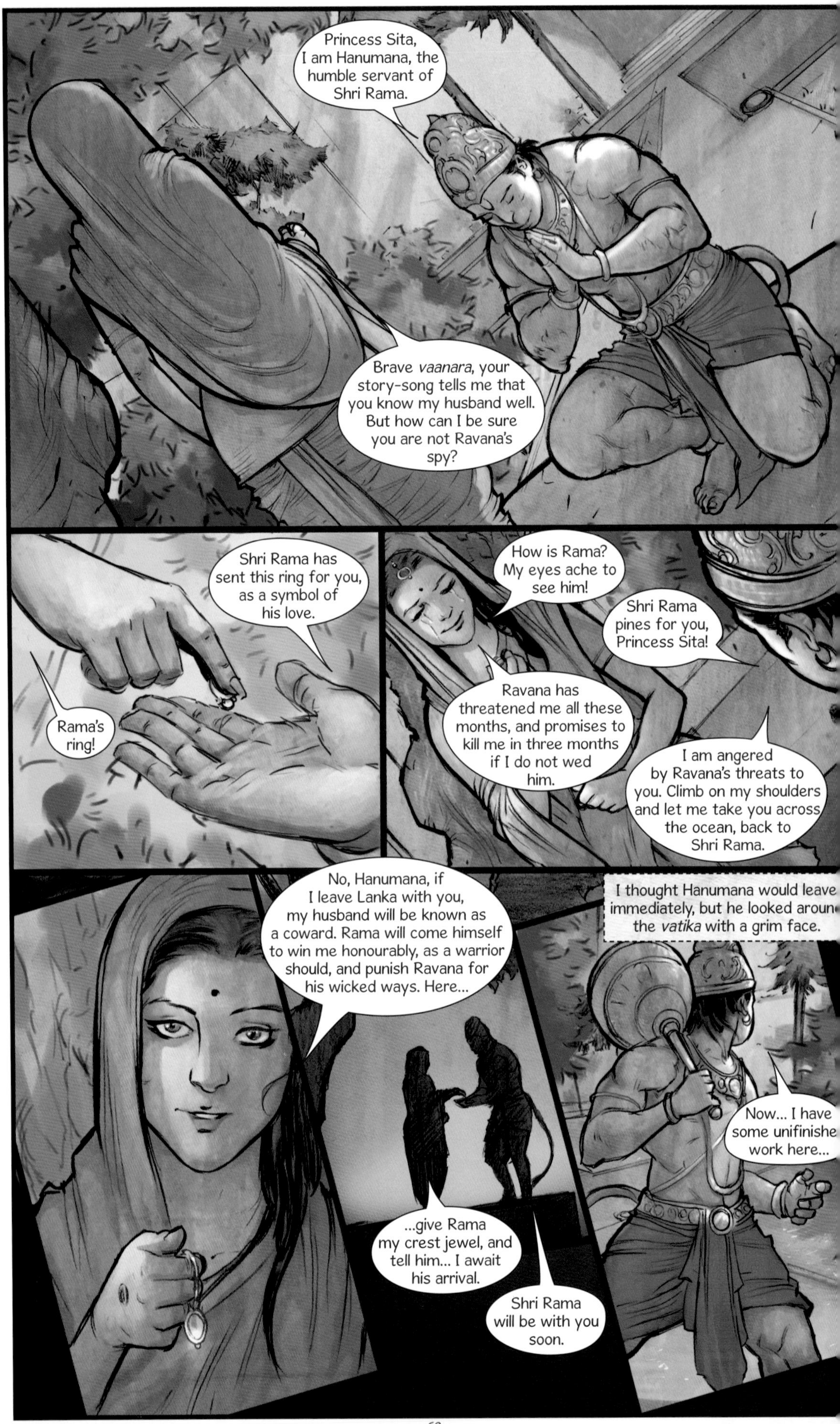
Princess Sita, I am Hanumana, the humble servant of Shri Rama.
Brave *vaanara*, your story-song tells me that you know my husband well. But how can I be sure you are not Ravana's spy?
Shri Rama has sent this ring for you, as a symbol of his love.
Rama's ring!
How is Rama? My eyes ache to see him!
Shri Rama pines for you, Princess Sita!
Ravana has threatened me all these months, and promises to kill me in three months if I do not wed him.
I am angered by Ravana's threats to you. Climb on my shoulders and let me take you across the ocean, back to Shri Rama.
No, Hanumana, if I leave Lanka with you, my husband will be known as a coward. Rama will come himself to win me honourably, as a warrior should, and punish Ravana for his wicked ways. Here...
...give Rama my crest jewel, and tell him... I await his arrival.
Shri Rama will be with you soon.
I thought Hanumana would leave immediately, but he looked aroun the *vatika* with a grim face.
Now... I have some unifinishe work here...

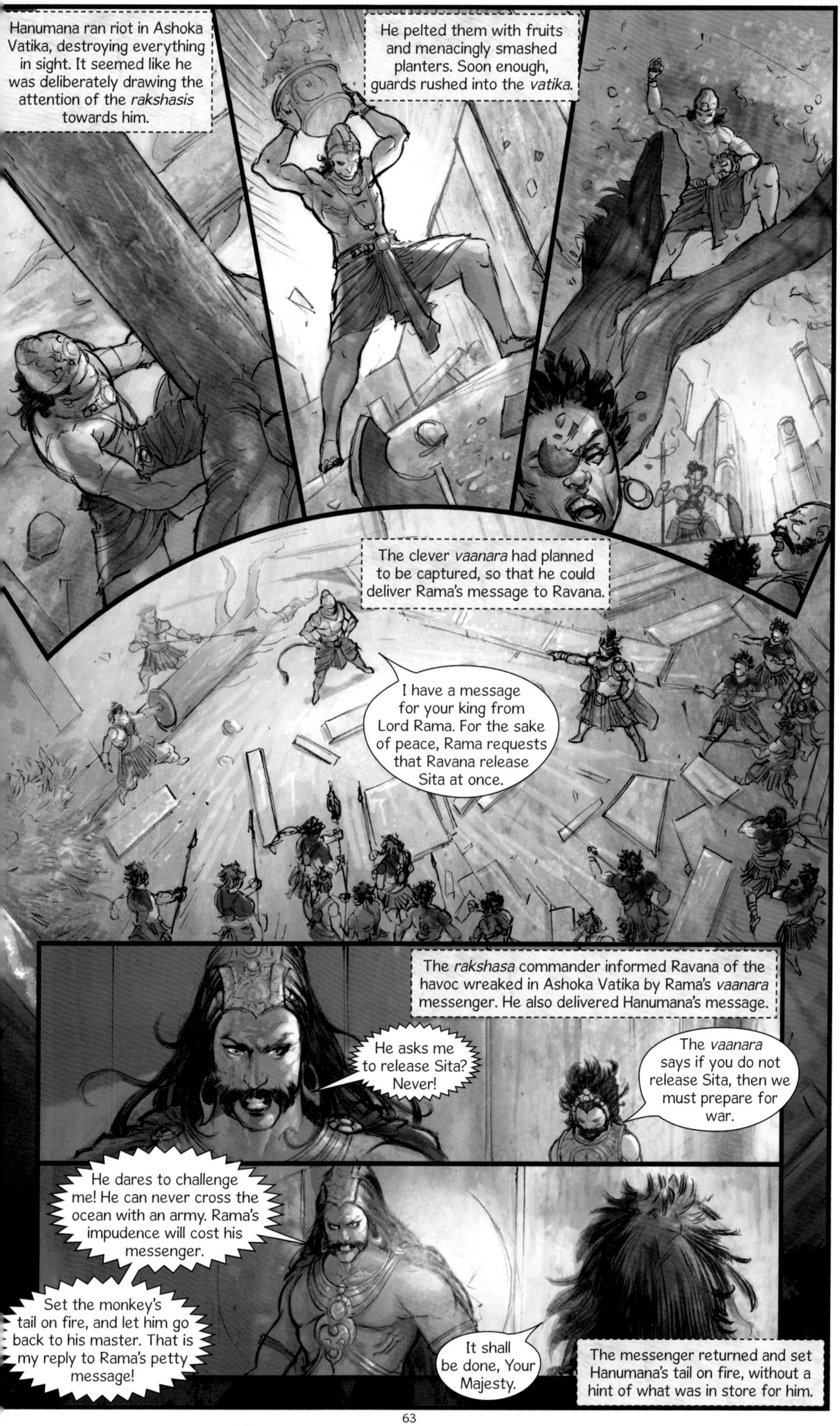

Hanumana ran riot in Ashoka Vatika, destroying everything in sight. It seemed like he was deliberately drawing the attention of the *rakshasis* towards him.
He pelted them with fruits and menacingly smashed planters. Soon enough, guards rushed into the *vatika*.
The clever *vaanara* had planned to be captured, so that he could deliver Rama's message to Ravana.
I have a message for your king from Lord Rama. For the sake of peace, Rama requests that Ravana release Sita at once.
The *rakshasa* commander informed Ravana of the havoc wreaked in Ashoka Vatika by Rama's *vaanara* messenger. He also delivered Hanumana's message.
He asks me to release Sita? Never!
The *vaanara* says if you do not release Sita, then we must prepare for war.
He dares to challenge me! He can never cross the ocean with an army. Rama's impudence will cost his messenger.
Set the monkey's tail on fire, and let him go back to his master. That is my reply to Rama's petty message!
It shall be done, Your Majesty.
The messenger returned and set Hanumana's tail on fire, without a hint of what was in store for him.

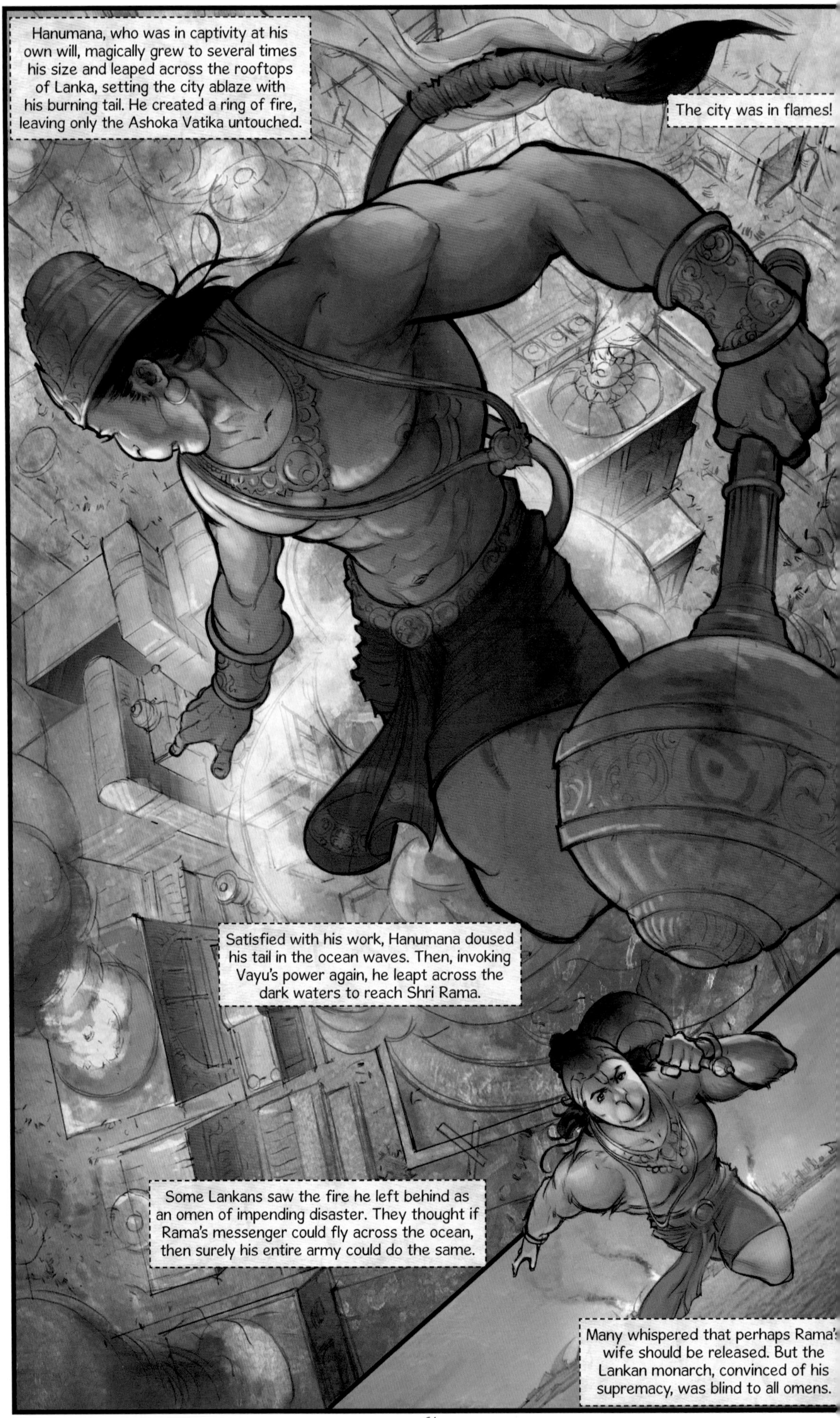
Hanumana, who was in captivity at his own will, magically grew to several times his size and leaped across the rooftops of Lanka, setting the city ablaze with his burning tail. He created a ring of fire, leaving only the Ashoka Vatika untouched.
The city was in flames!
Satisfied with his work, Hanumana doused his tail in the ocean waves. Then, invoking Vayu's power again, he leapt across the dark waters to reach Shri Rama.
Some Lankans saw the fire he left behind as an omen of impending disaster. They thought if Rama's messenger could fly across the ocean, then surely his entire army could do the same.
Many whispered that perhaps Rama's wife should be released. But the Lankan monarch, convinced of his supremacy, was blind to all omens.

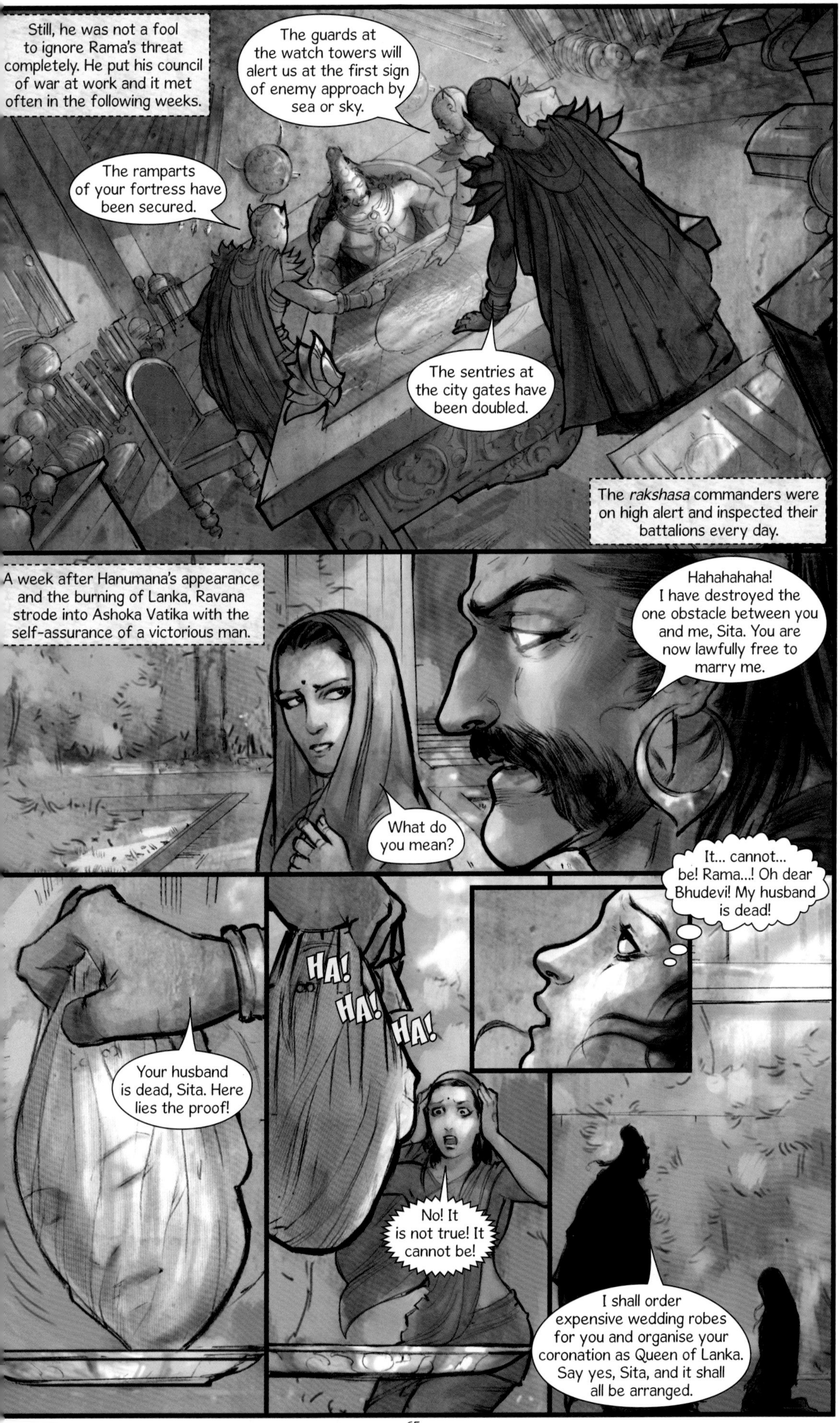
Still, he was not a fool to ignore Rama's threat completely. He put his council of war at work and it met often in the following weeks.
The guards at the watch towers will alert us at the first sign of enemy approach by sea or sky.
The ramparts of your fortress have been secured.
The sentries at the city gates have been doubled.
The *rakshasa* commanders were on high alert and inspected their battalions every day.
A week after Hanumana's appearance and the burning of Lanka, Ravana strode into Ashoka Vatika with the self-assurance of a victorious man.
Hahahahaha! I have destroyed the one obstacle between you and me, Sita. You are now lawfully free to marry me.
What do you mean?
Your husband is dead, Sita. Here lies the proof!
HA! HA! HA!
No! It is not true! It cannot be!
It... cannot... be! Rama...! Oh dear Bhudevi! My husband is dead!
I shall order expensive wedding robes for you and organise your coronation as Queen of Lanka. Say yes, Sita, and it shall all be arranged.

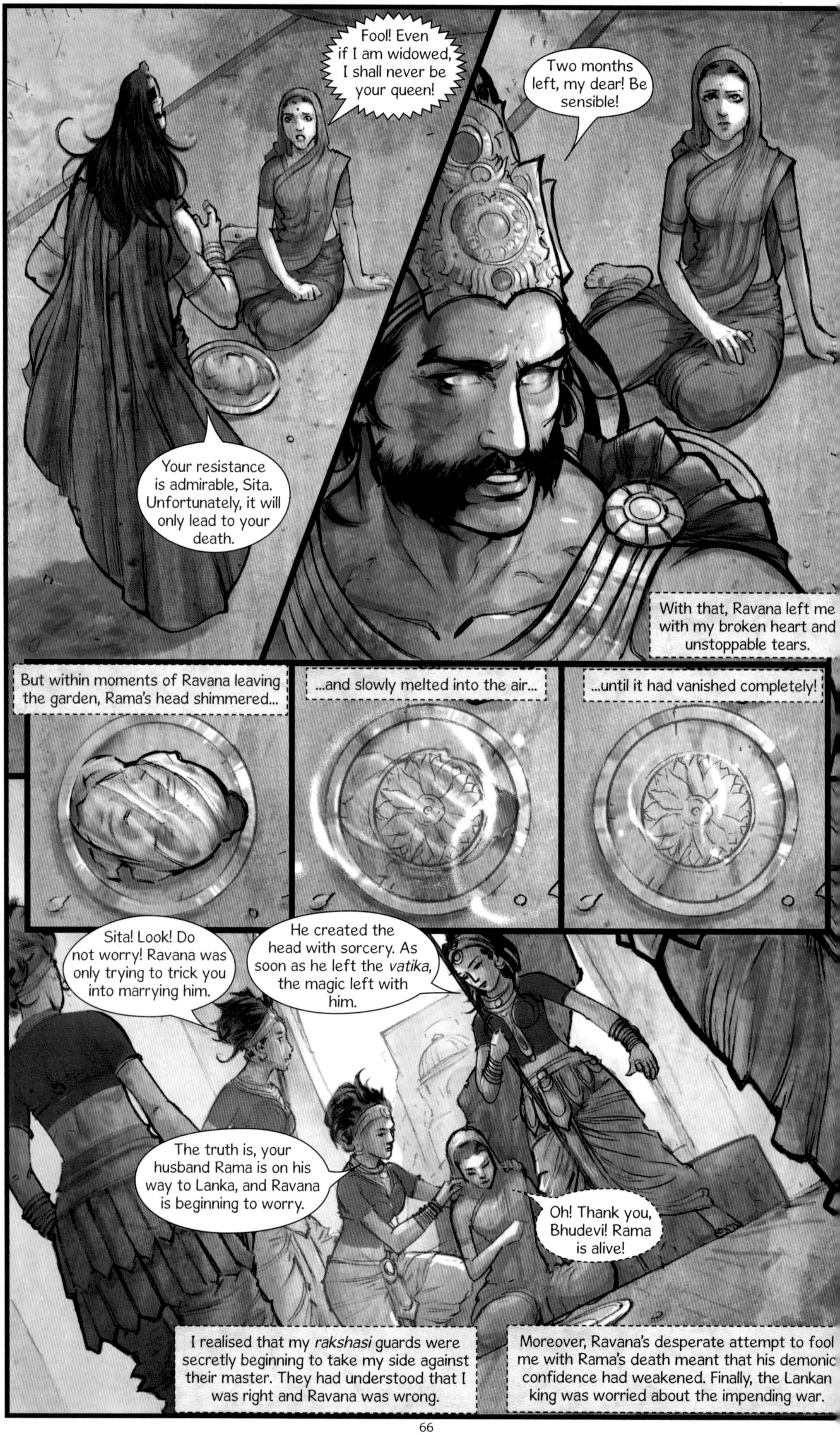
Fool! Even if I am widowed, I shall never be your queen!
Your resistance is admirable, Sita. Unfortunately, it will only lead to your death.
Two months left, my dear! Be sensible!
With that, Ravana left me with my broken heart and unstoppable tears.
But within moments of Ravana leaving the garden, Rama's head shimmered...
...and slowly melted into the air...
...until it had vanished completely!
Sita! Look! Do not worry! Ravana was only trying to trick you into marrying him.
He created the head with sorcery. As soon as he left the *vatika*, the magic left with him.
The truth is, your husband Rama is on his way to Lanka, and Ravana is beginning to worry.
Oh! Thank you, Bhudevi! Rama is alive!
I realised that my *rakshasi* guards were secretly beginning to take my side against their master. They had understood that I was right and Ravana was wrong.
Moreover, Ravana's desperate attempt to fool me with Rama's death meant that his demonic confidence had weakened. Finally, the Lankan king was worried about the impending war.

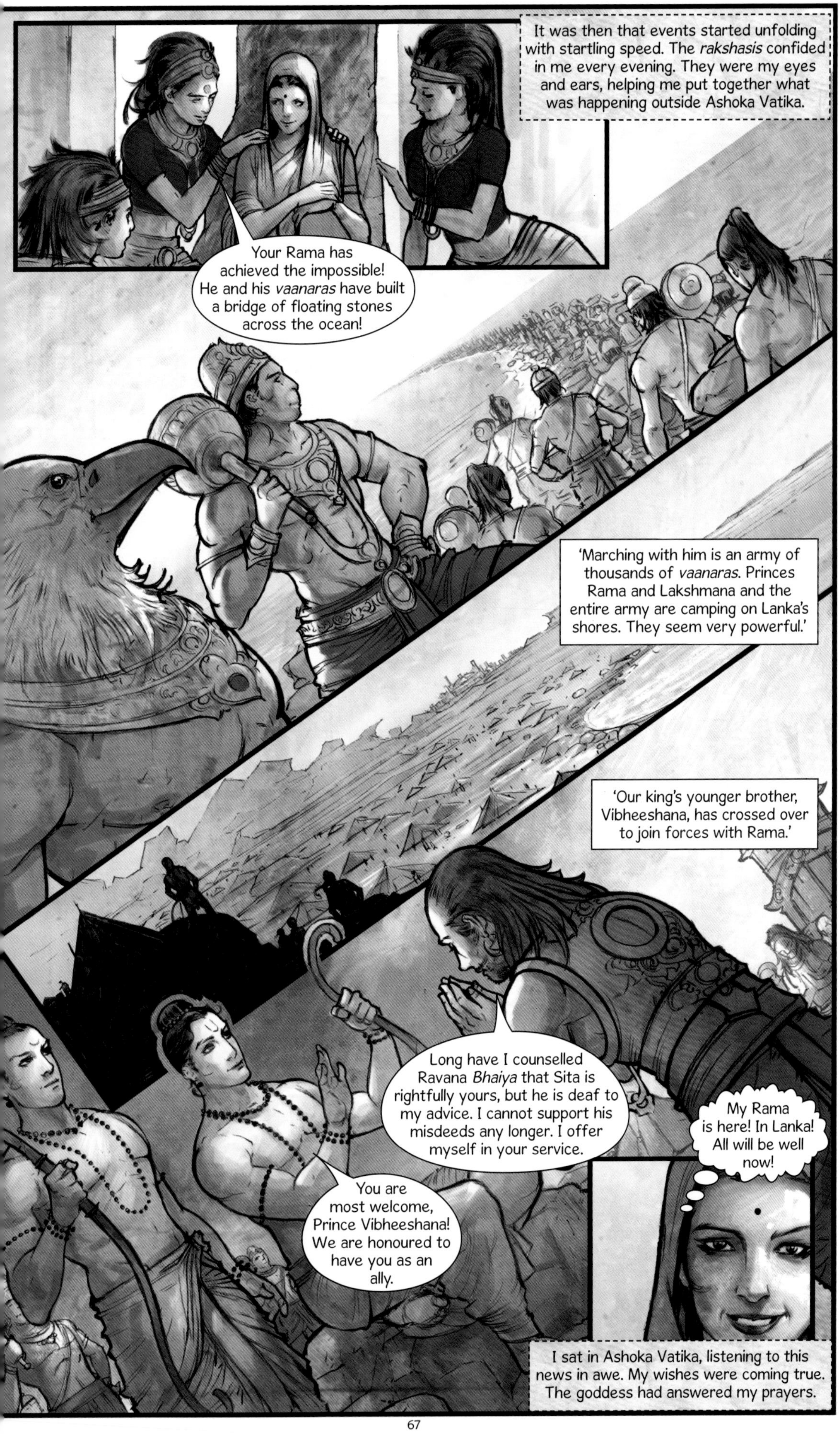

It was then that events started unfolding with startling speed. The *rakshasis* confided in me every evening. They were my eyes and ears, helping me put together what was happening outside Ashoka Vatika.
Your Rama has achieved the impossible! He and his *vaanaras* have built a bridge of floating stones across the ocean!
'Marching with him is an army of thousands of *vaanaras*. Princes Rama and Lakshmana and the entire army are camping on Lanka's shores. They seem very powerful.'
'Our king's younger brother, Vibheeshana, has crossed over to join forces with Rama.'
Long have I counselled Ravana *Bhaiya* that Sita is rightfully yours, but he is deaf to my advice. I cannot support his misdeeds any longer. I offer myself in your service.
You are most welcome, Prince Vibheeshana! We are honoured to have you as an ally.
My Rama is here! In Lanka! All will be well now!
I sat in Ashoka Vatika, listening to this news in awe. My wishes were coming true. The goddess had answered my prayers.

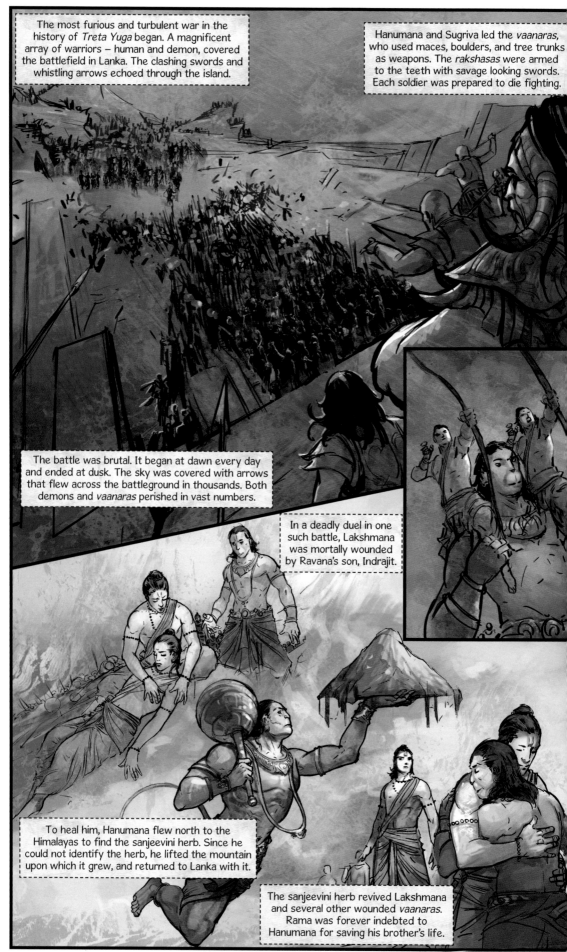

The most furious and turbulent war in the history of *Treta Yuga* began. A magnificent array of warriors – human and demon, covered the battlefield in Lanka. The clashing swords and whistling arrows echoed through the island.

Hanumana and Sugriva led the *vaanaras*, who used maces, boulders, and tree trunks as weapons. The *rakshasas* were armed to the teeth with savage looking swords. Each soldier was prepared to die fighting.

The battle was brutal. It began at dawn every day and ended at dusk. The sky was covered with arrows that flew across the battleground in thousands. Both demons and *vaanaras* perished in vast numbers.

In a deadly duel in one such battle, Lakshmana was mortally wounded by Ravana's son, Indrajit.

To heal him, Hanumana flew north to the Himalayas to find the sanjeevini herb. Since he could not identify the herb, he lifted the mountain upon which it grew, and returned to Lanka with it.

The sanjeevini herb revived Lakshmana and several other wounded *vaanaras*. Rama was forever indebted to Hanumana for saving his brother's life.

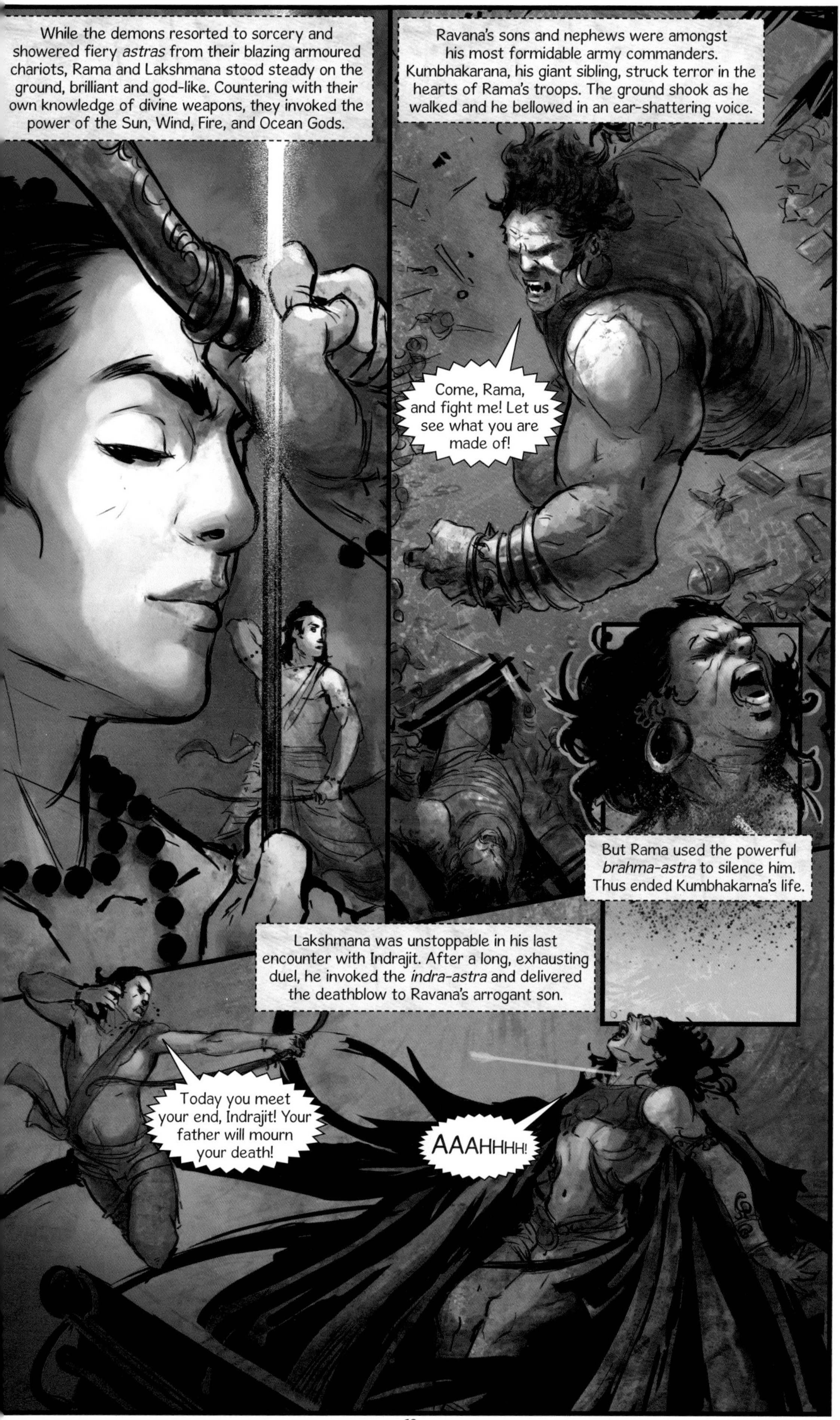
While the demons resorted to sorcery and showered fiery *astras* from their blazing armoured chariots, Rama and Lakshmana stood steady on the ground, brilliant and god-like. Countering with their own knowledge of divine weapons, they invoked the power of the Sun, Wind, Fire, and Ocean Gods.
Ravana's sons and nephews were amongst his most formidable army commanders. Kumbhakarana, his giant sibling, struck terror in the hearts of Rama's troops. The ground shook as he walked and he bellowed in an ear-shattering voice.
Come, Rama, and fight me! Let us see what you are made of!
But Rama used the powerful *brahma-astra* to silence him. Thus ended Kumbhakarna's life.
Lakshmana was unstoppable in his last encounter with Indrajit. After a long, exhausting duel, he invoked the *indra-astra* and delivered the deathblow to Ravana's arrogant son.
Today you meet your end, Indrajit! Your father will mourn your death!
AAAHHHH!

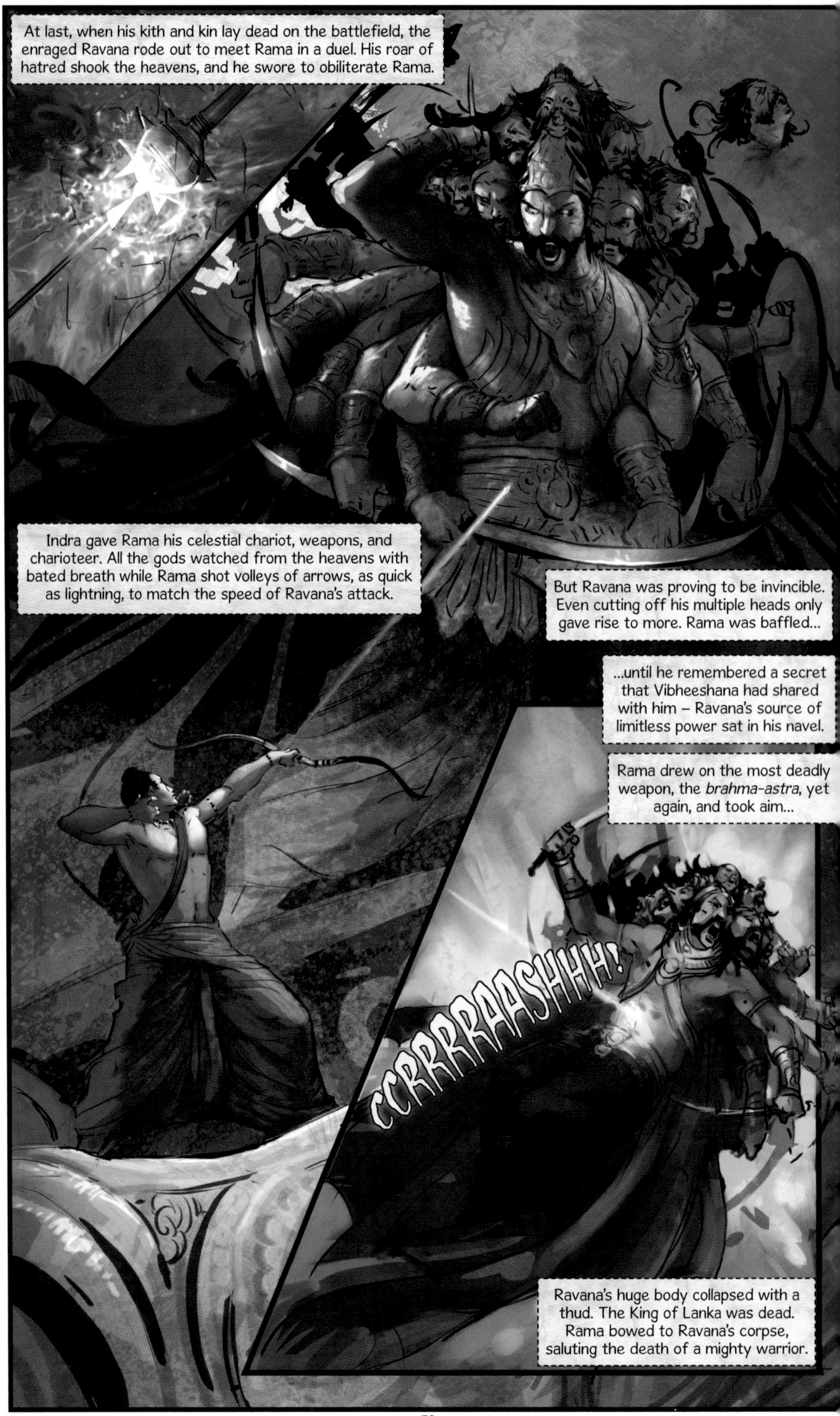
At last, when his kith and kin lay dead on the battlefield, the enraged Ravana rode out to meet Rama in a duel. His roar of hatred shook the heavens, and he swore to obiliterate Rama.
Indra gave Rama his celestial chariot, weapons, and charioteer. All the gods watched from the heavens with bated breath while Rama shot volleys of arrows, as quick as lightning, to match the speed of Ravana's attack.
But Ravana was proving to be invincible. Even cutting off his multiple heads only gave rise to more. Rama was baffled...
...until he remembered a secret that Vibheeshana had shared with him – Ravana's source of limitless power sat in his navel.
Rama drew on the most deadly weapon, the *brahma-astra*, yet again, and took aim...
CCRRRRAASHHH!
Ravana's huge body collapsed with a thud. The King of Lanka was dead. Rama bowed to Ravana's corpse, saluting the death of a mighty warrior.

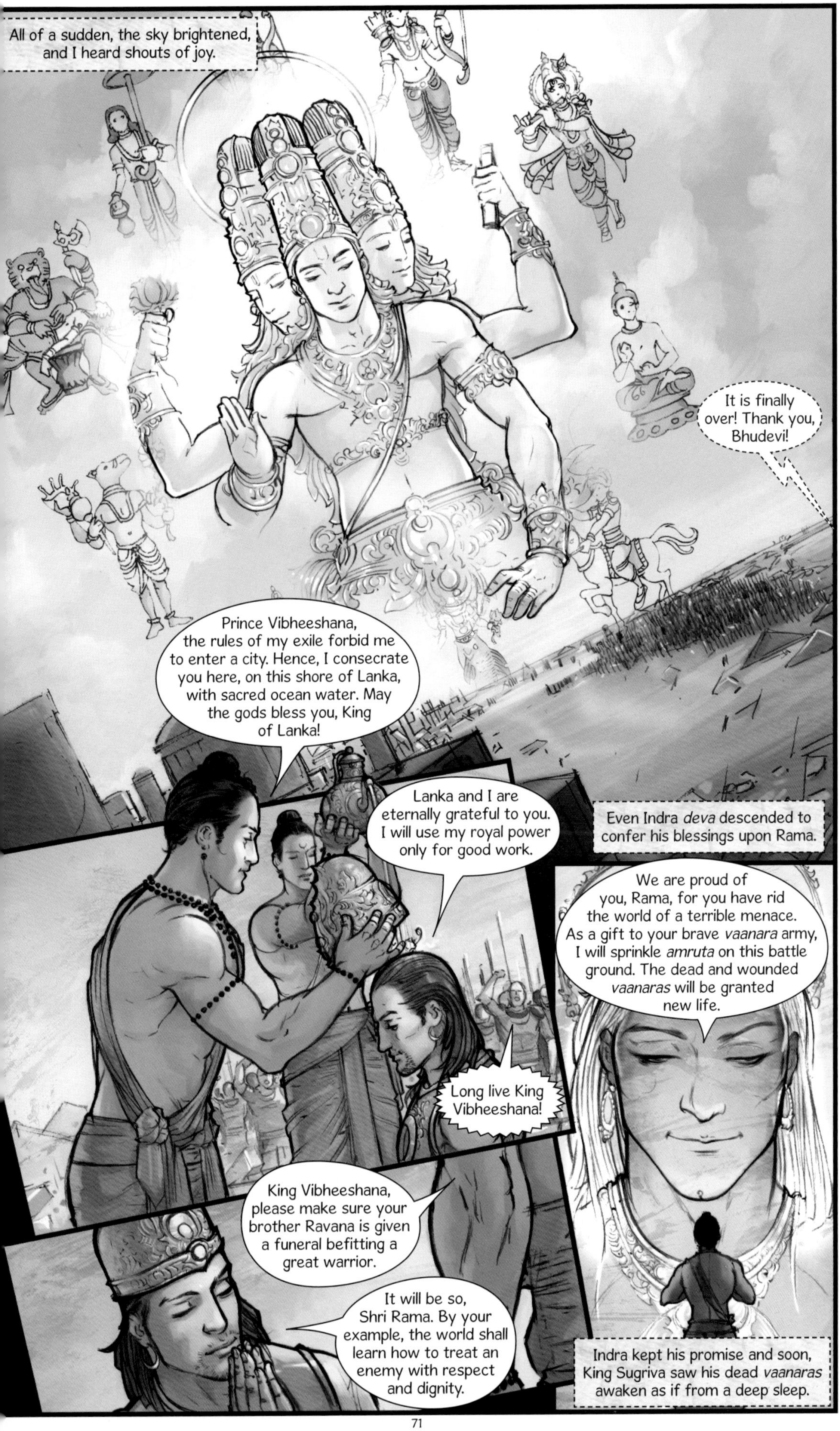

All of a sudden, the sky brightened, and I heard shouts of joy.
It is finally over! Thank you, Bhudevi!
Prince Vibheeshana, the rules of my exile forbid me to enter a city. Hence, I consecrate you here, on this shore of Lanka, with sacred ocean water. May the gods bless you, King of Lanka!
Lanka and I are eternally grateful to you. I will use my royal power only for good work.
Long live King Vibheeshana!
King Vibheeshana, please make sure your brother Ravana is given a funeral befitting a great warrior.
It will be so, Shri Rama. By your example, the world shall learn how to treat an enemy with respect and dignity.
Even Indra *deva* descended to confer his blessings upon Rama.
We are proud of you, Rama, for you have rid the world of a terrible menace. As a gift to your brave *vaanara* army, I will sprinkle *amruta* on this battle ground. The dead and wounded *vaanaras* will be granted new life.
Indra kept his promise and soon, King Sugriva saw his dead *vaanaras* awaken as if from a deep sleep.

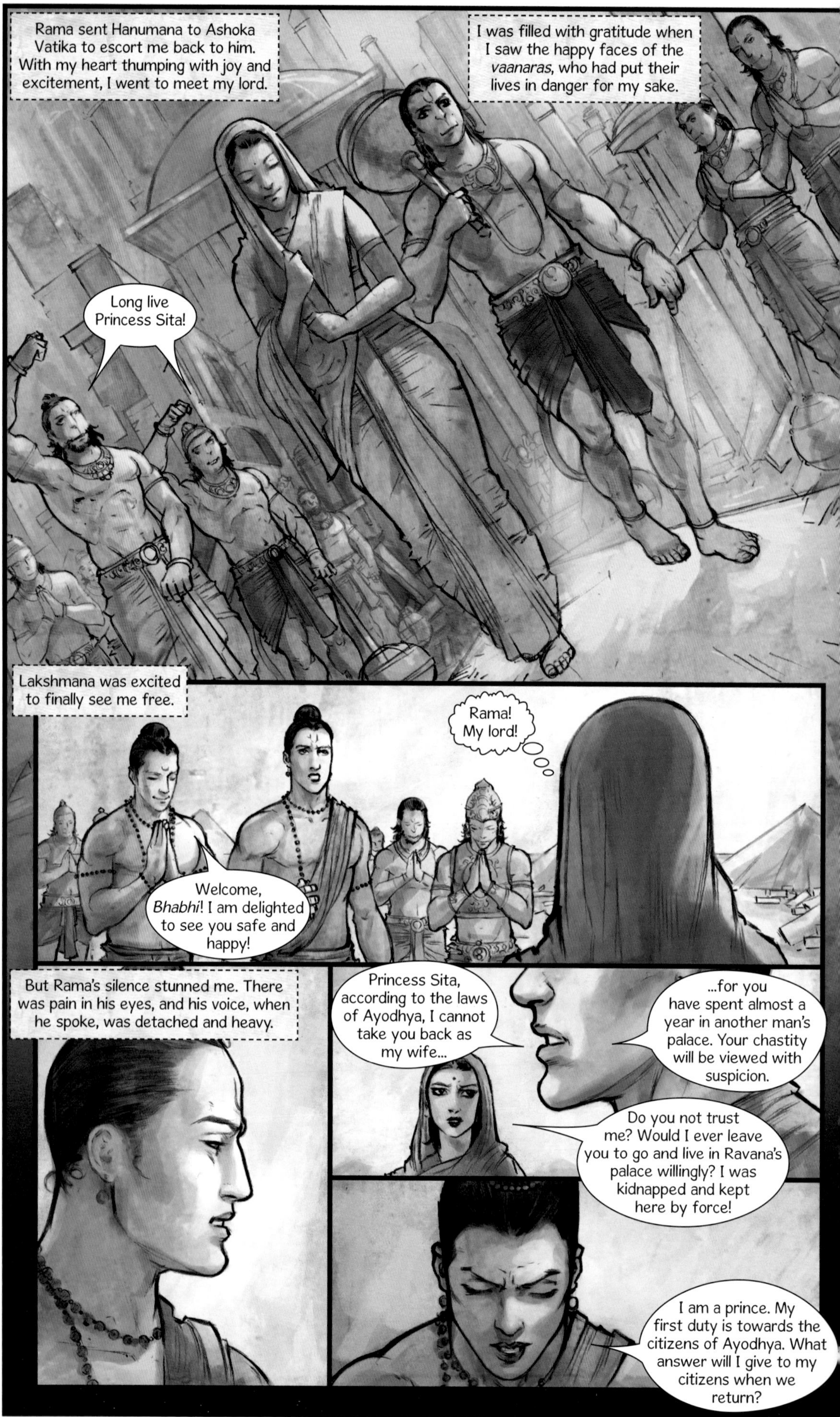
Rama sent Hanumana to Ashoka Vatika to escort me back to him. With my heart thumping with joy and excitement, I went to meet my lord.
I was filled with gratitude when I saw the happy faces of the *vaanaras*, who had put their lives in danger for my sake.
Long live Princess Sita!
Lakshmana was excited to finally see me free.
Rama! My lord!
Welcome, *Bhabhi*! I am delighted to see you safe and happy!
But Rama's silence stunned me. There was pain in his eyes, and his voice, when he spoke, was detached and heavy.
Princess Sita, according to the laws of Ayodhya, I cannot take you back as my wife...
...for you have spent almost a year in another man's palace. Your chastity will be viewed with suspicion.
Do you not trust me? Would I ever leave you to go and live in Ravana's palace willingly? I was kidnapped and kept here by force!
I am a prince. My first duty is towards the citizens of Ayodhya. What answer will I give to my citizens when we return?

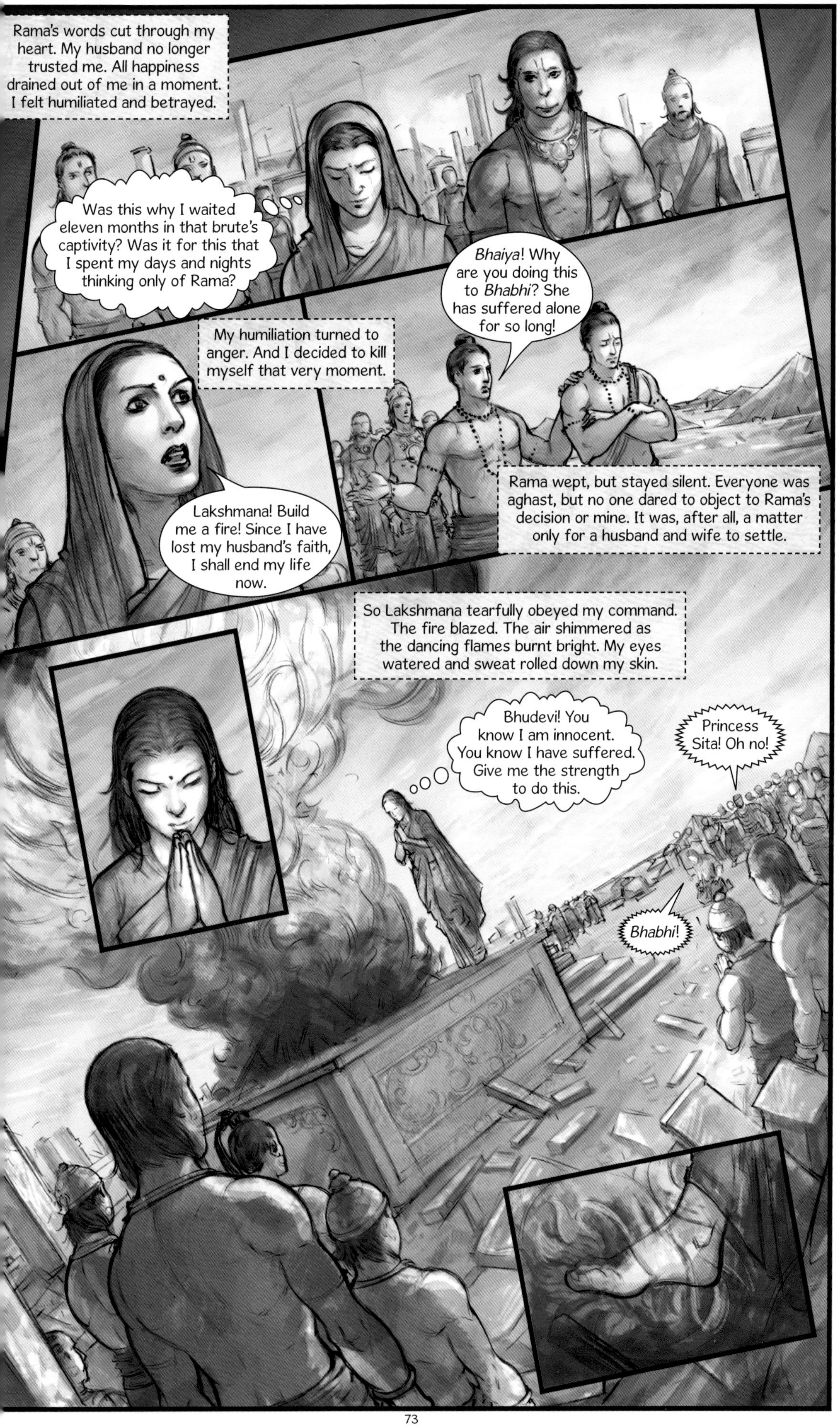
Rama's words cut through my heart. My husband no longer trusted me. All happiness drained out of me in a moment. I felt humiliated and betrayed.
Was this why I waited eleven months in that brute's captivity? Was it for this that I spent my days and nights thinking only of Rama?
My humiliation turned to anger. And I decided to kill myself that very moment.
Lakshmana! Build me a fire! Since I have lost my husband's faith, I shall end my life now.
Bhaiya! Why are you doing this to *Bhabhi*? She has suffered alone for so long!
Rama wept, but stayed silent. Everyone was aghast, but no one dared to object to Rama's decision or mine. It was, after all, a matter only for a husband and wife to settle.
So Lakshmana tearfully obeyed my command. The fire blazed. The air shimmered as the dancing flames burnt bright. My eyes watered and sweat rolled down my skin.
Bhudevi! You know I am innocent. You know I have suffered. Give me the strength to do this.
Princess Sita! Oh no!
Bhabhi!

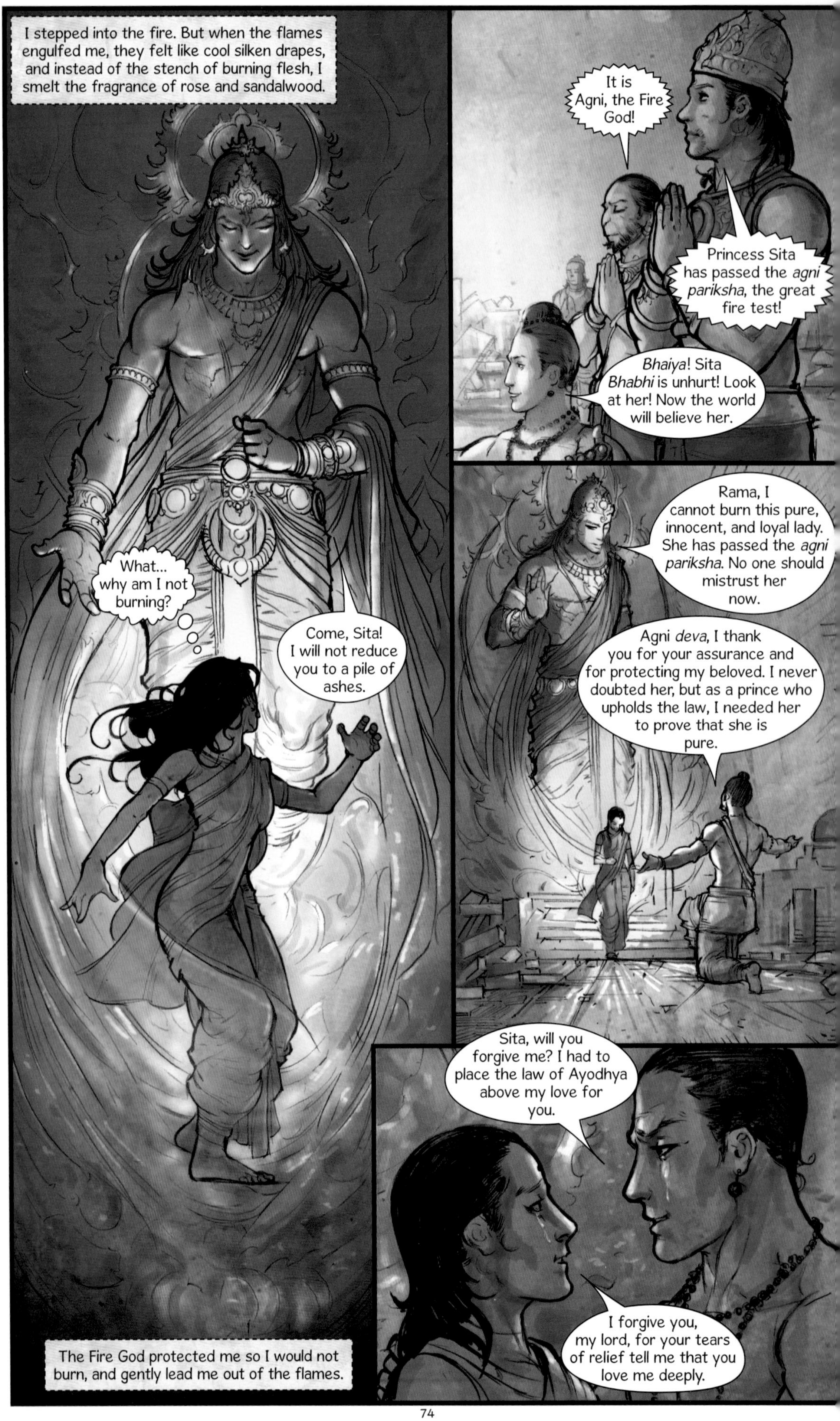

I stepped into the fire. But when the flames engulfed me, they felt like cool silken drapes, and instead of the stench of burning flesh, I smelt the fragrance of rose and sandalwood.
What... why am I not burning?
Come, Sita! I will not reduce you to a pile of ashes.
The Fire God protected me so I would not burn, and gently lead me out of the flames.
It is Agni, the Fire God!
Princess Sita has passed the *agni pariksha*, the great fire test!
Bhaiya! Sita *Bhabhi* is unhurt! Look at her! Now the world will believe her.
Rama, I cannot burn this pure, innocent, and loyal lady. She has passed the *agni pariksha*. No one should mistrust her now.
Agni *deva*, I thank you for your assurance and for protecting my beloved. I never doubted her, but as a prince who upholds the law, I needed her to prove that she is pure.
Sita, will you forgive me? I had to place the law of Ayodhya above my love for you.
I forgive you, my lord, for your tears of relief tell me that you love me deeply.

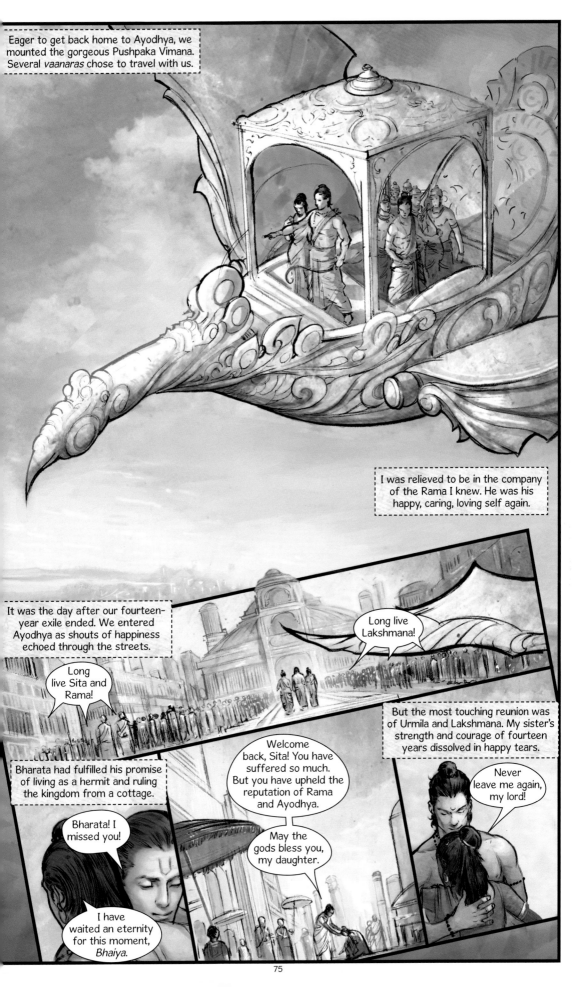

Eager to get back home to Ayodhya, we mounted the gorgeous Pushpaka Vimana. Several *vaanaras* chose to travel with us.

I was relieved to be in the company of the Rama I knew. He was his happy, caring, loving self again.

It was the day after our fourteen-year exile ended. We entered Ayodhya as shouts of happiness echoed through the streets.

Long live Lakshmana!

Long live Sita and Rama!

But the most touching reunion was of Urmila and Lakshmana. My sister's strength and courage of fourteen years dissolved in happy tears.

Bharata had fulfilled his promise of living as a hermit and ruling the kingdom from a cottage.

Welcome back, Sita! You have suffered so much. But you have upheld the reputation of Rama and Ayodhya.

Never leave me again, my lord!

Bharata! I missed you!

May the gods bless you, my daughter.

I have waited an eternity for this moment, *Bhaiya*.

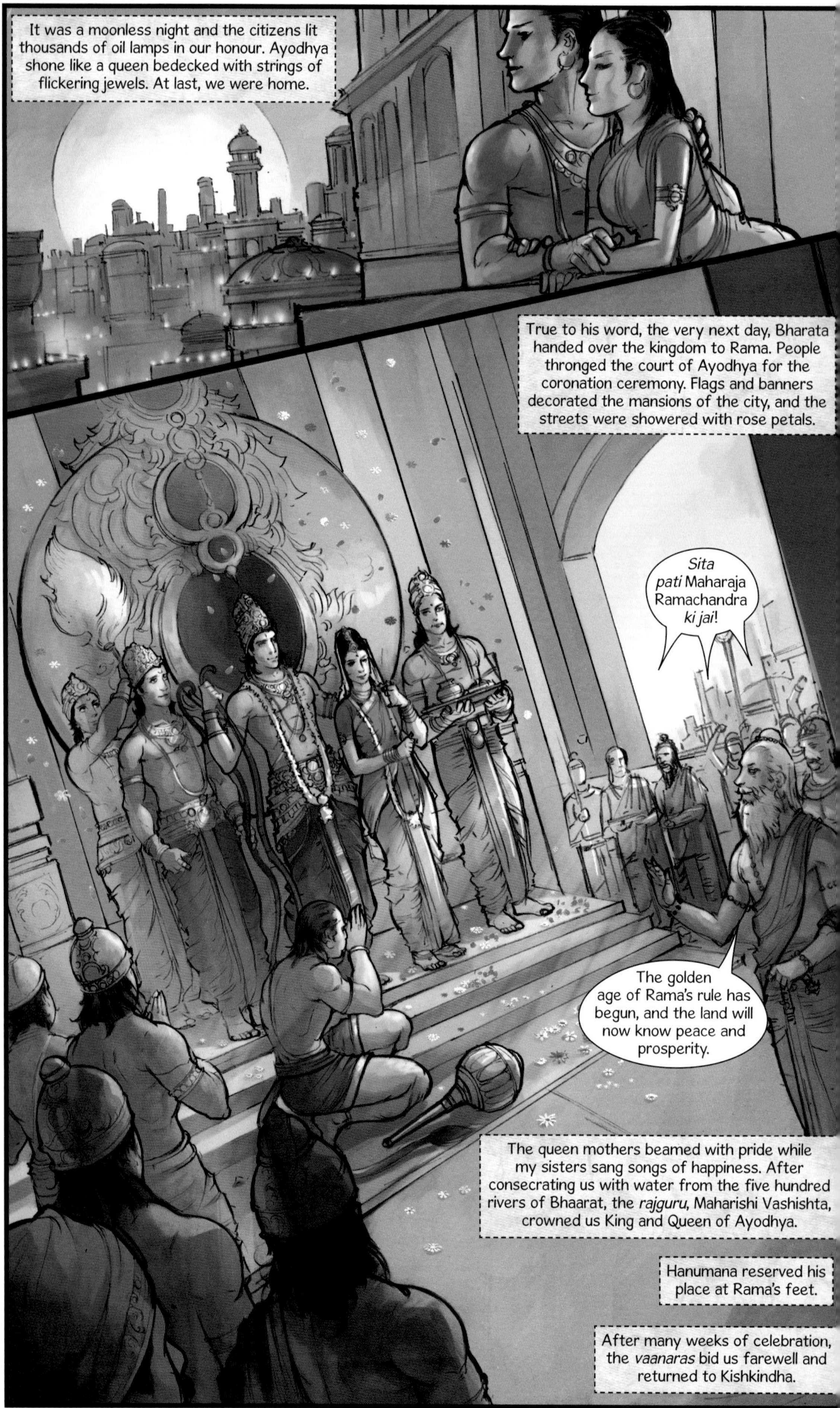

It was a moonless night and the citizens lit thousands of oil lamps in our honour. Ayodhya shone like a queen bedecked with strings of flickering jewels. At last, we were home.
True to his word, the very next day, Bharata handed over the kingdom to Rama. People thronged the court of Ayodhya for the coronation ceremony. Flags and banners decorated the mansions of the city, and the streets were showered with rose petals.
Sita pati Maharaja Ramachandra *ki jai*!
The golden age of Rama's rule has begun, and the land will now know peace and prosperity.
The queen mothers beamed with pride while my sisters sang songs of happiness. After consecrating us with water from the five hundred rivers of Bhaarat, the *rajguru*, Maharishi Vashishta, crowned us King and Queen of Ayodhya.
Hanumana reserved his place at Rama's feet.
After many weeks of celebration, the *vaanaras* bid us farewell and returned to Kishkindha.

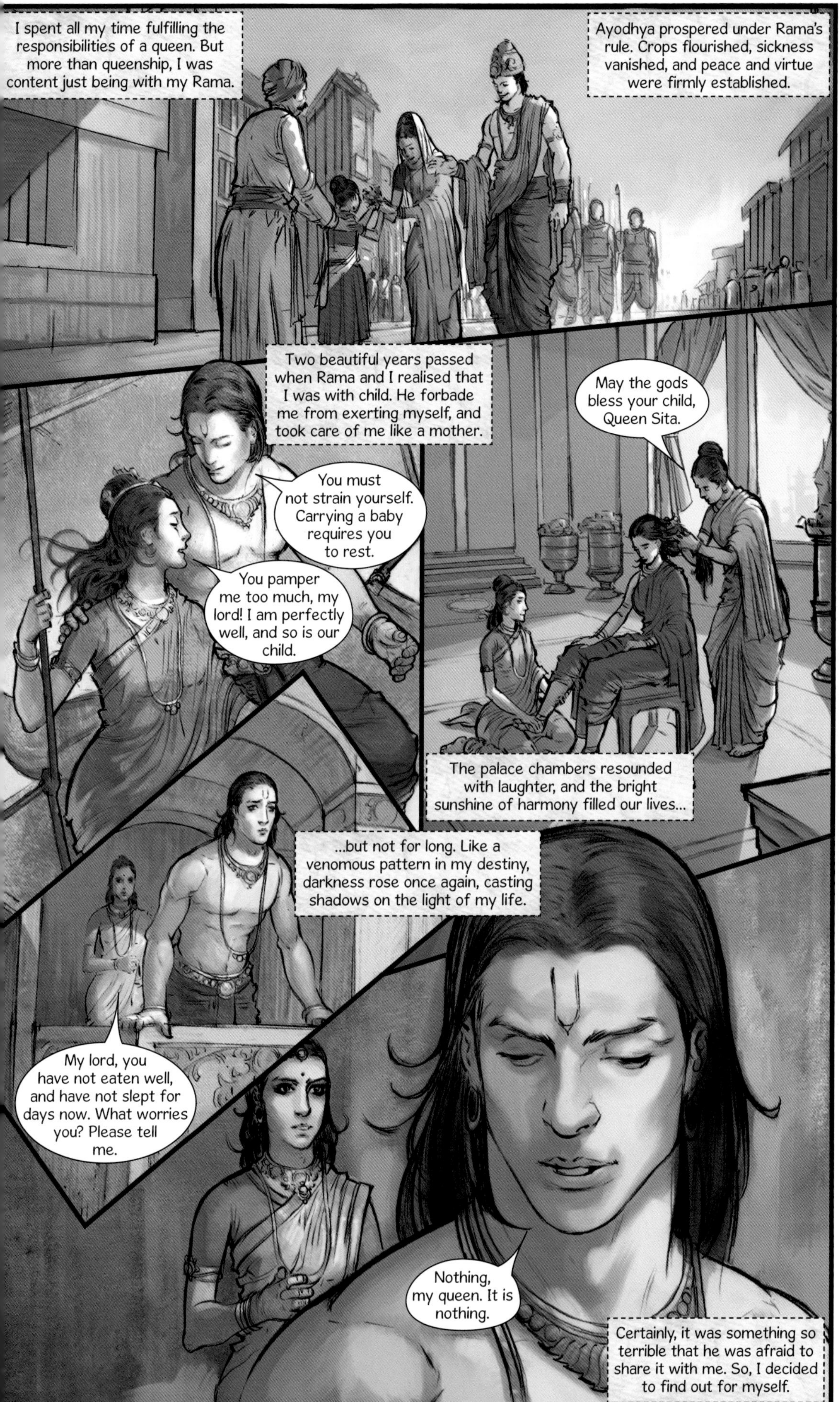
I spent all my time fulfilling the responsibilities of a queen. But more than queenship, I was content just being with my Rama.
Ayodhya prospered under Rama's rule. Crops flourished, sickness vanished, and peace and virtue were firmly established.
Two beautiful years passed when Rama and I realised that I was with child. He forbade me from exerting myself, and took care of me like a mother.
You must not strain yourself. Carrying a baby requires you to rest.
You pamper me too much, my lord! I am perfectly well, and so is our child.
May the gods bless your child, Queen Sita.
The palace chambers resounded with laughter, and the bright sunshine of harmony filled our lives...
...but not for long. Like a venomous pattern in my destiny, darkness rose once again, casting shadows on the light of my life.
My lord, you have not eaten well, and have not slept for days now. What worries you? Please tell me.
Nothing, my queen. It is nothing.
Certainly, it was something so terrible that he was afraid to share it with me. So, I decided to find out for myself.

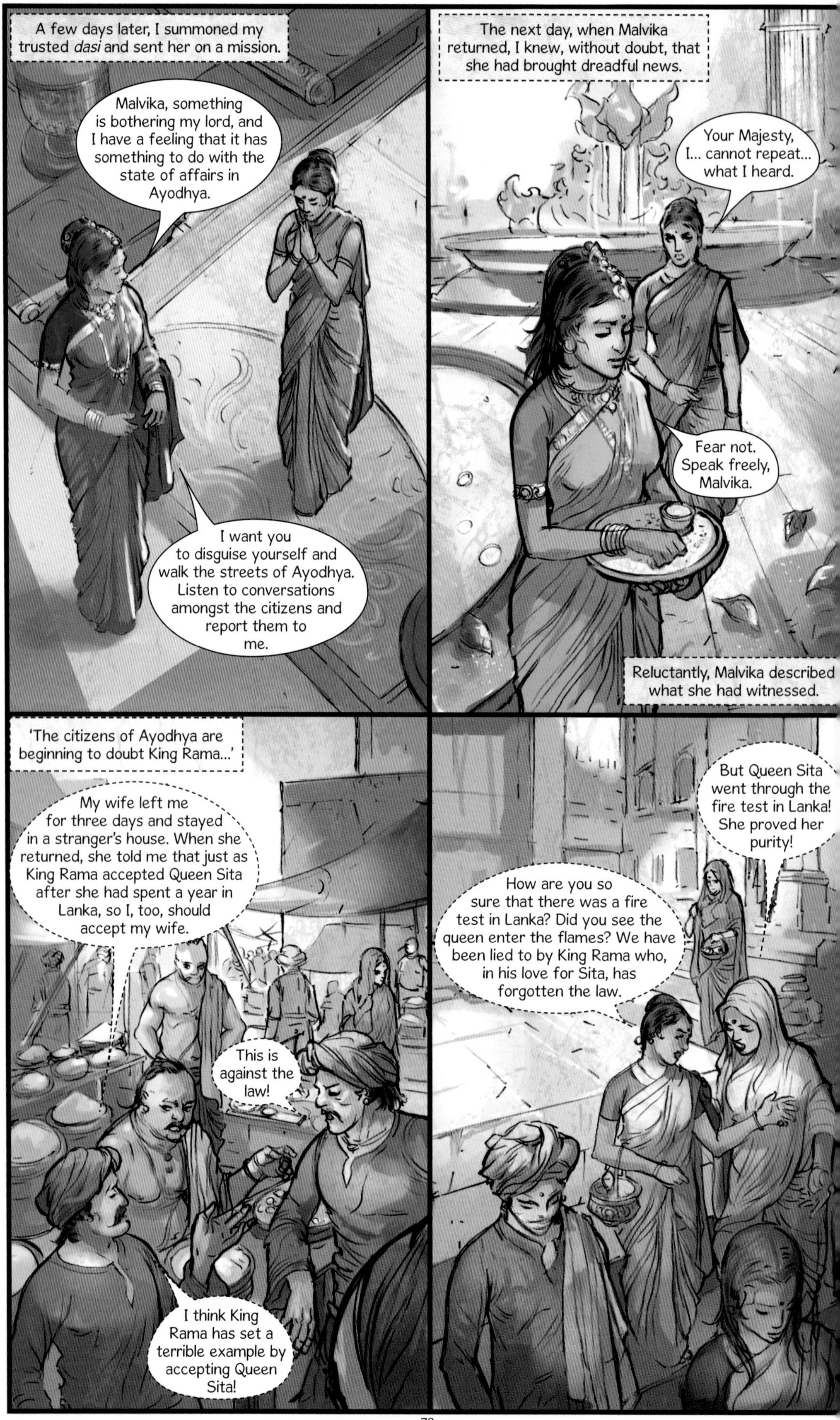

A few days later, I summoned my trusted *dasi* and sent her on a mission.
Malvika, something is bothering my lord, and I have a feeling that it has something to do with the state of affairs in Ayodhya.
I want you to disguise yourself and walk the streets of Ayodhya. Listen to conversations amongst the citizens and report them to me.
The next day, when Malvika returned, I knew, without doubt, that she had brought dreadful news.
Your Majesty, I... cannot repeat... what I heard.
Fear not. Speak freely, Malvika.
Reluctantly, Malvika described what she had witnessed.
'The citizens of Ayodhya are beginning to doubt King Rama...'
My wife left me for three days and stayed in a stranger's house. When she returned, she told me that just as King Rama accepted Queen Sita after she had spent a year in Lanka, so I, too, should accept my wife.
This is against the law!
I think King Rama has set a terrible example by accepting Queen Sita!
But Queen Sita went through the fire test in Lanka! She proved her purity!
How are you so sure that there was a fire test in Lanka? Did you see the queen enter the flames? We have been lied to by King Rama who, in his love for Sita, has forgotten the law.

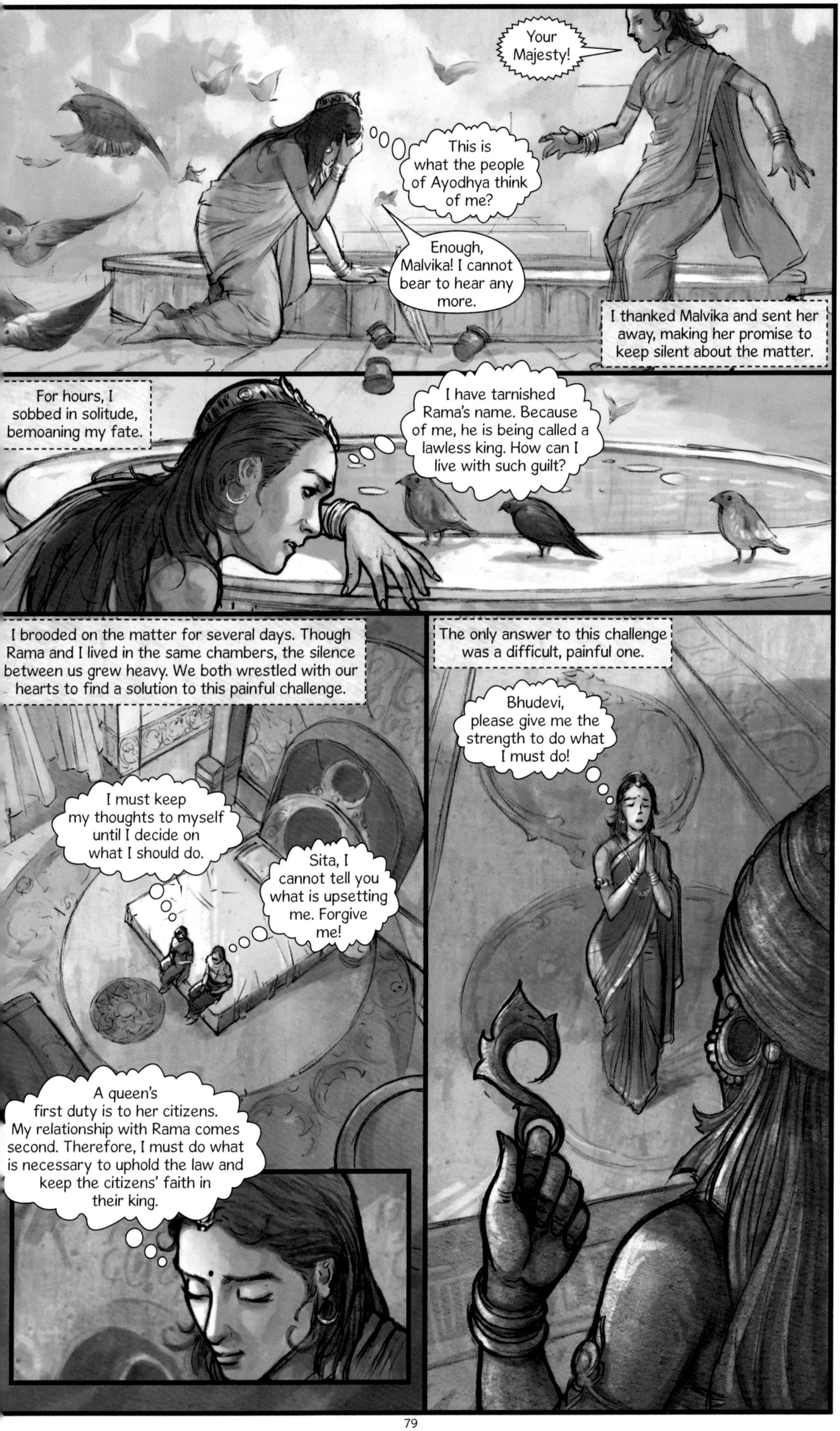
Your Majesty!
This is what the people of Ayodhya think of me?
Enough, Malvika! I cannot bear to hear any more.
I thanked Malvika and sent her away, making her promise to keep silent about the matter.
For hours, I sobbed in solitude, bemoaning my fate.
I have tarnished Rama's name. Because of me, he is being called a lawless king. How can I live with such guilt?
I brooded on the matter for several days. Though Rama and I lived in the same chambers, the silence between us grew heavy. We both wrestled with our hearts to find a solution to this painful challenge.
I must keep my thoughts to myself until I decide on what I should do.
Sita, I cannot tell you what is upsetting me. Forgive me!
A queen's first duty is to her citizens. My relationship with Rama comes second. Therefore, I must do what is necessary to uphold the law and keep the citizens' faith in their king.
The only answer to this challenge was a difficult, painful one.
Bhudevi, please give me the strength to do what I must do!

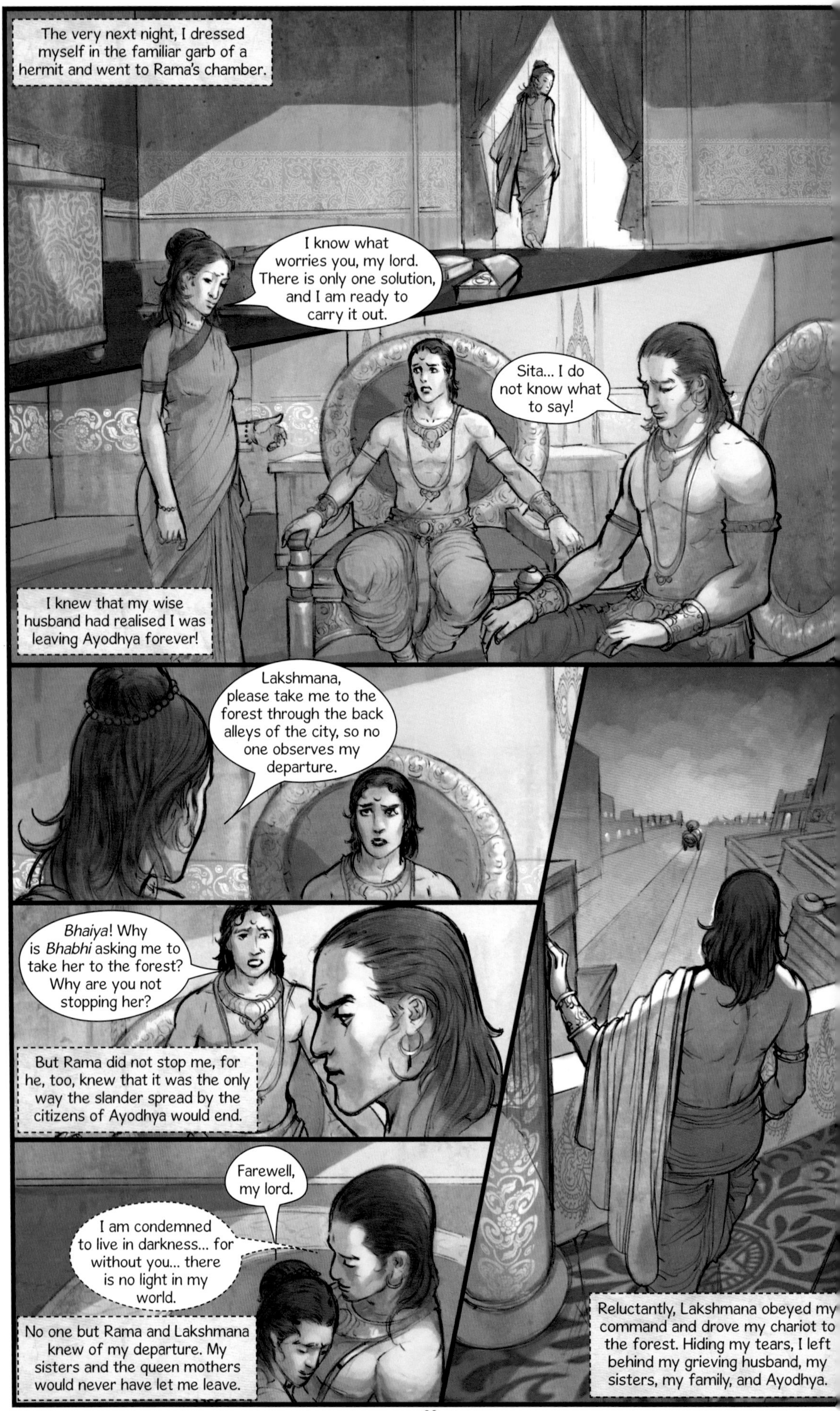
The very next night, I dressed myself in the familiar garb of a hermit and went to Rama's chamber.
I know what worries you, my lord. There is only one solution, and I am ready to carry it out.
Sita... I do not know what to say!
I knew that my wise husband had realised I was leaving Ayodhya forever!
Lakshmana, please take me to the forest through the back alleys of the city, so no one observes my departure.
Bhaiya! Why is *Bhabhi* asking me to take her to the forest? Why are you not stopping her?
But Rama did not stop me, for he, too, knew that it was the only way the slander spread by the citizens of Ayodhya would end.
Farewell, my lord.
I am condemned to live in darkness... for without you... there is no light in my world.
No one but Rama and Lakshmana knew of my departure. My sisters and the queen mothers would never have let me leave.
Reluctantly, Lakshmana obeyed my command and drove my chariot to the forest. Hiding my tears, I left behind my grieving husband, my sisters, my family, and Ayodhya.

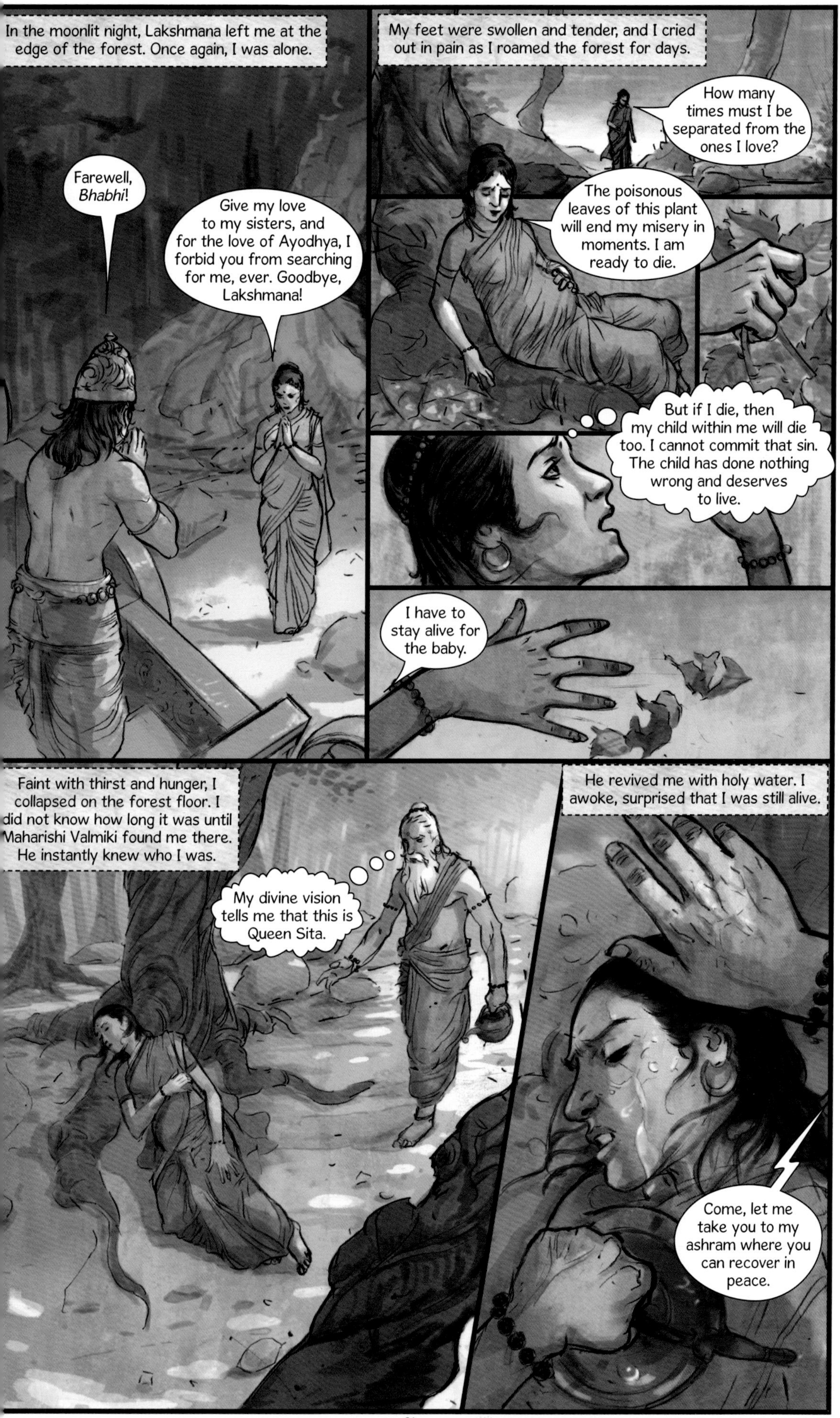

In the moonlit night, Lakshmana left me at the edge of the forest. Once again, I was alone.
Farewell, *Bhabhi*!
Give my love to my sisters, and for the love of Ayodhya, I forbid you from searching for me, ever. Goodbye, Lakshmana!
My feet were swollen and tender, and I cried out in pain as I roamed the forest for days.
How many times must I be separated from the ones I love?
The poisonous leaves of this plant will end my misery in moments. I am ready to die.
But if I die, then my child within me will die too. I cannot commit that sin. The child has done nothing wrong and deserves to live.
I have to stay alive for the baby.
Faint with thirst and hunger, I collapsed on the forest floor. I did not know how long it was until Maharishi Valmiki found me there. He instantly knew who I was.
My divine vision tells me that this is Queen Sita.
He revived me with holy water. I awoke, surprised that I was still alive.
Come, let me take you to my ashram where you can recover in peace.

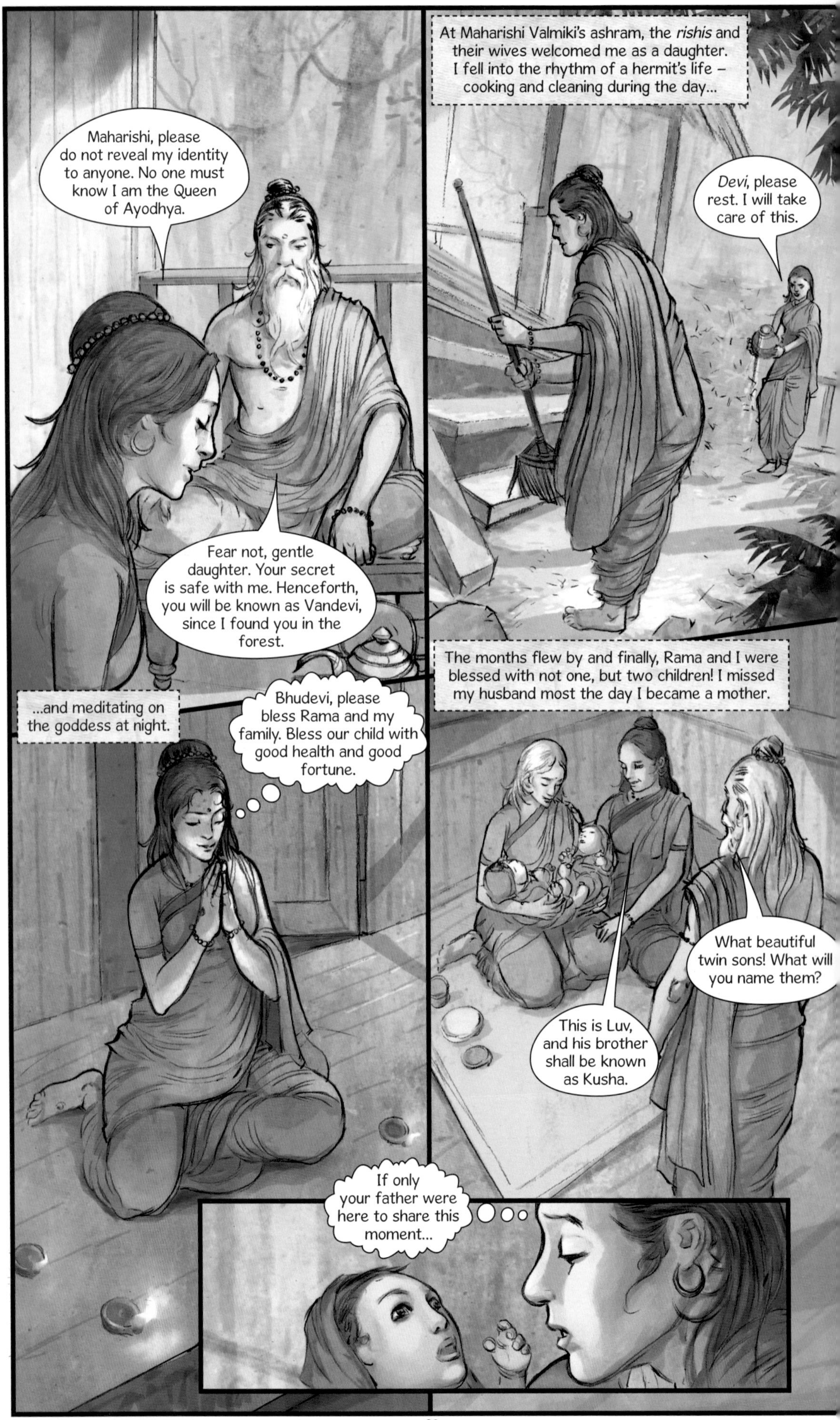
Maharishi, please do not reveal my identity to anyone. No one must know I am the Queen of Ayodhya.
Fear not, gentle daughter. Your secret is safe with me. Henceforth, you will be known as Vandevi, since I found you in the forest.
At Maharishi Valmiki's ashram, the *rishis* and their wives welcomed me as a daughter. I fell into the rhythm of a hermit's life – cooking and cleaning during the day...
Devi, please rest. I will take care of this.
...and meditating on the goddess at night.
Bhudevi, please bless Rama and my family. Bless our child with good health and good fortune.
The months flew by and finally, Rama and I were blessed with not one, but two children! I missed my husband most the day I became a mother.
What beautiful twin sons! What will you name them?
This is Luv, and his brother shall be known as Kusha.
If only your father were here to share this moment...

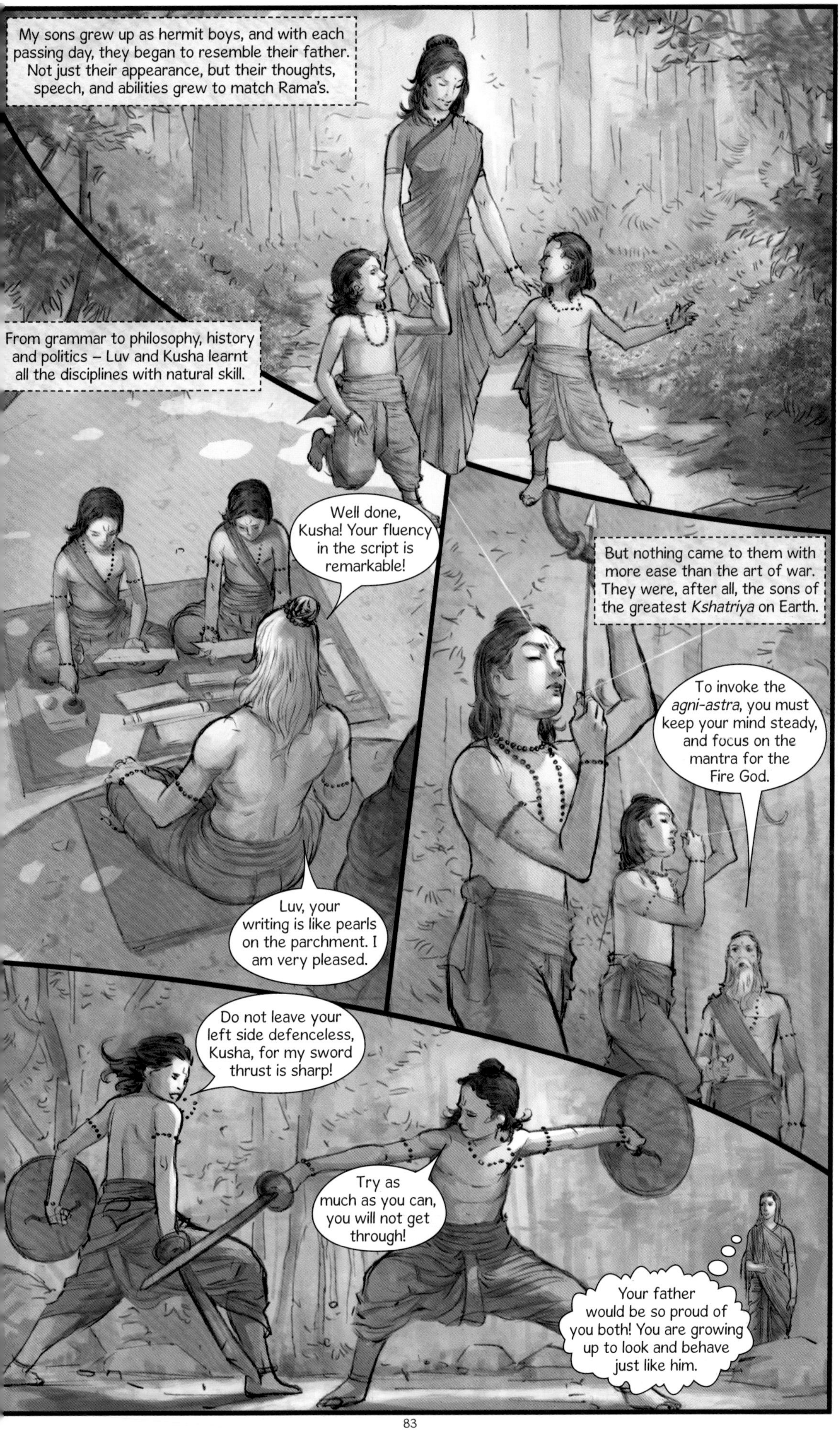

My sons grew up as hermit boys, and with each passing day, they began to resemble their father. Not just their appearance, but their thoughts, speech, and abilities grew to match Rama's.
From grammar to philosophy, history and politics – Luv and Kusha learnt all the disciplines with natural skill.
Well done, Kusha! Your fluency in the script is remarkable!
Luv, your writing is like pearls on the parchment. I am very pleased.
But nothing came to them with more ease than the art of war. They were, after all, the sons of the greatest *Kshatriya* on Earth.
To invoke the *agni-astra*, you must keep your mind steady, and focus on the mantra for the Fire God.
Do not leave your left side defenceless, Kusha, for my sword thrust is sharp!
Try as much as you can, you will not get through!
Your father would be so proud of you both! You are growing up to look and behave just like him.

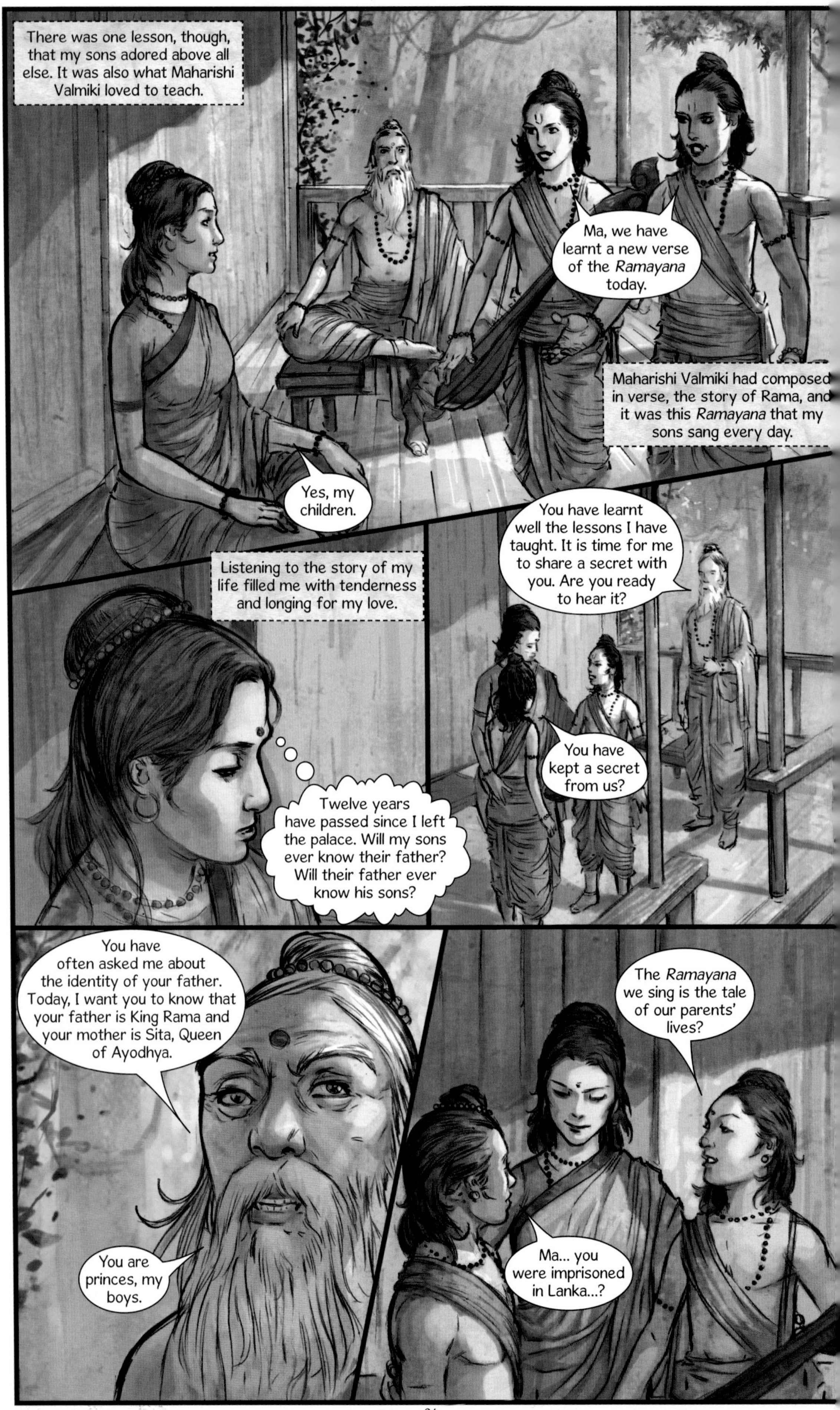
There was one lesson, though, that my sons adored above all else. It was also what Maharishi Valmiki loved to teach.
Ma, we have learnt a new verse of the *Ramayana* today.
Maharishi Valmiki had composed in verse, the story of Rama, and it was this *Ramayana* that my sons sang every day.
Yes, my children.
Listening to the story of my life filled me with tenderness and longing for my love.
Twelve years have passed since I left the palace. Will my sons ever know their father? Will their father ever know his sons?
You have learnt well the lessons I have taught. It is time for me to share a secret with you. Are you ready to hear it?
You have kept a secret from us?
You have often asked me about the identity of your father. Today, I want you to know that your father is King Rama and your mother is Sita, Queen of Ayodhya.
You are princes, my boys.
The *Ramayana* we sing is the tale of our parents' lives?
Ma... you were imprisoned in Lanka...?

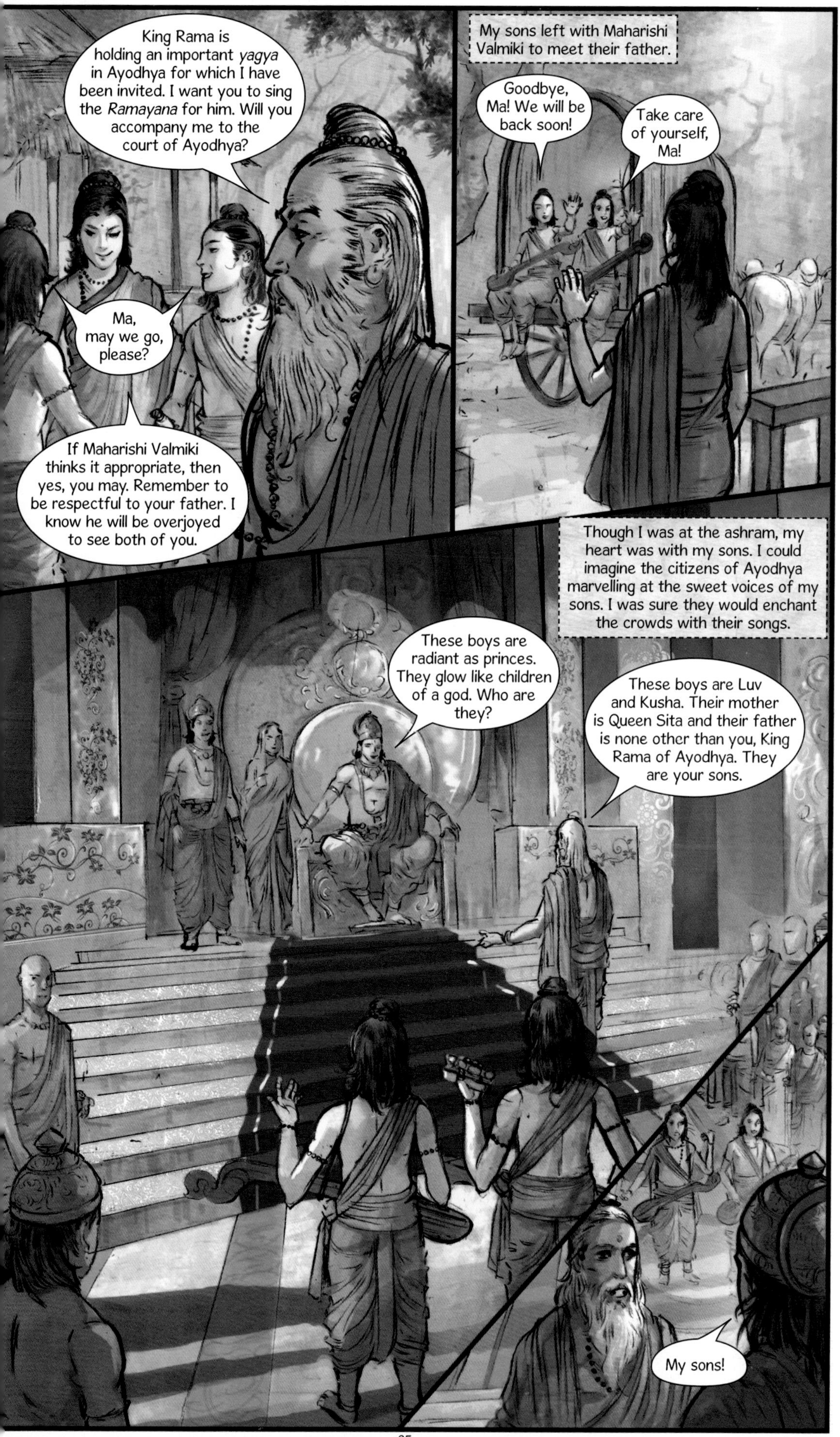
King Rama is holding an important *yagya* in Ayodhya for which I have been invited. I want you to sing the *Ramayana* for him. Will you accompany me to the court of Ayodhya?
Ma, may we go, please?
If Maharishi Valmiki thinks it appropriate, then yes, you may. Remember to be respectful to your father. I know he will be overjoyed to see both of you.
My sons left with Maharishi Valmiki to meet their father.
Goodbye, Ma! We will be back soon!
Take care of yourself, Ma!
Though I was at the ashram, my heart was with my sons. I could imagine the citizens of Ayodhya marvelling at the sweet voices of my sons. I was sure they would enchant the crowds with their songs.
These boys are radiant as princes. They glow like children of a god. Who are they?
These boys are Luv and Kusha. Their mother is Queen Sita and their father is none other than you, King Rama of Ayodhya. They are your sons.
My sons!

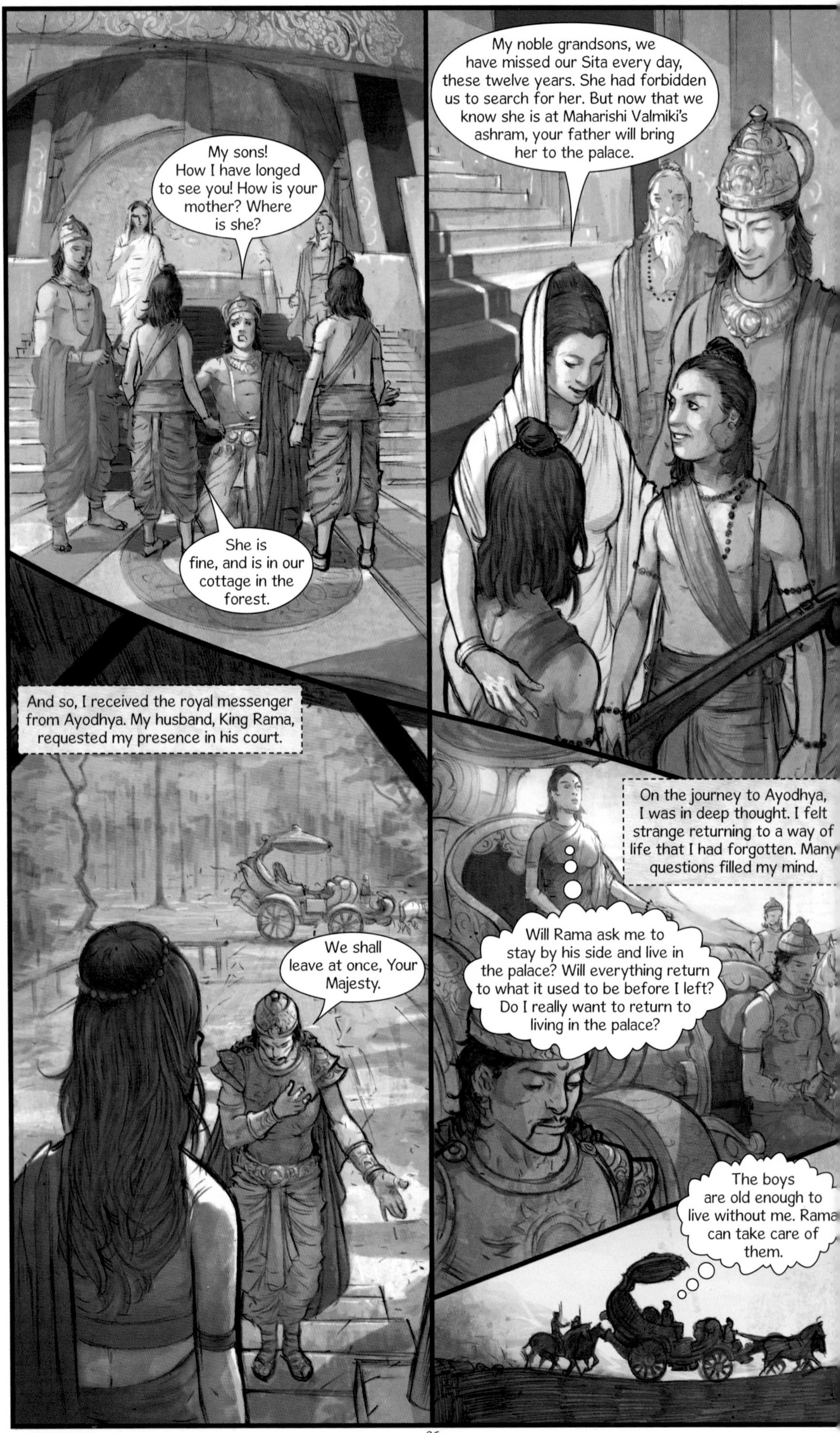

My sons! How I have longed to see you! How is your mother? Where is she?
She is fine, and is in our cottage in the forest.
My noble grandsons, we have missed our Sita every day, these twelve years. She had forbidden us to search for her. But now that we know she is at Maharishi Valmiki's ashram, your father will bring her to the palace.
And so, I received the royal messenger from Ayodhya. My husband, King Rama, requested my presence in his court.
We shall leave at once, Your Majesty.
On the journey to Ayodhya, I was in deep thought. I felt strange returning to a way of life that I had forgotten. Many questions filled my mind.
Will Rama ask me to stay by his side and live in the palace? Will everything return to what it used to be before I left? Do I really want to return to living in the palace?
The boys are old enough to live without me. Rama can take care of them.

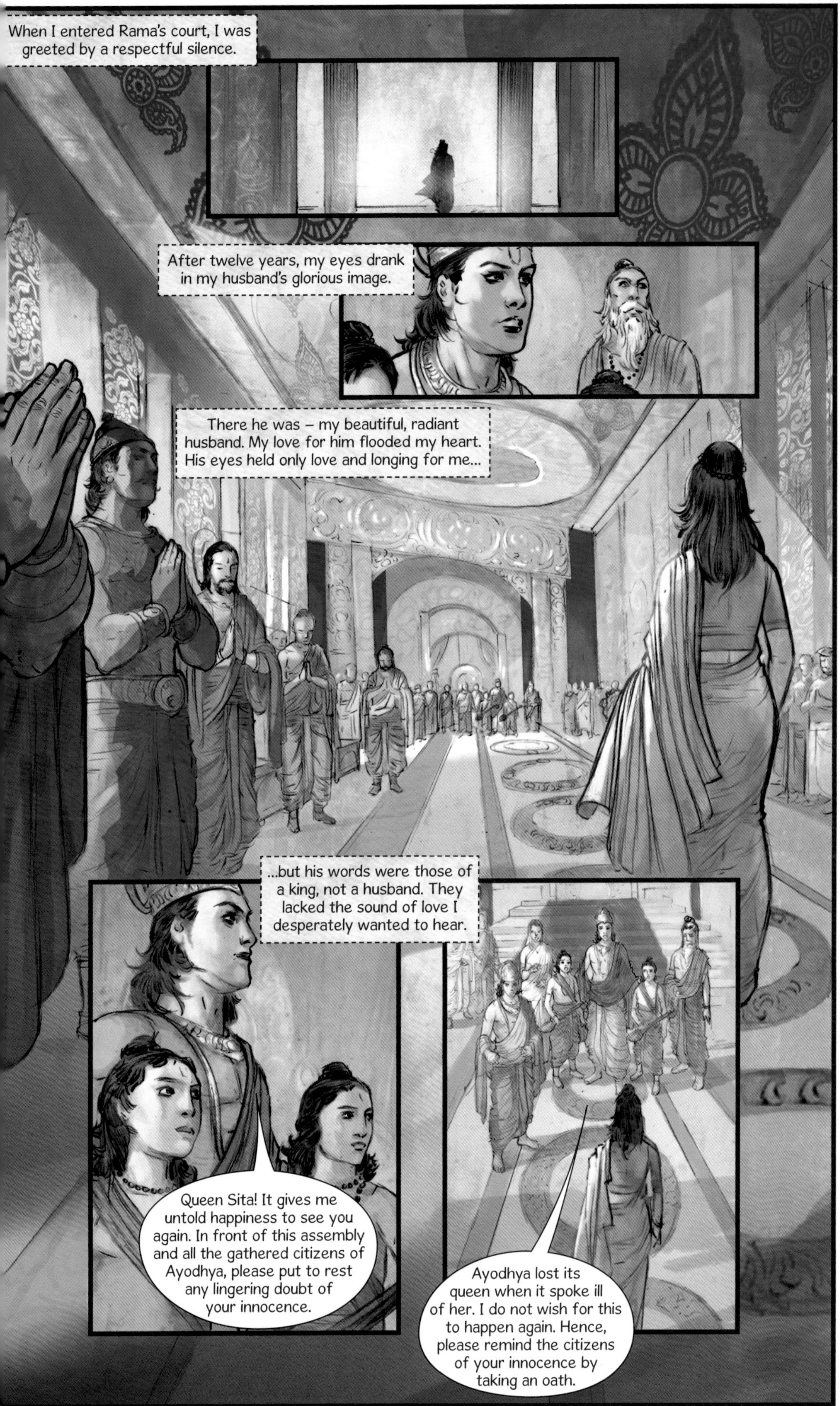

When I entered Rama's court, I was greeted by a respectful silence.
After twelve years, my eyes drank in my husband's glorious image.
There he was – my beautiful, radiant husband. My love for him flooded my heart. His eyes held only love and longing for me...
...but his words were those of a king, not a husband. They lacked the sound of love I desperately wanted to hear.
Queen Sita! It gives me untold happiness to see you again. In front of this assembly and all the gathered citizens of Ayodhya, please put to rest any lingering doubt of your innocence.
Ayodhya lost its queen when it spoke ill of her. I do not wish for this to happen again. Hence, please remind the citizens of your innocence by taking an oath.

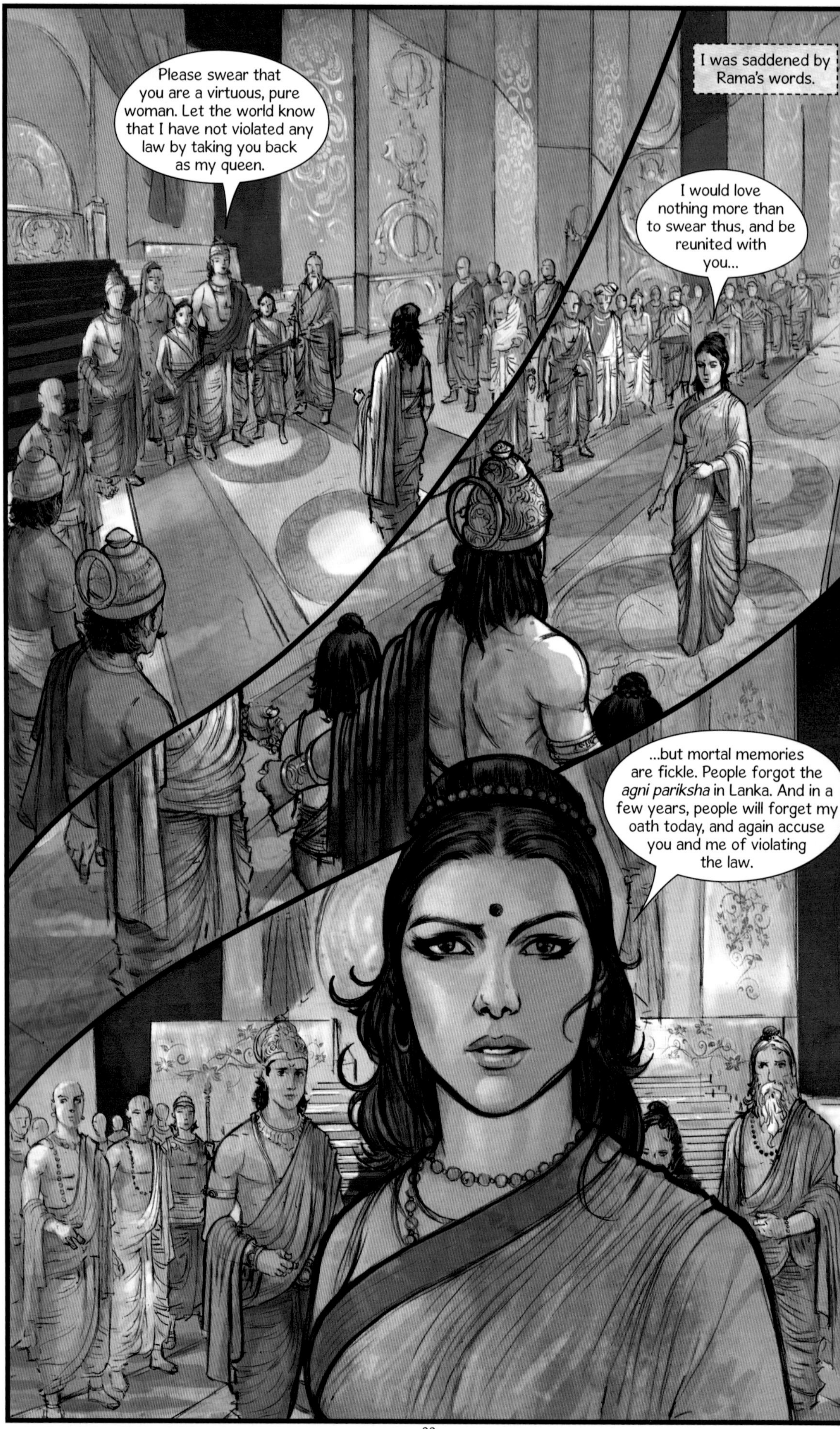
Please swear that you are a virtuous, pure woman. Let the world know that I have not violated any law by taking you back as my queen.
I was saddened by Rama's words.
I would love nothing more than to swear thus, and be reunited with you...
...but mortal memories are fickle. People forgot the *agni pariksha* in Lanka. And in a few years, people will forget my oath today, and again accuse you and me of violating the law.

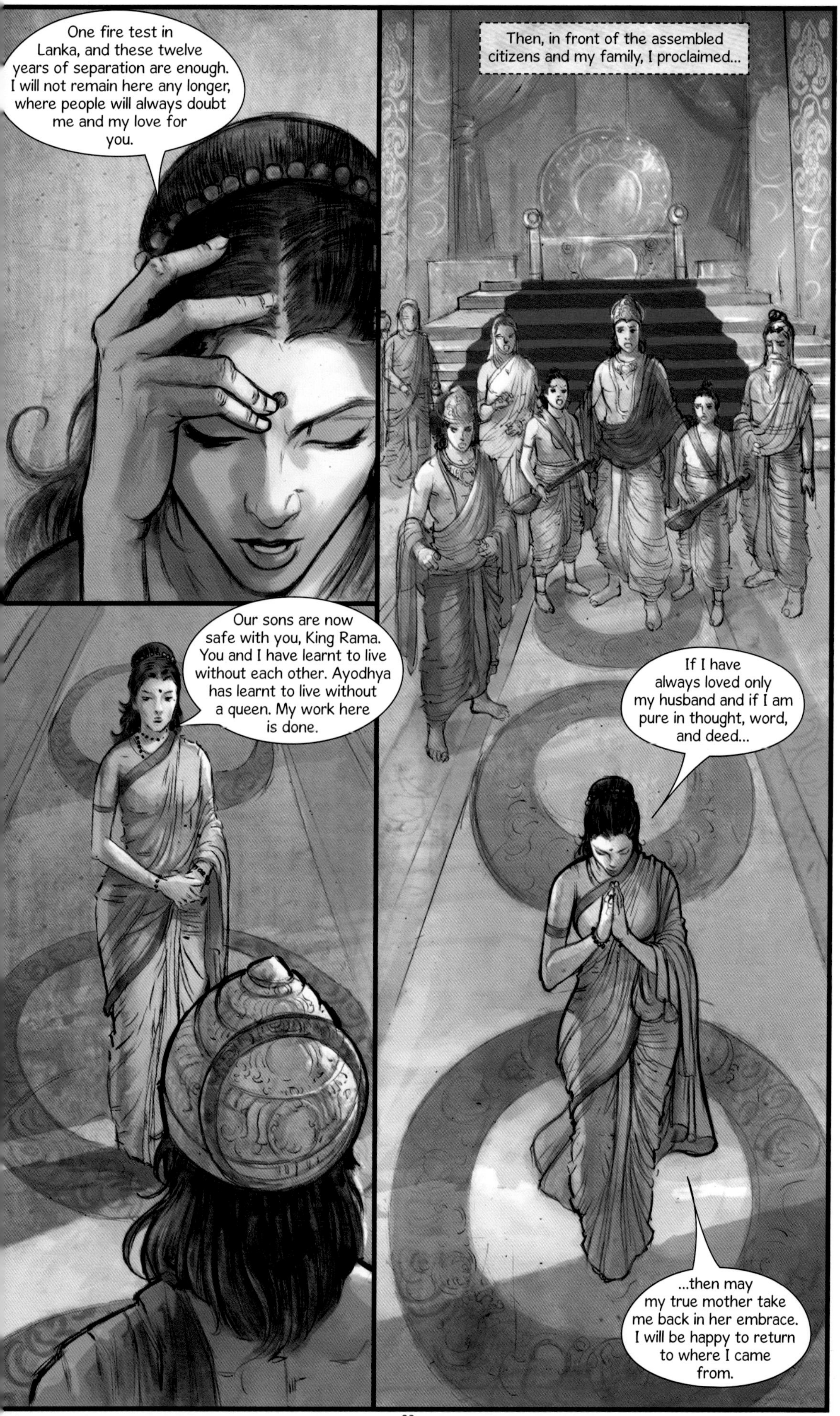

One fire test in Lanka, and these twelve years of separation are enough. I will not remain here any longer, where people will always doubt me and my love for you.
Then, in front of the assembled citizens and my family, I proclaimed...
Our sons are now safe with you, King Rama. You and I have learnt to live without each other. Ayodhya has learnt to live without a queen. My work here is done.
If I have always loved only my husband and if I am pure in thought, word, and deed...
...then may my true mother take me back in her embrace. I will be happy to return to where I came from.

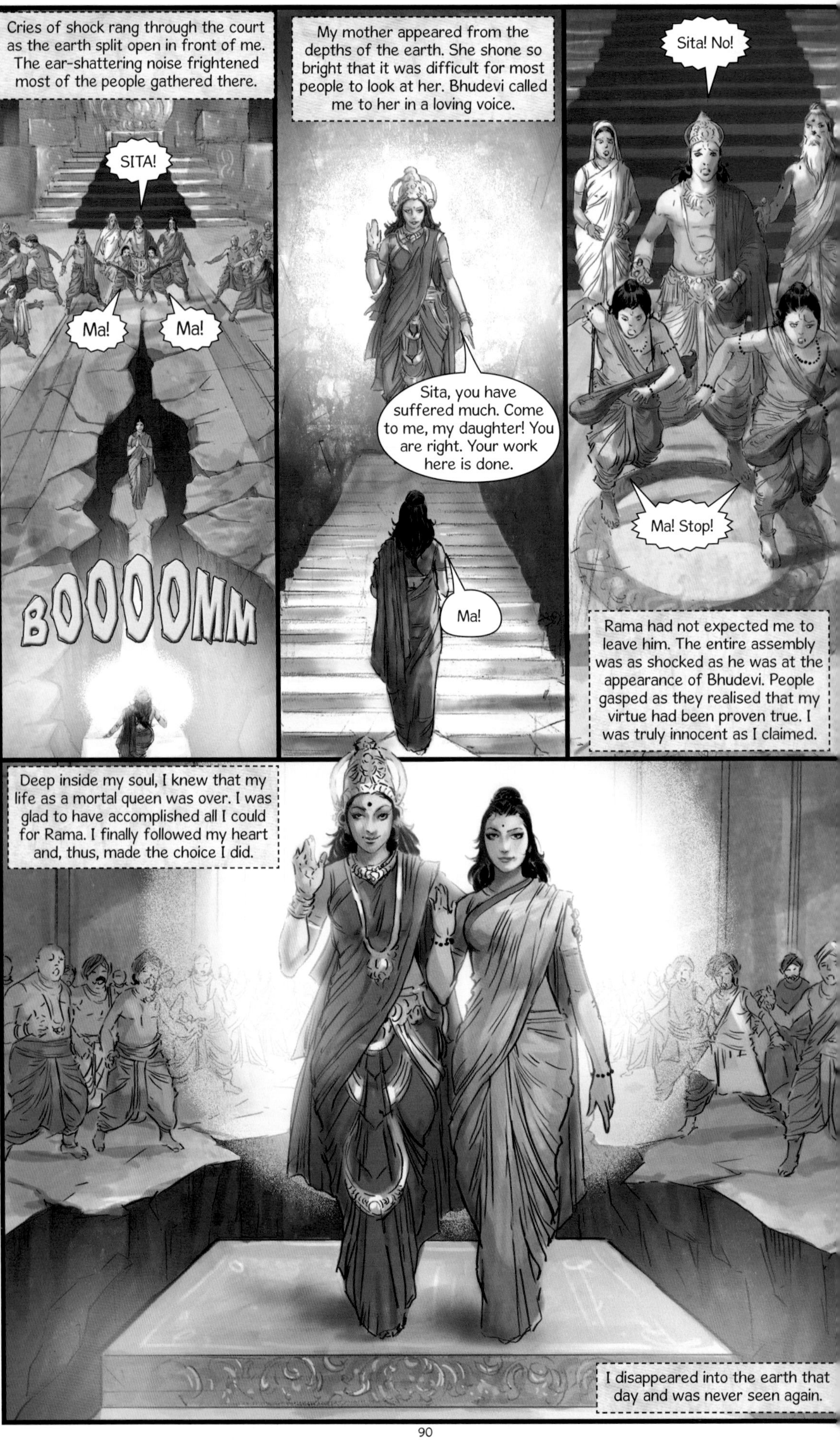
Cries of shock rang through the court as the earth split open in front of me. The ear-shattering noise frightened most of the people gathered there.
SITA!
Ma!
Ma!
BOOOOMM
My mother appeared from the depths of the earth. She shone so bright that it was difficult for most people to look at her. Bhudevi called me to her in a loving voice.
Sita, you have suffered much. Come to me, my daughter! You are right. Your work here is done.
Ma!
Sita! No!
Ma! Stop!
Rama had not expected me to leave him. The entire assembly was as shocked as he was at the appearance of Bhudevi. People gasped as they realised that my virtue had been proven true. I was truly innocent as I claimed.
Deep inside my soul, I knew that my life as a mortal queen was over. I was glad to have accomplished all I could for Rama. I finally followed my heart and, thus, made the choice I did.
I disappeared into the earth that day and was never seen again.

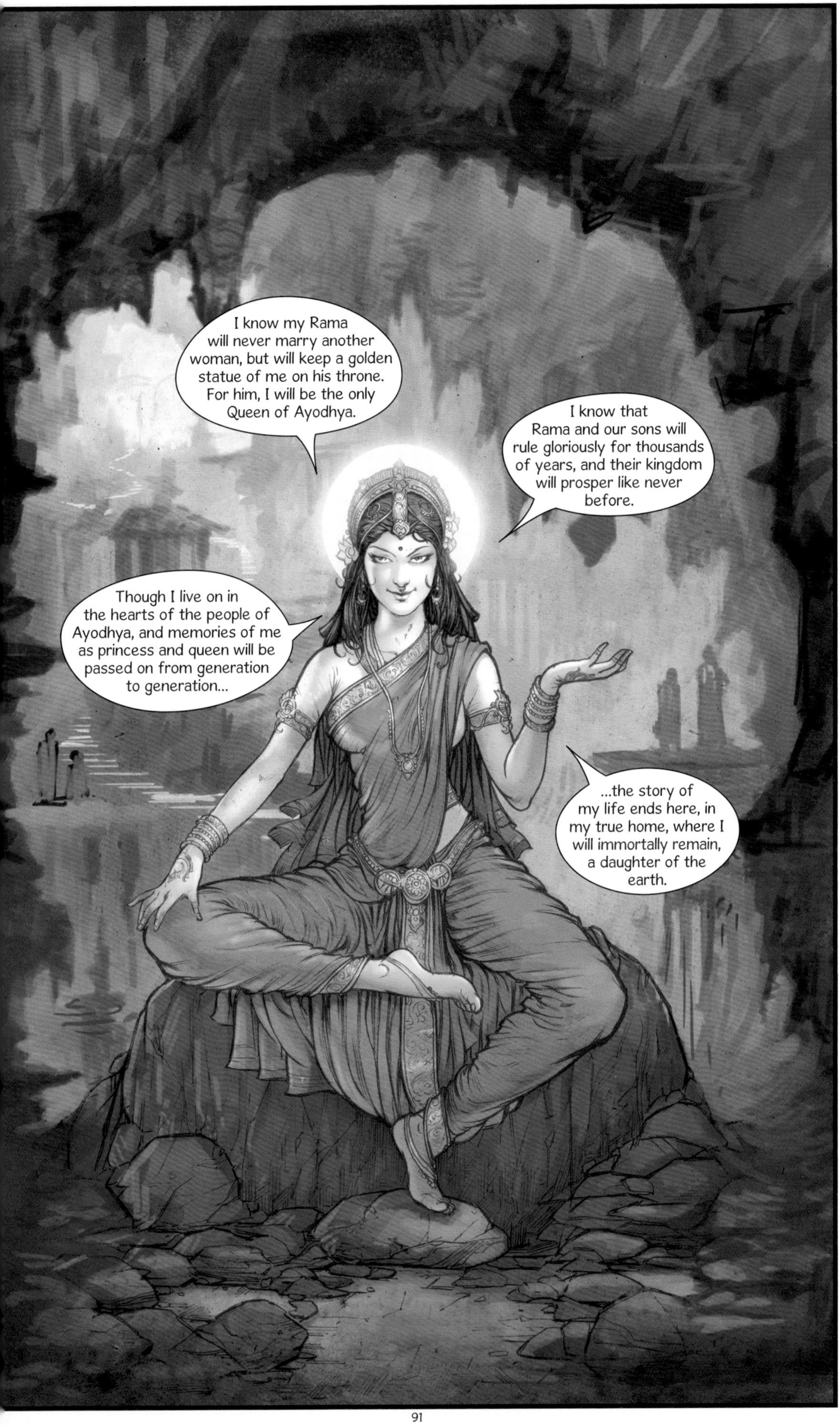
I know my Rama will never marry another woman, but will keep a golden statue of me on his throne. For him, I will be the only Queen of Ayodhya.
I know that Rama and our sons will rule gloriously for thousands of years, and their kingdom will prosper like never before.
Though I live on in the hearts of the people of Ayodhya, and memories of me as princess and queen will be passed on from generation to generation...
...the story of my life ends here, in my true home, where I will immortally remain, a daughter of the earth.

GLOSSARY

AGNI	The God of Fire
AGNI PARIKSHA	The fire test
ANGA	A kingdom of Bhaarat
APSARA	A celestial woman who is a dancer at the court of Indra
ASHOKA VATIKA	The garden of Ashoka trees
ASTRA	Weapon
BHAARAT	The ancient name of India
BHAIYA	A term of respect, meaning elder brother
BHUDEVI	The Earth Goddess
BRAHMA-ASTRA	Weapon carrying the power of Brahma (the God of Creation)
DAI-MAA	A nurse-maid or nanny
DASI	Maid servant
DEVA	A god
DEVI	A goddess
HIMAVAN	The personification of the Himalayas
INDRA	King of the gods, presiding over rain and thunder
INDRA-ASTRA	Weapon carrying the power of Indra
KHADAUN	Wooden footwear worn by hermits
KOSALA	A kingdom close to Videha. Ayodhya was the capital of Kosala.
KSHATRIYA	Person belonging to the warrior caste
LAKSHMANA REKHA	The magical line drawn by Lakshmana
LANKA	The island kingdom of the *rakshasa* king, Ravana
MANTRA	A powerful, sacred chant used to invoke a god
MANTRI-JI	Minister
MATA	A term of respect used for women, meaning mother

MITHILA	The capital city of the kingdom of Videha
NISHADHA	The name of a tribe
PAYAS	A traditional Indian dessert made of milk and rice
PUSHPAKA VIMANA	A luxurious flying chariot belonging to Ravana
RAJGURU	The spiritual teacher or preceptor of the royal family
RAKSHASA	Demon. A female demon is called a *rakshasi*.
RAMACHANDRA	Another name of Rama
RAMAYANA	The story of Rama and Sita, written in verse by Maharishi Valmiki
REKHA	Line
RISHI	Sage
SHRI	A title of respect added before a man's name
SITA	Literally means 'furrow'. Name of the daughter of Janaka and Sunaina. Wife of Rama.
SITA PATI	Husband of Sita
SURYAVANSHI	A royal dynasty, believed to be descended from the sun
SWAYAMVARA	A ceremony where the bride chooses her groom from amongst a gathering of men.
TILAK	The sandalwood/vermillion mark on the forehead
TRETA YUGA	The second great age. According to ancient Indian texts, there are four great ages or time cycles – Sat Yuga, Treta Yuga, Dvapara Yuga, and Kali Yuga.
VAANARA	A member of the intelligent and powerful monkey race
VATIKA	Garden
VAITARANI	The river of blood that flows in the Land of Death
VANDEVI	Goddess of the Forest. Also, Sita was known by this name in Valmiki's ashram.
VAYU	The God of Wind
VIDEHA	A kingdom ruled by King Janaka, father of Sita
YAJNYA/YAGYA	A ritual in which priests invoke the blessings of gods by pouring offerings into a fire.
YAMA	The God of Death and Righteousness

OF MYTHS AND LEGENDS

Long, long ago, even before language was created, people managed to tell stories by drawing and painting pictures on caves and walls. Later, when language was invented, people started writing on palm leaves. These stories have been passed on, retold, and interpreted in many ways by many people because everyone loves a good story! Nobody knows whether they are true or false, but they have been around as myths and legends.

LEGENDS

Legends are tales that, because of their tie to a historical event or location, are believable, although not necessarily true. However, over time, the story may have changed to take on some fantastical elements.

MYTHS

Myths are ancient stories that deal with supernatural beings, magic, and other fantastical elements. Some of them could be based on real events, but usually, myths were created to teach people something important and explain events such as earthquakes, the rising and setting of the sun, floods, etc.

Legends and myths are also adapted by different cultures in different ways. The best example would be the Thai version of the *Ramayana*. It is Thailand's popular national epic and is known as the *Ramakien* (which literally means 'Glory of Rama'). In the *Ramakien*, Sita is the daughter of T'os'akanth (Ravana). P'ip'ek (Vibhisana), the astrologer brother of Ravana, predicts that Sita will bring calamity. Ravana then has her thrown into the waters. She is later picked by Janok (King Janaka). While the main story is identical to that of the *Ramayana*, many other aspects were modified according to the Thai context. Elaborate murals depicting stories from the *Ramakien* can be seen at the Wat Phra Kaew temple in Bangkok.

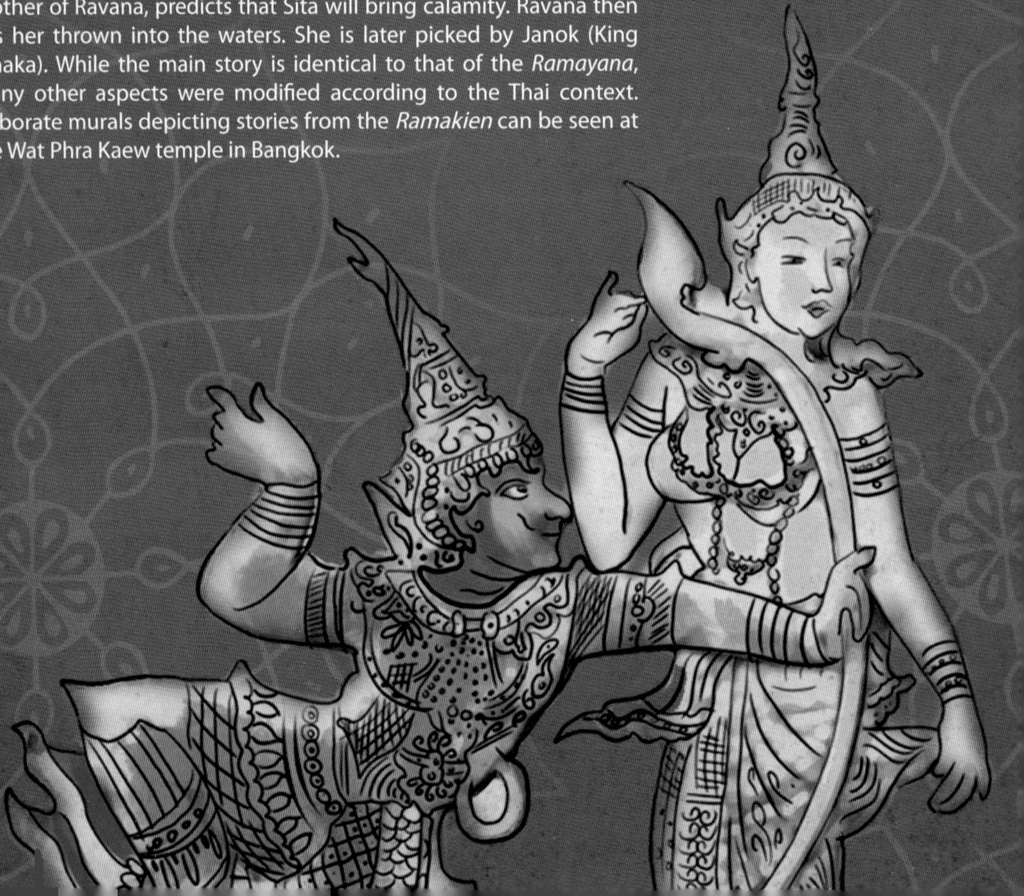

Now that we know the difference between the two, let's get to know some fascinating places that speak of the myths and legends around Sita.

Janakpur, Nepal

According to one legend, Janakpur is the birthplace of Sita, and also the site of Lord Rama and Sita's wedding. Dhanushadham, a locality in Janakpur, is believed to be the place where Rama broke the divine bow to obtain Sita's hand for marriage. Devotees still worship what is believed to be a fossilised fragment of the broken pieces of the divine bow.

Janaki-kund, Bihar

According to another legend, Sita was born in Sitamarhi, Bihar. It is said that much after Sita got married to Rama, King Janaka, constructed a tank and set up stone figures of Rama, Lakshmana, and Sita to mark this site. This tank is known as *Janaki-kund*.

Sita Mai Temple, Haryana

One very famous temple is the Sita Mai Temple in Karnal, Haryana. The temple is made in a simple style but the main feature is the elaborate ornamentation which covers the whole shrine, the pattern of which is formed by deep lines in the individual bricks. The shrine is said to mark the spot where Mother Earth swallowed Sita in answer to her appeal.

THE MANY NAMES OF SITA

As she was found in a furrow by King Janaka, he named her 'Sita', which literally means 'furrow'. Just like other major figures in Hindu legends, Sita is known by many names. As the daughter of King Janaka, she is known as Janaki; as the princess of Mithila, Mythili or Maithili; and as the wife of Rama, she is also known as Ramaa.

DID YOU KNOW?

Yama Zatdaw is the Burmese version of the *Ramayana*. It is considered to be Mayanmar's national epic. There are nine known pieces of the *Yama Zatdaw* in Myanmar. The Burmese name for *Ramayana* is *Yamayana*, where Rama is known as 'Yama' and Sita as 'Thida'. Interestingly, 'Yama' is the God of Death in India!

Also from Campfire

Ravana is the story of a demon who dared to challenge the gods, and almost got away with it. So what was it that proved to be the downfall of someone as powerful as Ravana? Was it only the desire for a woman? Or was it something more, rooted in the incidents of his life, in the history of his race? Ravana's tale is one that never fails to inspire awe and fear.

Based on an episode from the *Ramcharitmanas* by Tulsidas, the story described here needs little introduction to readers familiar with the Indian epic of Ramayan. Hanuman is strong and invincible, but he is also a brave and loyal follower of Ram, and is able to overcome all crises through his single-minded devotion.

Evil is back on earth in the guise of Kansa. To vanquish him, Lord Vishnu is born again in his eighth avatar – Krishna, defender of dharma. As Krishna fights evil, he observes that the struggle of good against evil pits him not against shape-shifting monsters, but kings, and brave warriors. Will Krishna be able to triumph over the darkness and restore dharma?

Adapted from the ancient Indian epic, the Mahabharata, this is the story of an astonishingly outspoken woman, abandoned at every turn, and forced to make the difficult choice between revenge and compassion.